Love Finds You™

IN

Wildrose

NORTH DAKOTA

Love Finds You™

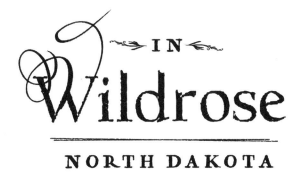

~⇜ IN ⇝~

Wildrose

NORTH DAKOTA

TRACEY BATEMAN

summerside
PRESS™

Summerside Press™
Minneapolis 55438
www.summersidepress.com

Love Finds You in Wildrose, North Dakota
© 2012 by Tracey V. Bateman

ISBN 978-1-60936-592-9

Scripture references are from the Holy Bible, King James Version (KJV).

The town depicted in this book is a real place, but all characters are
fictional. Any resemblances to actual people or events are purely
coincidental.

Cover design by Lookout Design | www.lookoutdesign.com
Interior design by Müllerhaus Publishing Group | www.mullerhaus.net
Cover photo by Susan Fox / Trevillion Images

*Summerside Press™ is an inspirational publisher offering fresh,
irresistible books to uplift the heart and engage the mind.*

Printed in USA.

Dedication
....

For Jesus, the lover of my soul

Acknowledgments

....

Rusty, you cook, clean, and rub my arms at
the end of a really long day of writing.

Thank you for being steady. You're a perfect match for me.

Thanks to Lori Ranfeld, who listens. This book
might not have happened without you.

Thanks to Rachel Meisel, who offered prayer
and support as I wrote this book.

Wild Prairie Rose near Wildrose, ND

WILDROSE, NORTH DAKOTA, WAS A GREAT NORTHERN RAILROAD town site founded in 1909. It absorbed the old post offices of Paddington and Montrose. It was planned that the Montrose name would be transferred here, but there was already a stop named Montrose on the Great Northern Railroad line, so officials of the railroad selected a new name noting the wild roses in bloom at the site. Until 1916, it was the terminus of the railroad line and billed itself as the largest primary grain market in the United States. A peak population of 518 was reached in 1930. Today the town boasts only about 110 residents.

Tracey Bateman

Prologue
....

Wildrose, North Dakota, 1913

She took her son's hand and allowed him to help her down from the wagon.

"Are you okay here by yourself until Pa comes to find you?" he asked. "He said he wouldn't be long."

"Of course. Go find your friends."

The image of his pa, he looked down at her. "You sure, Mama? I don't mind waiting."

She gave him a dismissive wave. "Go. The girls already ran off to find their friends; you may as well too. I'm fine here alone."

At eighteen years of age, Roland would be off to college next year. And the year after that, her youngest would too. The years had gone by much too quickly.

The mayor stood in front of the post office as the crowd milled about, waiting to watch the historic moment. In his hand, he held a pink flower. "Citizens, neighbors, and friends," he started in that grandiose manner that had always irritated Rosemary—even when he was the mayor of Paddington, which had recently joined with the town of Montrose. Today the two towns were being absorbed into one: Wildrose. A new town didn't mean a new mayor.

"Today we become incorporated into one village," he said. "Wildrose, North Dakota."

She clapped along with the crowd as her husband came alongside her and touched her elbow.

"My wild rose," he said in her ear. "They finally got smart and named a town after you."

Her face warmed at his teasing. She tapped her fingertips on his arm. "Don't be silly." The town had almost been called Montrose, until one of the railroad officials caught sight of the wild roses blooming and decided that would make a better name for the town. But of course her husband had always called her his "wild rose," so he liked to tease her about it.

He slipped his arm around her as they listened to the mayor christen their town. Rosemary couldn't help but think what a difference such a few short years had made. The crowd around her faded as her mind took her back twenty years to the day she arrived in Dakota Territory.

As she loved to tell the children, "It was the coldest wind I'd ever felt in my life...."

Chapter One

. . . .

North Dakota, 1895

Bone-weary and half-frozen, Rosemary Jackson stepped down from the wagon into the kind of swirling snow that even the hardiest of men would have called a blizzard back in Kansas. But this weather was like nothing she'd ever experienced, especially in the middle of April. The wind sliced into her cheeks, and she was almost certain that if she looked into a mirror she'd find cuts and bruises from nature's assault.

Rachel had warned her that the weather up here in Dakota Territory was harsh and raw, but no one could have possibly prepared Rosemary for a spring blizzard of this magnitude.

Mr. Bakker, the freighter who had allowed her to ride with him from Williston the past forty miles, left her baggage in the back of his wagon and made a beeline for the warmth of the little log cabin—the first shelter they'd come across in six hours since the snow began to twist and swirl. Thankfully, Mr. Bakker had been able to keep his horses on course, though the going had grown slower and slower as the blinding snow accumulated, and with the wagon wheels threatening to bog down more than once.

For the first time, she wondered if she had done the right thing by leaving her home in Kansas. After all, the school board had offered her a teaching position after Pa's death. But Rosemary's mind had been set on seeing her sister again. She hadn't even thought twice before thanking them kindly and refusing the offer.

The front door swung open, and a broad-faced woman with a toddler on her generous hip ushered Rosemary inside after the driver. "Gracious me," she said with a thick accent that Rosemary surmised was German. "Please come quickly and close the door. Ve do not vant the cold coming in vith you. Nor the snow."

She stared at Rosemary with something akin to pity in her bright blue eyes. "You must be frozen in your body. Come vith me." Turning to a red-faced little man with a blond beard and a thick mop of blond hair, she deposited the child in his arms. "Varm up the soup while I take care of the little girl."

Inwardly Rosemary flinched. At twenty years of age, she was often still mistaken for a child. She was small—a good two, even three inches shorter than most of the girls she had gone to school with back before she earned her certificate of commencement. Rachel was just as small of stature, but it had never bothered her the way it bothered Rosemary.

The German woman escorted her to the far end of the one-room cabin and pulled aside the curtain that had been hung for privacy. "Now, let's get da clothes off and get you varm. Vhere are your bags, Fräulein?"

Rosemary had packed a valise with her Bible, an extra dress, and a nightgown. The rest of her things were in the trunk. And of course there were still crates to come. But those had been shipped and wouldn't arrive for some time. "Still in the wagon."

A deep frown drew the woman's eyebrows together. "Dat man did not bring it in? I vill give him a piece of my mind, yes, I vill."

"I c–can't blame him." Rosemary had been in just as much of a hurry to get inside, and she hadn't been the one fighting the horses for the past ten miles. She unwrapped her scarf and pulled it from her face. The woman's eyes went wide with recognition.

"Frau Tate, vat are you doing so far from home?"

Rosemary smiled at the mistaken identity. "You're thinking of my sister, Rachel—the r–real Mrs. Tate." She slipped off her gloves and extended her hand. "I'm M–miss Jackson, her s–sister." Her body felt the chill through and through, and although she willed herself to stop shivering, it refused to obey.

The German woman's face split into a wondrous smile. "You are the image of one another."

"T–twins."

Her large, work-roughened hand enfolded Rosemary's, and the woman gave it a hearty shake that nearly yanked her arm from the socket. "I am Frau Fischer, and my Heinrich you haf met when you come in. Gracious, your hand is like icicle."

Rosemary hadn't exactly "met" Frau Fischer's Heinrich, but that point was moot for now. The important thing was that these kind folk appeared to be willing to put them up while the snow prevented safe travel.

"Pleased to meet you, Frau Fischer."

Rather than release her, Frau Fischer covered Rosemary's hand with both of hers. "I too am pleased to meet you, Fräulein Jackson." The calloused palms moved swiftly across Rosemary's skin, coaxing the feeling back into her fingers.

"Call me Rosemary," she said, relieved to discover that she would not be permanently frozen, as her body began to warm up. "If you and my sister are neighbors, then I'm your neighbor now too. And I prefer the friendliness of using given names."

"And you vill call me Agnes."

"All right, Agnes."

The two exchanged the sort of smile reserved for strangers who already knew they could be friends if given half a chance.

"Frau and Herr Tate's homestead is ten more miles north of here. Too far to visit often. Dat Herr Tate, he is fine man. Vork very hard."

Rosemary nodded. "Finn worked for Pa back in Kansas on our ranch. It's where he and Rachel met." Now that her fingers were no longer freezing, they were beginning to burn. At least they weren't frostbitten. "Pa wanted to keep him on as foreman, but Finn had an itch to start his own farm."

"It is the vay of man. He must plow his own land. Raise his own herd. This is goot. It is God's vill."

Yes, Rosemary supposed it was good. If only he hadn't wanted to fulfill God's will so far from home.

Agnes Fischer patted Rosemary's shoulder as though understanding her unspoken thoughts. "Come, come. Ve should get your vet skirt off so you do not catch death." Agnes handed Rosemary a thick quilt. "Cover vith this vhile I go and put some vater on the stove so you may vash."

"I'd appreciate it." She felt as though she hadn't cleaned up in a month. How heavenly an actual bath would be. But she guessed she'd have to wait until she arrived at Rachel's house for that.

Rosemary's fingers still trembled as she clumsily worked at her

buttons. By the time Agnes returned, Rosemary had wrapped the quilt around herself and was becoming drowsy as she grew warmer.

Agnes smiled her approval. She handed over a wool dress. "This is my Marta's. She is just about your size. The blue vill match your eyes—just like Marta's."

"Thank you." Rosemary clutched the dress to her chest.

Agnes waved away her thanks and took Rosemary's wet things from the stool by the bed where Rosemary had set them. "I vill hang these by the fire to dry."

"I hate for you to go to so much trouble for me," Rosemary said. "I'll hang them up as soon as I'm dressed."

"Nonsense, Fräulein." She shook her head. "I vill not mind." Agnes patted the bed. "You lie here and rest vhile the vater heats on the stove. My Heinrich and Herr Bakker are taking care of the horses. Heinrich vill carry in your valise."

"Will we be going on to my sister's homestead in the morning?"

Agnes hesitated then shook her head. "The snow is still coming down very hard."

As if to accentuate her words, the wind gusted outside, howling and shaking the little cabin to its foundation.

"How long, do you think?"

Agnes shrugged. "Perhaps if the snow stops by morning, who knows. Two, maybe three days? Or maybe a veek. But do not vorry. It vill not be so bad here. My children, they are all five vell-behaved.

"Voman!" Herr Fischer called. "The vater is hot for the little girl."

"My Heinrich, he does not holler so much." She rolled her eyes. "Only sometimes."

Rosemary watched Agnes duck around the curtain and felt

17

ashamed. Here this woman was doing her best to make her feel comfortable, and she felt like complaining about being forced to stay for a few days.

Agnes returned moments later, carrying the water.

Rosemary stood up. "Thank you for everything, Agnes." She released a sigh. "I don't mean to sound ungrateful."

A kind smile played at the corners of Agnes's lips. "There is no need for apologizing." She set the bowl of warm water on the dresser. "You vish to see Rachel. It is to be understood. I vould also so love to see my own sisters."

Tears threatened Rosemary's eyes, but she refused to surrender. Instead she smiled. "Thank you. I appreciate the warm water and the dress—and the food."

"You vash and get dressed and I vill dish you up some supper. You are hungry, *ja*?"

"Yes, thank you. That sounds lovely."

"Do not worry, Rosemary. A veek vill go by much faster than you know."

Rosemary reached out and touched Agnes's arm. "I'm sure it will be fine. I just miss Rachel so much. We haven't seen each other in three years." She smiled at her hostess. "Papa used to tell me to look in the mirror if I missed her so much. The problem was, I could tell us apart even if he couldn't." She let out a little laugh at her unsuccessful attempt to lighten her mood.

"I vill tell you apart. Already, you are Rosemary and she is Rachel. Both beautiful, but vith different eyes." Agnes headed toward the curtain, leaving Rosemary to wonder what she meant. Rachel's eyes were identical to hers, just like the rest of their physical

appearance. She didn't have the opportunity to question the woman, as she seemed to be in a hurry to get to the other room. "The food vill be ready soon. You rest. I come and get you when it is hot."

"Thank you." After the curtain closed behind Agnes, Rosemary let the quilt drop and then slipped the blue wool dress over her head. A wave of sadness washed over her as she buttoned up the front. She had been so sure she would be seeing Rachel tomorrow. She had been on one train after another for a week until her arrival in Williston. And it had taken another three days to find a freighter willing to let her ride as far as possible in the direction of Finn and Rachel's homestead. The three years without Rachel had been the most miserable of her life. Waiting another week felt like a lifetime.

By the time she was dressed, Rosemary could hardly keep her eyes open. As hungry as she felt, exhaustion was winning the battle between the two basic needs. She stretched out on the bed and barely heard Agnes slip back around the curtain. She hovered over the bed and clicked her tongue in disapproval before patting Rosemary's leg. "It is all right. You vill not become ill from one missed meal. Tonight you vill sleep. Tomorrow you vill eat."

"I don't want to put you out of your bed," Rosemary said, slurring her words.

"Do not vorry," Agnes said. "Marta and Elsa will sleep in the bed vith you, and Herr Bakker vill sleep on the floor by the fire. You sleep. I vill haf bed. My Heinrich vill haf bed. Children vill also haf bed in the loft."

Too weary to argue, Rosemary murmured a thank-you she hoped reached her lips. She didn't awaken when the children were placed in her bed, but in the morning, when the smell of frying pork tempted her awake and made her stomach rumble, two cold feet were pressed firmly against her back and only part of her body was covered with the quilt.

Her stomach sank as she recognized the sound of the howling wind outside and felt the chill through the cracks in the wood. There was no point in trying to go back to sleep, so she carefully slid out of bed, so as not to wake the two children, and ducked around the curtain. Mr. Fischer and Mr. Bakker sat at the table, their feet stretched toward the stove. Clearly, the two men had already taken care of the chores outside.

Agnes stood in front of the stove, frying ham and stirring a pot. On her hip rested the child she'd been holding the night before when they arrived. She looked up from the stove and scowled. "You should still be in bed, Fräulein." She shook her head as understanding dawned on her face. "Those children of mine sleep every vich-a vay. I should not haf put them to bed vith you."

"I slept fine." She grinned. "Until I woke up with icy feet on me. I'm sorry to take your bed, though."

"It does not matter. Ja, Heinrich?"

He grunted, and Rosemary had a pretty good idea that Heinrich wasn't as generous about lending his bed to strangers as his wife was.

"Well, I insist upon sleeping elsewhere and giving you back your bed tonight." Rosemary joined her in the kitchen area. "How can I help?"

"Oh no. You are guest. Sit. Sit. I get you coffee?"

"I'm not an invited guest. I'm a drop-in guest who has imposed upon you due to the weather, so please, let me help."

Agnes hesitated for only the briefest moment before agreeing. She handed over the spatula. "Goot. I vill tend the children."

The men ignored Rosemary as she pushed the slices of ham around the pan to keep them from scorching. As she watched the fat sizzle at the edges of the meat, her thoughts flowed to Rachel and the letter she had received just after Christmas.

I am beside myself with worry over Pa. However, I am afraid coming to you is impossible now. Finn has offered to purchase fare for my travel after the spring thaw, bless him. I have enclosed a letter for Pa. And darling Rosemary, please know that when Pa's time comes, Finn and I will welcome you with open arms into our home.

Thinking of those open arms brought a bittersweet smile to her lips. She lifted the slices of meat onto the platter and stirred the oats. Had Rachel received the letter she'd penned three weeks ago after Pa's death? Pa had taken care of everything important ahead of time, so all that was left for Rosemary to do was to give him a decent burial in the cemetery next to Ma and then make her arrangements to travel. And with nothing else to stay for, she'd left Kansas within two weeks, with the school board's assurance that, should she decide to come home, the teaching position would be hers.

But she'd rather die than go back and live out her life as an old-maid teacher. If Pa had only trusted her enough to let her run the ranch as she'd begged him to... But short of her finding a husband and marrying before his death, Pa had never intended to leave the place to her. So there had been nothing to do but the next best thing: come to Rachel and Finn.

"Papa! Elsa pulled my hair!" The cry came from the bed where Rosemary had slept.

Rosemary's stomach clenched as Heinrich expelled a sigh and got up from his chair. She watched as he walked across the room and opened the curtain. "Vat is this about pulling hair?" he bellowed.

Rosemary's pa had never been one to yell. He was firm but soft-spoken—a trait shared by Rachel. Rosemary had been more inclined to raise her voice when riled. But that didn't mean she wanted to hear a grown man intimidate his children in such a way. She waited for the forthcoming reprimand.

"Must you be now tickled?" he bellowed.

Both girls began to squeal and giggle, and Rosemary relaxed. She smiled at the sound of the father playing with his children, and her thoughts went back to one of the first letters she had received from Rachel.

The Germans from Russia are hardworking, well-bodied, hardy folk who cook the oddest food, which I have to admit I've developed an affinity for. There are 160 acres for the taking, if one can endure the hardship for five years. Mostly the Germans keep to themselves, but we've befriended a few, in particular Herr and Frau Fischer. They have four children and Agnes is with child again. I must say, I like them quite well.

Again Rosemary smiled. She could hear Agnes moving around in the loft with the boys. And the girls were still wrestling with their pa. She could well believe Rachel had grown to love this noisy, lovable family after the years of quiet in their large, nearly empty home. Pa had never been one to enjoy the boisterous antics of children, and Rosemary couldn't imagine him wrestling and playing the way Mr. Fischer was making his girls giggle so hard they were losing their breath.

By the time the meal was ready, the children had all appeared, dressed with hair smoothed, and were sitting at the long table on their best behavior.

"Now, my children," Heinrich grunted out, "you must all say goot morning to Fräulein Jackson, who is the sister of Frau Tate, and Herr Bakker, who drives the freighter to bring supplies to Herr Morehouse's General Store in Paddington."

The two boys, ten and eleven years old, were the image of their father despite their hair. Thick white-blond hair topped Heinrich Jr.'s head. He was the elder of the two and his eyes remained sober, as though he knew the responsibility that comes from being the eldest son. Afonso, the only red-haired child of the five, held out his hand. Rosemary saw the willful spirit in Afonso's eyes though his body remained still, and he said, "Goot morning, Fräulein Jackson. You are very pretty like Frau Tate."

"Why, thank you, Afonso." Rosemary couldn't contain her laugh as she shook his hand.

He shrugged and looked away, eyeing the food on the table.

Heinrich Jr. stretched out his hand as well. "It is a pleasure to meet you, Fräulein." Rosemary reached across the table and shook his cool hand. He met her gaze with a frank sincerity that drew Rosemary.

Elsa's pretty blue eyes were full of spirit, but she offered a shy smile. Rosemary met her gaze and grinned. "I have already met your very cold feet, my little friend."

Elsa pressed her lips together to hide her smile, but her eyes couldn't contain a thing. Rosemary liked her immediately. Even more so when the little girl said, "I thank you for the warmth of your back."

Delighted and surprised by the girl's words, Rosemary couldn't resist the urge to toss back her head and laugh as Agnes scolded her precious daughter.

The eldest child, Marta, cleared her throat. "Pleased to meet you, Fräulein Jackson," she said, lowering her lashes. "Pleased to meet you, Herr Bakker." Her face reddened as she addressed the driver, and Rosemary suspected that the girl, on the verge of womanhood, did not have many occasions to be in the company of men other than her father.

"Pleased to meet you too, little lady," Mr. Bakker said, oblivious to her discomfort. He winked and her blush deepened.

Rosemary smiled at Marta, whose face still glowed from the experience. "I'm also very pleased to meet you, Marta. And thank you for loaning me your dress last night. I'm afraid I fell asleep while still wearing it." It was a little tight across the chest, but otherwise it fit her perfectly.

"It was my pleasure, Fräulein."

Heinrich glanced around the table and the children instantly fell silent. "Ve shall ask the Lord's blessing now, before ve eat."

Rosemary closed her eyes, thankful for the stillness that even the simplest prayer of thanks could bring.

When the meal was over, Heinrich nodded to Marta, who stepped over to the mantel and took down a book. She brought it to Heinrich.

"We read from the Vord of God," he said, eyeing first Herr Bakker then Rosemary. He opened and began to speak in a language that Rosemary assumed was German.

"In English, please, Heinrich," Agnes gently chastised. "Our guests do not understand."

He muttered an apology and began to read in halting English from the Twenty-third Psalm. The first two verses were so difficult for him to read, Rosemary felt sorry for him. She lifted a finger. Heinrich's eyebrows rose but he stopped reading. "Fräulein?"

"I know this passage by heart, and I would love to hear it read in your language." She swallowed, suddenly feeling foolish and hoping she hadn't offended or embarrassed her hosts. "It's just that...God is so big and He knows us all in our own language and land. After all, He's the one who confused the languages in the first place."

Rosemary's face burned as the children stared at her with wide-eyed amazement, but when she met Agnes's gaze, the woman's wide, leathery face had softened to beautiful. "Heinrich, German, please. Our guest made the asking."

Her husband muttered something in German, and Rosemary was almost positive it had nothing to do with the Twenty-third Psalm. But as he lifted the Bible and began to read again, she closed her eyes, drinking in the cadence, the beauty of those familiar words spoken in another language, and peace flowed over her. When he closed the Bible, she smiled. "Thank you, Herr Fischer," she said. "That was lovely."

He studied her for a second before he nodded and lifted his coffee cup to his lips.

Agnes clapped her hands together. "Breakfast is finished," she told her children. "Boys—upstairs and do lessons."

"Yes, Ma," the two muttered.

Agnes turned to Marta. "You and Elsa vill please clean up the dishes now, and then you may do lessons also."

"Of course, Mama."

Rosemary stood and reached for her plate. "May I help?"

Agnes shook her head and waved her back to her seat. "The time after breakfast I haf my tea and the girls clean the dishes. It is our..." She frowned as though searching for the word.

"Routine?"

"Yes! That is it. It is our routine. And you vill haf tea with me vhile Heinrich and Herr Bakker tend to the vood." She turned to her husband. "Ja?"

He stood and kissed her on the forehead. "Ja, Agnes."

Mr. Bakker stood. "Thank you for the breakfast, ma'am," he said to Agnes. "I appreciate the hospitality."

"It is our pleasure."

The two men left, and Agnes handed the baby to Rosemary so she could prepare the tea. The girls cleared the table and began the process of washing up the dishes in the basin on the counter by the stove. The method by which the girls washed the dishes fascinated Rosemary. She had been using a pump and sink for several years,

but this kitchen made her feel as though she'd stepped back in time twenty-five years. It looked almost primitive. She could only assume that someone had drawn water from a well outside.

Agnes set two cups on the table along with a bowl of sugar cubes and then dropped into her chair with a grunt. "Now ve haf our tea and ve get to know one another."

Before Agnes could stir sugar into her tea, the baby began to fuss.

Rosemary bounced her, feeling completely inept. "I'm sorry. I'm afraid I know so little about children."

"Do not be sorry, Rosemary," Agnes said gently. "Some things about babies a woman must learn. Besides, only I can quiet her when she is hungry."

Agnes took the baby, unbuttoned her blouse, and discreetly covered herself with the shawl she had about her shoulders.

"How old is Gerta?" Rosemary asked, trying not to show her discomfort at sitting there while Agnes nursed the child.

"My Gerta." She gave a soft sigh. "She is almost one year. Soon to be veaned. But not quite yet."

"She's a beauty."

Agnes beamed under the praise. "The Lord haf been goot to Heinrich and me. Strong, healthy children and goot-looking too."

Rosemary smiled and lifted her cup to her lips.

"Ah, Rachel vill be pleased for you to help her with her new little one."

Setting the cup back on the table, Rosemary met her gaze. "What do you mean? Is Rachel...?"

"I am afraid I haf given avay secret." Agnes's eyes lit with merriment. "She carried her baby through the summer and fall. She must haf given birth in the vinter sometime. We haf not seen nor heard from any of our neighbors in a vhile. But I believe you vill be greeted by a sister and her child."

Tears came to Rosemary's eyes. Rachel's last two letters had arrived in the fall and winter. She must have known she was going to have a baby, but she hadn't said a word. Was that the main reason she hadn't come home to see Pa?

Clearly, her sister hadn't wanted to worry them, with Pa so sick. That was just like Rachel, thinking of others before herself. But Rosemary couldn't help but believe that Pa might have been happy to hear the news that he was going to be a grandfather.

"A baby for Rachel. I can hardly believe it." Rosemary's arms ached to hold her niece or nephew. The news of the baby would make waiting the rest of the week for the snow to clear that much more difficult to bear.

Chapter Two

. . . .

Finn held his bundle close, feeling the baby's sweet breath on his throat as he wandered up to the counter at Morehouse's General Store.

"That last storm nearly did us in," the proprietor said to the fellow standing in front of him. "Glad you could make it when you did."

"I'm glad myself," the man said. "Got caught over by those Germans a few miles thataway. Spent almost a week listening to that foreign talk. I was never so glad to put a place behind me. *Ja* this and *ja* that. People ought to learn English if they want to come to this country."

Finn's back went up at the slur against his friends. "You mean the Fischers?"

The man turned and gave him a once-over. "That's right."

"What were you doing over that way if you're bringing goods from Williston?" Finn kept his gaze level, mindful of the baby in his arms, and tried not to look as irritated as he felt at the implied criticism of his friends. No use in starting something he couldn't finish.

Though the distance from his homestead to the town of Paddington and to the Fischers' homestead was the same, they were in two different directions, so he knew the fellow had driven miles out of his way.

"What's it to you?" the freighter asked.

Finn shrugged. "Nothing. Just wondering why a man would go out of his way, that's all. Besides, I happen to know the Fischers and think a lot of them—even if they are Germans. Seems to me when a man spends a week taking advantage of another man's hospitality, he oughtn't speak ill of him or his family."

"Finn's right. No need to be so all-fired unfriendly, Bakker," Mr. Morehouse admonished, shoving a book toward the freighter. "Make your mark."

"Just don't like folk in my business, that's all."

"Well, it so happens that it *is* Finn's business what you were doin' at the Fischers' homestead."

"How so?" Bakker asked. And Finn had to admit, he was curious about Mr. Morehouse's comment as well. Bakker made his mark and shoved the ledger back across the counter. The storekeeper opened his register, pulled out some bills, and handed them over.

"The woman who hired you to drive her is this man's kin. Or his wife's, anyway. It's his homestead where she's heading."

The storekeeper's words hit Finn hard in the gut, as he realized they could only mean that Rosemary had arrived. So much had happened, he'd forgotten all about her until this second.

He looked at the freighter. "Was the woman's name Rosemary Jackson?"

"That sounds about right. Small of stature but pretty as a picture. If I didn't have a wife at home already…"

Finn's ire rose. "Watch it." He forced himself to relax and speak amicably. "The woman. Did you take her to my homestead?"

The man shook his head. "Ground was still a mite soft, so I

came on this way. Your German friend is taking her to your place tomorrow."

Panic shot through Finn, and then shame.

He had no time to dwell on it, as Mrs. Morehouse was stepping into the store from a back room. She spied the baby and reached out. "Let me have that baby. Where is your pretty little wife?"

"I—um—left her at home." The truth was more than he could bear to share.

Mrs. Morehouse's eyes widened and she chuckled. "She must be a brave woman to allow a man to bring her baby into town without her."

Finn searched for a lie. "It's washing day. The baby needed linens."

"I guess so. She needs a change right now, Mr. Tate." The woman held on to her good humor. "Gracious, she's also spit up. I hope you've brought a fresh gown."

"She does that quite a bit." Finn felt his embarrassment warm his ears. "I—must have left them in the…"

She waved him away and laughed. "Don't you worry. Your wife should have known better than to let you bring her in the first place. I have some fresh gowns and linens in the back." She glanced down at the baby. "Gracious, what was your ma thinking, to leave you with a man?"

Finn choked down a groan. He closed the distance between himself and the woman holding his child. "Give her to me."

"Oh dear." Mrs. Morehouse frowned. "I meant no offense. My comments were meant in jest alone, I assure you."

"Give her to me." Finn knew he was behaving abominably, but

he couldn't offer the explanation the woman deserved. He took his child, left his items on the counter, and walked out of the store with his wailing baby in hand.

He knew she'd spit up again. He knew she was too thin and the milk she got seemed to make her sick, but what could he do? Finn set her in the basket on the wagon seat. Climbing up beside her, he released the brake and turned the wagon toward the doctor's clinic.

Frustration filled him when he reached the office only to find a note on the door. HAD TO GO TO WILLISTON FOR SOME SUPPLIES. IF DELIVERING BABY—GO SEE MRS. JAMES. OTHERWISE, I HOPE YOU CAN WAIT. BACK IN THREE DAYS, WEATHER PERMITTING.

Finn heaved a breath and shook his head. His mind went to Rosemary. If the freighter knew what he was talking about, Rosemary would be arriving at Finn's homestead tomorrow. Well, he didn't really have a choice. The baby had to see the doc even if that meant Rosemary had to go straight back to the Fischers'. And he hoped she would.

The baby's wails had reached a fever pitch. Finn pulled out the jar of still-cool milk. He opened the top, sniffed to make sure it hadn't turned, and pulled out the feeder. He lifted her from the basket, snuggled her close, and slipped the nipple into his daughter's mouth. Her crying stopped as her stomach filled, but he knew that, within minutes, half of it would come back up. Finn sat in the wagon as the townsfolk—most of whom he'd never seen before—walked past, staring at him, curiosity in their eyes. Finn supposed he was something of a spectacle. Mrs. Morehouse hadn't mentioned his own unkempt appearance: his uncut hair, unshaven face, clothes that hadn't been washed in months. Only the need for supplies had

brought him out. That and knowing his baby girl—Rachel's baby—was much too thin for three months old. Much too small. And they wouldn't be able to see the doctor for days.

Exhaustion had weakened every muscle and dulled his senses. He had lost all ability or desire to do anything but take care of the baby, and his home reflected that. Only he hadn't cared until now.

What would Rachel's sister think of him? Everything was gone because of him, and all he had left was a sick child, a filthy home, and a wife he hadn't been able to save.

* * * * *

By the second morning after Rosemary arrived at the Fischers', the snow had completely stopped, and the temperature rose enough to start melting the blizzard's foot of snow. It was as though winter had tightened its grip for one last stand before spring won the tug-of-war and winter moved on. For the rest of the week, each day brought more melting, and by the time Rosemary had stayed a full seven days, the ground was almost ready to support a wagon without bogging down in thick mud.

Agnes had volunteered Heinrich to drive Rosemary the rest of the way to Finn and Rachel's homestead. Itching to move on, Mr. Bakker had readily accepted the offer. He was already late in making his deliveries to the general store, which was a different direction from the homestead and five miles farther. His grumbling had nearly driven them to distraction over the past week. Rosemary stayed a day longer to give the ground a chance to dry a little more before Heinrich drove her the last ten miles.

The morning dawned bright and the sun rose with blinding beauty, promising to spread its warmth as the day progressed. Eight days had now passed since that first night she'd straggled into the warm log cabin, half-frozen and wearier than she'd ever been. She had grown to love this raucous, lively family of Russian Germans more than she would have thought possible—and despite the fact that she was desperate to get to Rachel, her heart tightened at the thought of leaving Agnes, Heinrich, and the children.

To pass the time, Rosemary had helped with the children's lessons and read to them from the Bible, and at midweek, Agnes had taught Rosemary how to make apple strudel. Her first couple of attempts had been utter disappointments. But, determined, Rosemary had refused to stop until late one night, after supper was all cleaned up and the children were sound asleep. While Heinrich slept behind the curtain and Gerta slept next to him in the cradle and Mr. Bakker's snores shook the house almost as violently as the blizzard, she and Agnes sat at the table savoring warm apple strudel that she, Rosemary Jackson, had cooked from start to finish, all alone. She would never forget that special time.

But now, as much as she hated to leave her new friend, she was anxious to lay eyes on her sister again.

A weepy Agnes grabbed her and hugged her hard.

"You come back and I vill teach you to make sauerkraut and sausage."

"I promise I will. Thank you for everything," she said. "I hope to see you again very soon."

Agnes's eyes were red from tears, and she swallowed hard. "Ve will haf service ven the preacher comes, and Herr Tate vill bring

you and Rachel and the new little one." She pulled away and composed herself. "Come, children, and say goot-bye to our new friend, Fräulein Jackson."

Heinrich helped her into the wagon after all the good-byes were said. Agnes set a basket in her lap. "For lunch today. Sausage and rolls. From last night's supper." She indicated a crate in the back of the wagon. "I haf wrapped up bread, and there are two jars of jam. And strudel. Also, the gowns my Gerta is too big to wear, I send to Rachel for her new babe."

"Thank you, Agnes," she said, taking the lunch basket. "Thank you for everything."

Marta approached and held up a folded linen with beautiful embroidery. "This is for you."

Setting the basket on the seat beside her, Rosemary took the cloth, curious. Then she couldn't resist unfolding it to reveal a lovely full apron. Little flowers were stitched with delicate detail along the pocket.

"Why, Marta, your work is exceptional. What are these flowers?"

Marta's eyes lit with pleasure at the praise. "Wild roses. You will soon find them growing everywhere, and maybe you will not be so impressed."

"My Marta does beautiful vork." Agnes was so emotional already that her pride in her daughter brought on another rush of tears.

"Ah, Mama," Marta said, placing her arm about her mother's shoulders. "We will see our Rosemary again soon. Ten miles is not so far. Is it, Papa?"

"Not so far, ja. Still, we should get going; the ground is still muddy. It vill be slow." His gaze rested with affection on his wife, and then he nodded to Marta. "Take your mama into the house and make her a nice cup of tea."

"Yes, Papa."

Marta lifted a hand of farewell then turned and did as her pa had instructed. Rosemary clutched the apron to her chest. Her eyes filled, and she looked quickly away. After all, what did she have to be sad about? She would see Agnes and Marta and the other children again soon. She sniffed as her nose began to burn with the effort of staving off the tears.

Without a word, Heinrich handed her a handkerchief.

"Thank you," she whispered and dabbed at her eyes and nose.

The air still held the kind of chill that Rosemary would have considered a winter day back home, but Agnes had assured her that this was indeed spring come to the plains and she should enjoy the sun on her face even if the chill necessitated a heavy shawl. She shivered and wrapped her red shawl more firmly around her as Heinrich slapped the reins and spoke to the horses.

Heinrich wasn't much of a talker. That, combined with his need to hang on to the team as it struggled against the mud that sucked at the wheels for the first two hours, made for a silent, slow, and somewhat tense trip. The ten miles, which normally would have taken only two or three hours, dragged on until four hours had passed since they left the Fischers' home, and still they hadn't arrived at the homestead. At noon, Heinrich commanded the mules to stop near a grove of trees next to a still creek. Here, it seemed, the snow had not been as brutal. "Ve vill haf lunch now," he announced.

Glad for the opportunity to stretch her legs, Rosemary didn't wait for Heinrich to help her down from the wagon. He carried a

blanket and spread it out next to the creek. He took his food and said a quick prayer. After a few bites, Rosemary drummed up the courage to ask, "How much farther until we reach Finn and Rachel's homestead?"

He swallowed and pointed. "Very soon. Maybe thirty minutes, if the road stays not so vet."

Only a few minutes left to go and they had stopped for lunch? If Heinrich had asked her opinion before he'd stopped, Rosemary would have opted to keep going. But she wouldn't complain. She was too grateful to do anything but smile. In merely one hour she would see Rachel again. The other half of herself. She would hold her sister's child. The excitement twisting her stomach stole her appetite.

Heinrich glanced at her mostly untouched plate. "You do not like the sausages, Fräulein?" As many times as Rosemary had given him permission to use her given name, he couldn't seem to bring himself to do so. "I vill not tell Agnes." He chuckled.

"They were wonderful last night at supper, Heinrich. But I am so nervous and anxious to see Rachel, my stomach isn't feeling so well."

He nodded, cramming his last three bites into his mouth at once. "Ve go," he said around the food.

"Oh, no. Please don't hurry your lunch. I've waited this long. It's not much longer." But he had already gotten to his feet and reached down to help her up. Rosemary was so touched by his kindness, it was all she could do not to embrace him. But she knew he'd be mortified by anything more than a thank-you, so she forced herself to keep her gratitude simple.

Within minutes they were back in the wagon and moving once

more. Rosemary barely noticed the chill in the air now, or the slushy mud that sucked at the wheels and jerked the wagon as the mules strained to keep them moving forward. Rosemary forced herself to keep from jumping down and running ahead.

"Soon," she said silently, fighting back tears of joy. She would be reunited with Rachel and her family. For the first time in months, she felt as though she were truly not alone.

Chapter Three

. . . .

Finally, after what felt like hours upon hours, Heinrich lifted his arm and pointed. "There."

Rosemary followed his finger with her eyes. On the horizon a tiny house stood, forlorn and gray. The sight of such a dismal dwelling made her frown. "There?"

She kept her gaze on the horrific little soddy, already imagining the dirt floors. Why hadn't Rachel warned her? But Rosemary knew the answer. Rachel probably felt like a queen in a palace. As long as she was by Finn's side, she didn't care where she lived. Anger at Finn flared inside her. He had promised Pa that Rachel would have a proper home. Feeling Heinrich's eyes on her, she turned and met his gaze.

"It's not the sort of home I expected. She never told me." She thought again of the modern house she had left in Kansas— the same one Rachel had left only three years ago.

"A man does not feel like a man if his woman is dissatisfied with the home he is able to provide for her."

The simple statement cut deep. Heinrich clearly understood how she was feeling.

"So you're saying I shouldn't mention it?" She gave him a wry smile, knowing for certain that Rachel would never have shown Finn that she wanted more than he could give her.

His expression remained sober. "It would be kind."

"Don't worry, Heinrich. I won't hurt him." She breathed slowly to calm her wayward emotions. "But thank you for reminding me. Pa always told me I didn't need to share every thought or show every feeling. I guess I didn't learn so well."

"You are still young. You vill learn." He winked at her...and even though he had to have been at least a decade younger than Pa, the paternal gesture was so reminiscent of him that she had to quickly avert her gaze to hide a rush of tears.

The image on the horizon didn't improve as they approached. On the contrary, the sod barn and little chicken house only made things worse. There was nothing here to praise, though she'd spent the last few minutes trying desperately to formulate a positive response.

An enormous sheepdog greeted them with a series of warning barks as Heinrich halted the mules. Rosemary wondered how on earth the strange-looking dog could see through the gray fur covering its eyes. As he looked up at her his tail started to wag, and Rosemary let out a laugh. "You're not much of a watchdog, are you?" He gave her a little whine and practically vibrated off the ground while she climbed down from the wagon. She couldn't resist reaching down to pet the floppy creature.

Glancing at the house, Rosemary anticipated Rachel's appearance in the doorway and kept her gaze fixed there. Her smile turned to disappointment when the door remained closed.

"Do you suppose they're gone?" she asked, turning to Heinrich.

"It could be so. General store, maybe." He shrugged. "I do not know."

"Well..." Rosemary smiled past her disappointment. "I'll just go on in and surprise them when they get home. Do you think that would be okay?"

"You are invited. And Rachel is your sister. You are family." He gestured toward the house and absently rubbed his knuckles over the dog's head. "You vill be velcome here. Do not vorry." He jerked his head toward the back of the wagon. "You vant I should get your things?"

"Yes, please. Maybe someone is home and just hasn't heard us yet." But she doubted it. The house seemed too still. Lonely, almost. Rosemary stepped forward, the dog at her hip whining and vying for her attention. When he nudged her so hard that he made her stumble, she laughed and grabbed him on both sides of his enormous head. "Goodness, boy. You're a needy mutt." His pink tongue slipped out, but she jumped back quickly. "None of that, mister or miss, whichever the case may be."

A chuckle rumbled from Heinrich's chest as he followed her, carrying the trunk across his back. Rosemary looked at the tiny dwelling and wondered how on earth all her things would fit inside. Several more crates were being shipped and would have to be picked up in Williston once they arrived, but for now, she had only brought clothing, books, and a few items she felt might be special to Rachel. Mama's china, for one. Rachel had always loved it. Rosemary had packed it in the trunk among her clothing and quilts to keep the pieces from breaking, but she had been determined not to leave Ma's china to the mercy of the men loading the packing crates. It would have most certainly arrived in pieces.

Uncertainty stopped her at the soddy door. Rather than walk into someone's home—even her beloved sister's—unannounced, she raised her knuckles and rapped, paused and then rapped again.

"Fräulein..." Heinrich's tone sounded strained under the weight of the trunk.

"I'm sorry," she breathed, reaching for the handle. Straightening her shoulders, she slowly pushed the door open and walked inside.

Rosemary gasped. "This is not... It can't be Rachel's home," she choked out.

Fear filled her, turning every muscle hot and cold and weakening her limbs. The little sod home was untidy at best. The bed was not made, dishes were piled up and filthy, filling the room with the stench of rotting food. Dirty clothing was strewn about. A cradle in the corner made her groan. What had happened here? Where were Rachel and Finn and their child? The images running through her mind brought terror to her heart.

Heinrich cleared his throat. "I should take the trunk back to the wagon, Fräulein?" he asked gently.

Rosemary shook her head. "I can't imagine what is happening here, but the animals are being cared for. Or the cow and chickens seem fine anyway." And the dog. Although he might have been catching rabbits or prairie dogs.

"These are Rachel's things." She pointed to the floor next to the bed. "She brought that rug from our house. Papa gave it to her from Mama's parlor. She would never have left it."

"I vould not vish to frighten you, Fräulein, but there are bad men who vould…"

"No!" She spun around. "Don't say anything else, Heinrich. Just put my things next to the door. I will make this place livable, and when Rachel and Finn get home, they'll have a perfectly reasonable explanation for why the house is in such disarray."

His chest heaved from the exertion of carrying her trunk, but even though he was out of breath, his tone left no doubt as to his resolve. "Fräulein, I cannot leave you here alone. It may be dangerous."

Rosemary had enough resolve of her own to not be intimidated by a strong man, even if she knew deep down that she should go back to Agnes and leave a note for Finn and Rachel as to her whereabouts. Finn would come for her. But as she looked around, she knew she'd never be able to bring herself to leave Rachel's home. She could not walk away without knowing what had happened here. "I'm not going anywhere, Heinrich." Raising her chin, she looked up and shot him a glare she hoped conveyed her determination. "If you try to take me by force, it will be kidnapping and that's illegal."

He shook his head, silently condemning her decision. "I vill go to bring the rest of your things."

"Thank you, Heinrich."

She didn't know why Rachel's home was in such a state, but Rosemary had no intention of leaving it the way she'd found it. If, God forbid, something terrible had occurred, she would know soon enough. If the explanation were less fearsome, the little soddy still needed to be scoured.

But where to start? She looked about, organizing her thoughts around the mess as she prayed frantically for her sister's safety and for speedy understanding of why she had discovered the place in such disarray.

The washtub sat on the floor, filled with dirty dishes. *Always a good place to start,* she decided. Rosemary emptied it and looked around. There was no kitchen pump, so there would have to be a well or at least a creek nearby. She thought of the creek where she and Heinrich had eaten lunch and hoped to goodness that it wasn't Rachel and Finn's water source.

She slung her shawl about her shoulders, preparing herself for the enormous task at hand. Grabbing the washtub, she headed out the door, glad to be leaving the putrid air inside the closed-up little one-room home.

Standing in the yard, she looked for the well, assuming Finn had even dug one. So much around here looked dismal and undone. That wasn't like Finn. Back in Kansas, he'd been the best of all Pa's hands. Why hadn't he done more to make his homestead livable?

Rosemary thought back to Rachel's letter telling her to come when Pa passed on. Just where Rachel had expected her to sleep, Rosemary couldn't imagine. Gracious, there was barely enough room for one person to live, let alone three adults and an infant. There was nowhere to even hang a curtain for privacy like the Fischers had in their cabin.

Heinrich met her as he was coming back from the wagon with the two remaining bags and the basket of apple strudel. The remaining sausages he tossed to the dog.

"Have you seen the well?"

"It is behind the barn, Fräulein."

Rosemary smiled and started to walk in that direction.

"Vait. I vill get the water for you. " He glanced at the tub and shook his head. "Ve find bucket. It vill perhaps be in the kitchen."

Feeling foolish, Rosemary nodded, her face warming. "We had a pump in the kitchen back home." She shrugged. "I never had to draw my own water."

He patted her shoulder as he walked by. "Bring the tub back into the house and ve can fill with vater. Two, maybe three times from vell."

And she had thought she could run Pa's ranch, had he left it to her? She didn't even know how to draw water to fill a tub of dishwater.

Heinrich carried the tub back inside. Rosemary located the bucket on the floor and picked it up, sloshing putrid water onto her skirt. She wrinkled her nose as she handed the bucket to Heinrich. "I don't know what's in there, but it's pretty nasty."

"I vash it fine. Do not vorry."

She watched him go, grateful he was there to take care of the water, then unbuttoned each sleeve at the wrist and folded her sleeves up to her elbows, bracing herself for her extensive task ahead.

The counter was so cluttered with dirty dishes that the first thing she did was stack the small wooden table with all the dishes that would fit. The pots she stacked under the table.

"It isn't as though the dirt floor is going to get scratched," she muttered to herself. She found some soap shavings and, with a dirty knife, shaved them even smaller into the tub.

Heinrich came in with the bucket and dumped fresh well water into the tub. "You will not heat the vater?"

"I'd rather," Rosemary admitted. "But all the pots are dirty. I'll have to scrub at least one of them first." She stopped for a breath and looked around. How could anyone possibly live here?

The task ahead seemed greater than the amount of strength she possessed, but she hadn't been taught to quit. She would work until no strength remained, rest, and then start again. Rosemary worked the soap until it dissolved, and by the time Heinrich returned with the second bucket of water, she was ready to tackle the mountain of dishes.

She glanced at Heinrich as he dumped the bucket and noticed with a start that his face was paler than usual and his eyes were watering. "Heinrich?" Rosemary said, alarm beginning to build. "What is it?"

"Fräulein," he said in a subdued tone, "you must sit down before I speak of vat I haf discovered."

Fear clutched at her heart, clenching her stomach and weakening her knees until she had no choice but to sit in one of the chairs by the table. "What is it? N—not Rachel?" She barely whispered the dreaded words.

"I feel so sorry that I must inform you, Fräulein—there is a grave with a marker. I do not read English goot, so I cannot say vat is the vords."

Rosemary couldn't bear to hear his halting words any longer. She jumped to her feet. "Show me, Heinrich. Just show me what has you so upset." Without waiting for him to lead the way, she rushed out the door toward the well, ignoring his cries. "Fräulein, vait! You should not go alone."

But it was too late. She ran a few yards past the well and came to a sudden stop. A wooden marker was half-buried in the ground.

Tears stung her eyes. She knew. Deep down, she knew who rested in the grave. Dropping to her knees, she slowly raised her gaze and read.

1875–1895
Rachel Tate
Beloved wife and mother

Rosemary fell across her sister's grave. Deep, guttural sobs exploded from her.

"Rachel!" she screamed as the pain grew too unbearable for one human heart to handle. "Rachel!" Her sister's smile taunted her as an apparition in the deepest recesses of her mind. Every smile, every laugh, every tear. Every whispered dream and heartbreak shared in secret—they all paraded through her memory until she thought she might go insane.

Agony wrenched the cries from her throat, and when she had no more voice, she cried silently until the tears stopped flowing altogether.

Chapter Four

·····················

Rosemary lay across her sister's grave for what seemed like hours. She had no will to move, not even when she heard Heinrich speaking to the animals.

Spent, weary, sick at heart, she began to think about Rachel's child and husband. A sense of responsibility for those Rachel had loved weighed upon her heart.

Finn obviously hadn't left for good. He had allowed the house to become uninhabitable by all standards of decency, but beyond that, it was just a matter of waiting for him to return from wherever he had gone. Then she would confront him with the condition of his home. There was no grave marker for a baby and no mention of a child on Rachel's marker. Considering those facts, and the soiled baby things she'd found inside, Rosemary could only surmise that the baby had lived.

Despite all the uncertainty surrounding her new lot in life, there was one thing she knew without question: her sister would expect her to make sure the baby was cared for. Pulling herself up from the earth, she felt strong arms raise her to her feet. "Thank you, Heinrich," she barely managed through a swollen throat. He handed her the handkerchief she had returned to him earlier.

"Let's get you back into the vagon, Fräulein. I take you back to Agnes. She vill know how to make you feel better."

"Oh, Heinrich, I'm not going anywhere. How can I?" Rosemary's lungs shuddered as she tried to remember what a normal breath felt like. "I have to be here for my sister's baby. When Finn gets back, we'll decide what is best. It's the least I can do for Rachel."

Heinrich looked conflicted. "I must leave soon, to tend my own chores at home. Please, you should return with me. My Agnes, she vill holler, 'Vhy did you not bring Fräulein back with you, Heinrich? You are a fool man vith no brains.' "

He looked so forlorn, Rosemary couldn't help but smile.

"Tell her I'm the one without brains and that I refused to return with you."

He shook his head, but Rosemary knew he was resigned. "She vill not believe me."

"I will be fine if you'll help me split some wood before you go?"

"This I haf done while you…" His voice trailed off and he glanced toward Rachel's grave.

For the first time, Rosemary noticed the smell of smoke. "You built a fire already?"

He nodded.

His thoughtfulness brought another rush of tears to her eyes. "Thank you, Heinrich. I'll be fine from here on. Even if Finn doesn't return for a couple of days, I can make do. I have the strudel and the bread and jam your dear wife sent. The cow will give me milk, and there are chickens for eggs."

Heinrich still frowned, but he gathered a breath and exhaled,

lifting his shoulders. Clearly, the man wasn't convinced by her reassurance.

"I have more than enough work to keep me busy for quite some time." She stepped inside the house as if to prove her point. "Don't you agree?"

"Ja. There is much vork to do here. But you should not be alone, Fräulein. It is not safe." He frowned. "Do you haf a gun?"

Rosemary hadn't even considered protection, but now that Heinrich brought it up, she nodded. "I have Pa's six-shooters in my trunk and plenty of bullets."

"Please, get them before I go. I vish to be assured they are goot."

After Heinrich had inspected the pearl-handled pistols and assured himself that they were loaded and ready to protect her from harm, he reluctantly headed outside. Rosemary followed him to his wagon. She would keep her chin up and not dissolve into the tears that threatened.

"You vill make me promise, ja?"

"Not until I know what it is." She smiled.

"If Herr Tate does not return in one veek, you get horse from the barn and come back to Agnes and me."

She hated to admit it, but if Finn didn't return within a week, it most likely meant he wasn't coming back. With this in mind, Rosemary agreed. "I promise."

He patted her shoulder awkwardly and nodded. "Goot," he said, climbing onto the wagon seat. He gathered up the reins and looked down at her. "Perhaps Agnes, she vill not take the broom to my back for leaving you alone." He winked.

She watched him leave, vaguely aware of the dog sitting at her feet, his body pressed tightly against her thigh. Absently she reached down and scratched his head. "Well, boy, I guess I'd better get busy. That pigsty isn't going to clean itself."

After three hours of backbreaking work, she stopped long enough to take a loaf of bread from the basket Agnes had sent. She eyed the strudel but couldn't bring herself to enjoy a treat while she mourned Rachel. After a quick meal of bread and milk, she returned to work. At dusk, she took the oil lamp from the stove. She had just replaced the globe when the dog's barking alerted her. She grabbed a pistol in one hand and the lamp in the other and stepped outside.

A man had dismounted and held his horse by the reins, walking it toward the barn.

"Hold it!" she called out. "Step into the light of the lamp."

Even in the twilight, she could see him raise his hands. "No need to be afraid," he called. "What are you doing in the Tates' homestead?"

"That's my business," she said, keeping her eyes on the approaching form. "That's far enough. I can see your face now." And that's all she needed to see. Pa had taught her that a man's intention always showed in his eyes before he made a move.

The man's eyes narrowed and his chin jutted forward. Then his jaw dropped. "Miz Tate? But how can that... It ain't possible. Is it?"

At least that clued Rosemary in that he probably wasn't a threat. "Mrs. Tate was my sister. I've just arrived today from Kansas."

"Oh, I'm sorry. But she..." His gaze slid toward the grave.

"I know." Rosemary's voice was still hoarse, but she had found Rachel's stash of tea and honey and was starting to regain a little volume. "I saw the marker." She tucked the pistol inside the band of her skirt. "My name is Rosemary Jackson. And you are?"

"Silas Freeman. I'm Finn's neighbor."

"Can you tell me what happened to my sister, Silas? And where are her husband and the child?"

Apparently realizing she wasn't going to shoot him, Silas relaxed. His eyes showed his sadness. "The wife and I thought a lot of Rachel. She just never got strong again after the baby came. I don't know the whole story, but the weather was too bad for Doc Richards or one of the women to help when the time came. Finn did the best he could, but not long after the baby came, Miz Tate got a high fever and it just never went away."

Rosemary's lips trembled as she fought back tears. "When was that?"

"Couple, maybe three months back. I'm real sorry, ma'am. It must have been hard to come up on the place like this—not knowin' and all."

If only she had been here for Rachel, perhaps she would have lived. She gathered a deep breath to compose herself then looked Mr. Freeman in the eyes. "Where are Finn and my sister's child?"

Silas shrugged. "I don't know, ma'am—er—miss. I'm sorry, but you look just like her."

"Yes, I know. And it's 'miss.' But if you're here, I assume it's because Finn asked you to feed the animals and tend his chores?"

"That's exactly right." He shoved his thumb toward the east. "My homestead is yonder, connected to this one. I expected he'd be back by tonight. I came by because I needed to speak with him."

"Finn is blessed to have such good neighbors close by."

"We filed our claims within a couple days of each other. My missus was close to Miz Tate." He shook his head. "I was sure hopin' to find Finn back here, though. Annie is hankerin' to pull up stakes and head back to Missouri."

"You mean sell out?" Rosemary had been raised by a rancher always looking to acquire more grazing land. The fact that a man was leaving 160 acres meant there was that much land for the taking.

"Your sister's passing hit her real hard. You see, she's havin' her first baby too, and now she's afraid that..." He averted his gaze, clearly uncomfortable with the subject and maybe a little afraid himself of the uncertainty of childbirth.

Rosemary set the lantern on the ground in front of the door. "I understand."

"Anyway, I might have to leave for a few days to take care of business, but I can't leave Finn's chores unattended after I told him I'd look after things."

"Well, you don't have to worry about that. I'm perfectly capable of milking a cow and feeding a horse and stealing eggs from chickens."

Even in the dim light of a waning sun, Rosemary recognized the relief that crossed his face. "I'd be obliged."

"May I be so bold as to ask—are you planning to sell the land?"

He scowled. "We still have two years left before we prove up, so it ain't really ours. I guess it never will be now."

Rosemary stifled a gasp. "But would you really leave, then? You must have cleared a lot of the land and..." She couldn't even fathom the choice this man was contemplating. One hundred sixty acres of land for nothing more than to live on the property for five years and building a home... It just seemed foolish to squander three years of hard work and living. Women had been having babies since the

beginning of time. The very idea irritated her to no end. What sort of foolish wife did he have at home?

"I might not have a choice." He frowned. "A man can't just turn his back on his wife. She's seen an awful lot of hardship and says she don't think she'll want to raise her family up here."

An idea began to form in Rosemary's mind, and she thought of the bank draft she carried for Rachel and Finn. Now that the baby had come, Finn had an heir. If he wanted to prosper the way her pa had prospered and leave something to his child, he would need more land than he currently homesteaded. She glanced up at Mr. Freeman. "So I take it you'd just pack up, lock, stock, and barrel. Is that right?"

His gaze narrowed. "Why do you ask?"

She shrugged. "Maybe Finn would buy you out and expand his property. You said it was just the homestead over, right? He could lease the land from you during the next two years, and when it's yours he could buy it outright."

He twisted his hat between his hands and shifted from one leg to the other. "I don't know, miss. That might not be right."

Right? Was this man daft? She was suggesting a way he could profit from leaving, keep his wife happy, and allow Finn the opportunity to expand his homestead. "Well, surely you wouldn't want to leave the fruits of all your hard work to some stranger who might do who knows what with it, would you? And why should Finn have to wait a full five years to own the land if you're willing to lease it to him in the meantime?"

A frown creased the farmer's brow, and he cleared his throat. "I reckon whatever business happens between me and Finn is our business."

Pasting on a smile, Rosemary nodded. Manly pride was setting in. She could see it a mile off. It was the same pride that had stopped her pa from handing over the ranch to her and instead selling it to the neighboring ranch. The only way to assuage a ruffled male ego was to be the soft-spoken woman that made him feel good about himself. "Of course you're right. Any business you have with Finn should be between the two of you, Mr. Freeman." She reached for the door. "I'll let you get to the chores so you can get on home to your Annie."

"It was mighty nice to meet you," Silas said, tipping his hat.

"Likewise." As he turned, she called after him. "Mr. Freeman? Have you ever tried apple strudel?"

"Only when the preacher comes through. The German women make it for the gatherings."

"Well, it just so happens that I've learned to make it from Frau Fischer. And I have some with me. Can I interest you in a slice?"

"Well...I don't know...."

"Please, it's the least I can do for the kind neighbor who was willing to do his own chores and then come by and do another man's as well."

Mr. Freeman smiled. "Well, it's my pleasure to help out ol' Finn, but if you insist, I'd be pleased to accept."

"Fine. Come and knock on the door when you're finished with the chores and I'll have plenty wrapped up for you to take home to your wife."

"Thank you, ma'am—I mean, miss. Sorry again."

"Please don't think anything of it."

Rosemary watched him walk toward the barn, her mind racing with possibilities. It wasn't that she'd want the couple to lose

their home without good reason. But if Mrs. Freeman had a desire to leave and her husband was willing to let her do it, then opportunity was presenting itself. And Pa had taught her long ago that one never passed up a good opportunity—at least not in business. The least she could do for Rachel was to look after the interests of her child, and that was precisely what she intended to do.

Chapter Five

....

Finn Tate knew he had no business bringing his baby girl back home. He had set out to go home after learning that Rosemary was coming, but the more he thought about his sick baby girl and the state of his house, the more he realized that the best thing he could do for Sarah would be to find her a good home with a ma who would love her the way Rachel would have. And he'd intended to do just that, as soon as the doctor examined his Sarah and assured him she would be all right.

He'd gotten them an inexpensive room over the saloon and had taken her to see the doctor that morning—actually, he had taken her for the past four days, each day expecting the doctor's return. But the doctor had had unexpected difficulty with his wagon, and the three-day trip had lengthened into a week-long ordeal. And by the time the doctor encouraged him to keep trying to get the milk down her and pray she grew to tolerate it better, Finn realized he couldn't let go of his little girl. He just couldn't do it. Not his Sarah Rose, his beautiful little girl, named for his mother and Rosemary.

That was another chore he had put off—writing a letter to Rachel's sister. He'd never really liked Rosemary that much. For all she looked like Rachel, the sisters couldn't have been more different. Rosemary had a habit of saying whatever came to mind, and if she didn't say it out loud, the expression on her face told a person exactly what she thought. He figured she'd be giving him an earful as soon as he saw her again.

If she had gone to the homestead that day as the freighter had indicated, she most likely would have turned straight around and gone back to the Fischers' home. He'd have to drive over there in a few days and tell her about Rachel. Let her see Sarah and send her back to Kansas or anywhere she chose. Anywhere but here. He couldn't bear to see her face every day and think of his wife.

Rachel was like a soft rose with gentle ways and quiet demeanor, while Rosemary was more like the wild roses that grew between the rocks and in the rough ground. But as much as he had not been looking forward to Rosemary coming to live with them after their pa finally passed on, Finn would have gladly endured her presence for the rest of his life to keep Rachel by his side. Wishing and regretting held no power to bring his wife back. The most he could do now was go back to the homestead and try to raise his daughter the way Rachel would have wanted.

At the fence marking the Freemans' property, Finn thought he might stop by and have a word with Silas, to find out how the animals were faring and to let Silas know he had returned, but the thought of facing anyone right now just seemed to require more effort than he had strength for.

He reached into the basket and felt the warm little body beneath the hand-stitched quilt. Sarah Rose squirmed a little at his touch. Love swelled inside of him until it threatened to burst through his

chest. He'd begun the ride home determined that he would be the best pa Sarah could have. The pa she deserved. As his mind wandered to home, shame filled him.

The soddy.

Rachel had kept the place spotless despite dirt floors and walls. She had added rugs and little hangings on the wall and crocheted coverlets for the chair. A tablecloth for the table. She loved the summer's wild roses that bloomed all over the fields. Knowing how she loved them, Finn had made sure a bouquet graced the table all summer long each of the three years they'd homesteaded.

Now, he never wanted to see another wild rose as long as he lived. And that included Rosemary.

As he neared the homestead, the sun was almost completely hidden, and the dusk that had fallen a few minutes earlier had surrendered to the approaching darkness. He frowned as a plume of smoke curled from the chimney. At first his heart did a funny little leap. He pictured his beloved wife with supper on the table for him and a warm cup of coffee with sugar, just the way he liked it. But he shoved away the dream as reality presented itself. Someone had made herself at home in his house. Apparently Rosemary hadn't hightailed it back to the Fischers' after all.

The smell of meat cooking and freshly baked bread tempted his stomach, reminding him that he hadn't eaten since the cold beans he'd attempted to swallow down sometime around noon. The cost of renting a room above the saloon for the week, plus buying milk for Sarah from folks in town, had left very little for food.

The door swung open, and Rosemary appeared in the doorway carrying a lantern and a pistol.

"Is that you, Mr. Freeman?"

"No. It's not." His breath caught as he recognized the soft face, the small but curvy frame, the silky dark hair that he could almost feel between his fingers even though it was upswept at present.... His mind swam a little. She looked so much like Rachel.

"Finn? It's you? Thank God you've come back. I've been here for almost a week, and I was beginning to despair that you'd ever return. As a matter of fact, I was planning to borrow your horse in the morning and go back to the Fischers'."

Carrying the basket containing his daughter, Finn walked cautiously toward the woman. Clarity was beginning to break through the confusion. "Rosemary." He should have known she wouldn't let a little thing like a filthy house and no owner keep her from making herself at home.

"Yes," she said softly. "I can only imagine how you must feel seeing me like this, looking so much like..."

No! everything inside of him screamed. *Don't say her name!*

"So," he said, brushing past her and entering the house, "you finally arrived." He set Sarah's basket on the table, noting immediately that not only did the house smell of something wonderful cooking in the oven, but Rosemary had cleaned it from top to bottom. It looked like Rachel's home once more.

"Yes," she said, her tone cautious. "Like I said, I arrived here a week ago. And a week before that I met the Fischers and was forced to impose upon their hospitality until the snow stopped and melted enough for Mr. Fischer to bring me here." As she spoke, her gaze had settled on the basket, and she inched closer to the baby. "Is this...?"

"Her name is Sarah Rose."

"Oh." The sound caught in her throat. She started to reach out but pulled back, turning to him. "May I hold her?"

As much as he wanted to rail against the unfairness of another woman holding his daughter when Rachel would never hold her again, he gave a jerky nod. "Did you milk the cow? Sarah's going to need to eat soon. There are baby feeders...." He frowned, looking about. He had no idea where they might be now that the place was clean.

"It's okay, Finn," she said, reaching inside the basket. "I cleaned them and put them away. And yes, I have a jar of milk outside staying cool."

"We have a cold cellar," he said. Did she think he hadn't done anything right by her sister?

"Yes, I found it. That's where I got the venison roast in the oven. From the looks of that cellar, there's enough smoked meat to last another month. Rachel mentioned what a fine hunter you are in one of her letters."

Hearing praise that had come from Rachel nearly did him in. So he had hunted well? Had been able to give her a proper home? Had kept her alive? He never should have taken her from Kansas. If he'd only done as Mr. Jackson wanted him to and agreed to stay on and run the ranch—eventually owning half when he passed on. Rachel would still be alive, and he would have means to provide for his family and Rosemary.

"She's not very big for two months, is she?"

"She's three months." Finn's defenses rose. Was she implying that he didn't know how to feed his daughter?

Rosemary frowned. "That's even smaller, then."

The concern in her voice matched the concern in Finn's heart. He shoved his fingers through his unruly hair. "She can't keep much milk down."

"Have you taken her to the doctor?"

"That's why I wasn't here sooner. He's been gone all week. I had to wait for him." He read the question in her eyes as she snuggled Sarah. "I thought I was overfeeding her and that's why she was throwing it up. I've never been around babies, Rosemary. I didn't know she wasn't eating enough."

Sarah nestled into Rosemary's arms, gave a sigh, and settled back into a peaceful sleep. Visibly moved, Rosemary's lips began to tremble. "She's so beautiful."

"Looks like her ma."

Rosemary turned to Finn, a hint of a smile touching her lips. "She looks like her pa too."

He couldn't take the sight of her anymore. Not looking like Rachel, sounding like Rachel, smiling like Rachel. "I'd best go take care of the wagon and get to the chores."

"The chores are done for the night." She kept her eyes focused on the baby. "But if you want to unhitch the wagon and take care of the horses, I'll have your supper on when you get back inside."

He hated the way she sounded. As if she belonged here, cooking at Rachel's stove, holding Rachel's baby. It wasn't right, her taking over.

"The baby probably needs to be changed."

Rosemary smiled, and when she looked at him, Finn noted how her eyes were bright with unshed tears. "Yes, I'll need a change too, I'm afraid. We're both soaked."

"I'll go and take care of the horses."

Outside, he gathered in a deep breath of fresh, cleansing air, trying to wrap his head around the new situation. It hadn't occurred to him that Rosemary might stay at his homestead. Not in the condition he had left it a week ago. But now that she was here, he had no idea how they were supposed to stay together without compromising her reputation.

He couldn't live in the barn. And he couldn't live in the house with her. That wasn't proper. The only thing that made sense was for Rosemary to just leave.

But he knew he would be in for a fight. Rosemary was stubborn. She wouldn't want to go, even if he told her to. The fact that she'd come meant Mr. Jackson had passed away, so she had nowhere else to go. Rachel had mourned her pa for months, knowing he was ill and she couldn't go to him. Finn knew the only consolation for his wife had been in knowing that her sister would soon join them. But what about Rosemary? Her pa and her sister were both gone. She had no other family. None but him and the baby.

He expelled a weighted breath as he moved toward the wagon. He didn't have to wonder what Rachel would expect of him. She would expect him to be nice to Rosemary and keep her close by— for Sarah's sake, if for no other reason. But how on earth could he do that?

The answer hit him. He could marry her. But the thought was ludicrously insane and immediately began a war inside him.

No. No, he couldn't marry her. He'd never marry again.

But it would be the proper thing to do.

But everything in him recoiled from the idea. Marry another woman? He shuddered at the very thought of it.

No rang loud and strong in his head, and he knew he couldn't do it. The pain of Rachel's death was too raw. His heart couldn't bear the idea of bringing another woman into Rachel's home to care for Rachel's child. Even if Rosemary was the one woman Rachel would have wanted for him.

But there had to be an alternative. Some way to satisfy Rachel's expectations. His mind traveled through the possibilities, every argument he could construct, as he unhitched the horses. He knew Rosemary needed a home. But why did he have to be the one to provide that home?

He looked up into the starlit sky, wondering if, somewhere up there, Rachel looked down on him. She'd be sorely disappointed at the mess he'd made of everything in life, when she had worked so hard to make it good and proper.

Even now, he could almost hear her soft voice speaking to him, reminding him of the night she'd begged him to find Sarah a good mama. *"A little girl needs a ma, Finn,"* she'd said. *"Rosie and I were almost grown when our ma died, but oh, how we missed and needed her. Pa tried to fill in the pieces for us, but no man can be a mother."*

"I can't do it, honey," he spoke into the vast darkness.

She had lain on her bed, pale and so very thin and weak. *"Rosemary has no one. The two of you would get on well, I think."* She had shuddered a sigh and bit her lip before going on. *"Perhaps it would be an adjustment; you're both so stubborn."*

He'd refused to let her speak any more about it. Refused to even consider the possibility that she wouldn't recover.

He could almost hear her soft voice telling him to marry Rosemary.

"Don't be mad at me, Rachel. I promise I'll take good care of Sarah, and I'll do my best by your sister. But don't ask me to marry another woman. There'll never be anyone for me except you."

The sky remained silent as he brushed down the horses and spread hay in the trough. He grabbed the quilts from the wagon and headed to the barn. He knew Rosemary expected him inside for supper, but he couldn't bring himself to go back and face her. She would undoubtedly want to discuss Rachel's death, Sarah's inability to keep milk down—and perhaps marriage had crossed her mind as well. He simply couldn't face it tonight.

He made a pallet in the farthest corner of the sod barn and stretched out, staring at the ceiling and trying to forget about his rumbling stomach. An hour passed. He was just about to shove down his pride and go to the house when the barn door opened. Rosemary entered, carrying a plate. Relief and dread washed over him.

"I thought you might be hungry," she said. "Sarah's all taken care of and sound asleep in her cradle. I hope you don't think I'm overstepping with her, but I diluted the milk with warm water and a little sugar. She took it fine and only spit up a little."

He nodded, letting her words bring some peace to his over-wrought nerves. "Thank you for caring for her. And for thinking of me."

"It's your food. All I did was cook it," she said, handing him the plate and a cup. "And your coffee." She smiled. "You used to drink it with sugar. I hope you still do."

"That's right. It's good of you to remember."

"My memory is one of my talents. Pa always said so."

"I take it he passed on?" He held his plate and set his cup on the ground next to him but didn't take a bite. It seemed insensitive to fill his stomach when Rosemary's eyes were filled with pain.

"Yes," she whispered. "You didn't receive my letter?"

"I haven't gone to the post office since…" He shrugged. "Why didn't you inherit the ranch? Rachel said your pa would never pass it on to you, but I thought surely he would."

"Rachel knew Pa well." Her face darkened, and she shrugged too. "Pa wanted a man running it. If you'd been there, he'd have left it to you and Rachel."

He heard the unspoken accusation. "And Rachel wouldn't be dead." Would there come a day when he didn't feel guilt over everything, past and present?

"I'm sorry." She gestured to his plate. "Please go ahead and eat. I know you must be famished."

"I am." The venison roast was the best thing he'd had to eat in as long as he could remember, and even that thought made him feel guilty. Rachel had been a wonderful housekeeper, but her cooking skills had left something to be desired. She'd lamented the burned dinners and undercooked breakfasts, coffee that was never quite right, and bread that didn't rise. Rachel was always looking to the horizon…dreaming.

Lost in thought, he hadn't noticed that Rosemary had made her way back to the door until she spoke. "If you are still hungry after that, come get more. I won't be sleeping for a while, so you won't disturb me."

"I'm obliged. I didn't realize how hungry I was." He sipped coffee to wash down a mouthful of bread.

"Rachel would want me to look after you and Sarah. She would do the same for me if it were the other way around."

Without waiting for his response, she ducked out of the barn, leaving Finn to wrestle with her words.

* * * * *

Rosemary's stomach quivered as she walked back into the soddy. There were so many things on her mind, so many words she wanted to say to Finn, but her brain refused to formulate even one of them.

She closed the door behind her and, as if pulled by a rope, she was drawn to the baby's cradle. Her heart rose to a height of love she'd never expected was possible, let alone felt. And as far as feelings went, this one had somehow evaded her for all her twenty years. To be sure, she had loved her ma and pa and Rachel, but this feeling was altogether different.

Kneeling beside the cradle, she thumbed a trail along the silky hair at the nape of Sarah's tiny neck. Oh, how Rachel would have loved this baby. She had always been the one to nurture kittens and calves. Any baby of any species Rachel considered hers to mother. It didn't seem fair that she should be gone before she could experience the joy of watching this incredible little creature grow into womanhood.

A rush of tears filled her eyes and spilled over. "How am I going to watch over her for you? We can't share this one room, Rach." But she knew Finn needed someone to watch over him. Someone to help put the pieces of himself back together. She hadn't realized how much he'd loved her sister until she started the process of cleaning up the soddy. Rachel's death might have destroyed him completely if not for baby Sarah. And now the baby was sick too.

"Please, God," she prayed as she looked down at her tiny niece, "show me what to do. How will I take care of Finn and watch over Sarah?"

Her mind raced to the land Mr. Freeman was about to desert. Had the two men spoken yet? She had wanted to bring it up in the barn, but her proximity to her sister's husband was disconcerting. She, who had never even been courted, stood a mere two feet from the man she had secretly watched for two months after he signed on to work at the ranch.

When Rachel rushed into their bedroom with her face ablaze and eyes bright, looking more beautiful than Rosemary had ever seen her, she knew Finn's attentions had not turned her direction but her sister's. That instant, Rosemary had put away all romantic notions of Finn Tate.

But the memory of her childish dreams of marriage to him filled her with shame.

She could go back to the Fischers' until she decided what to do. But how could she possibly watch over Sarah if she was as far away as a half-day's ride by wagon? Besides, their cabin was full as it was. She couldn't ask Heinrich and Agnes to make room for her.

The door opened, and she turned to find Finn standing there and holding his plate, looking like a little boy caught with a stolen pie. "I should have knocked."

"Don't be silly." She stood, casting a last glance at the baby. "It's your home. Besides, I needed to get busy. I could sit beside her cradle and do nothing but look at her for hours."

A hint of a smile touched his lips, and his expression softened. Rosemary caught her breath as his gaze trailed to his daughter. The tenderness in his eyes reflected her own heart. He turned to her as though hearing her unspoken thoughts. "She's something else, isn't she?"

"She's beautiful." Feeling exposed, she averted her gaze to the dishes he carried. "I haven't cleared supper yet. There's plenty more if you're still hungry."

"I wouldn't turn it down."

"Will you sit and eat at the table?" She took his proffered plate. "I'll bring the coffeepot."

Her stomach dipped as he moved past her in the cramped space. She hadn't seen Finn since he'd married Rachel and left immediately for Dakota Territory. Right now, he was sorely in need of a bath, a shave, and a haircut, but somehow she had to forgive his untidy appearance. The fact that he was this distraught over Rachel's death almost made her love him more. No, not love. It couldn't be love.

Shame filled her as she recognized the truth—her feelings hadn't changed for him one bit. Shame. Shame on her. A silent prayer poured from her heart. *Please don't let Rachel know I care for her husband in this manner.*

"Have you eaten?" Finn's voice broke through her traitorous thoughts. "I don't see another plate out."

Spearing a slice of venison roast onto the plate in her hand, she shook her head. She spooned juice from the pan over the meat and lifted the plate of bread in her other hand.

"I'll wait for you," he said as she set his meal in front of him.

It would have been foolish to argue. "If you want me to."

"Of course." He cleared his throat. "As long as we're sharing a meal, we may as well go ahead and discuss your plans."

Ah, so that was it. He was being cordial in an effort to get rid of her. The thought stung and, though she hated to admit it, angered her a little, after the week she'd spent cleaning up the pigsty he'd made of her sister's home. Now without appetite, she looked at her filled plate and knew she wouldn't eat any of it. Grabbing the coffee-pot as she turned, she went wordlessly to the table, poured coffee into his cup, then set the pot back on the stove, before taking the other chair across from him.

She hated to admit that the last thing she felt right now was thankful, but she folded her hands without allowing her elbows to touch the table. "Would you care to say the blessing?" she asked around the anger tightening her throat.

He hesitated, which made Rosemary wonder if he felt the same way she did. "I'd be pleased to."

"Lord," he prayed, "we thank You for…" He hesitated again, long enough that Rosemary glanced up. His eyes were on her. He shook his head. "If you want to say a prayer, I'll be reverent. But I can't just now."

Rosemary nodded. She closed her eyes. "We thank You for the meal before us, God. And we give thanks for Sarah." And because to thank Him for anything else right now seemed pretentious, she said, "Amen."

Chapter Six

....

The awkward silence between them seemed almost ridiculous, considering they were kin. Staring at Rosemary now, he couldn't help but think of Rachel. The two sisters, though the spitting image of each other, were as different inwardly as two pebbles from a brook. Always the responsible one of the two, Rosemary had helped her pa on the ranch, while Rachel had preferred to read dime novels—though she had sworn him to secrecy about those—and Lord Tennyson. Rachel surmised that their differences lay in the fact that, although born the same night, Rosemary arrived thirty minutes earlier. And she'd always taken on the role of older sibling…as silly as that sounded.

Somewhere deep down, she must have believed her pa would leave her the ranch, for Rosemary gave her thoughts to man's business and wasn't shy about sharing what was on her mind even when she disagreed. And her pa mostly agreed with her. Finn had been on the receiving end of that humiliation more than once. And though he had to admit that time usually proved her right, he still wasn't too keen on being outwitted by a woman.

Rachel, on the other hand, wanted nothing more than to become a proper wife and mother. She had made him happy, except for her lack of cooking skills, but he was willing to allow his stomach to suffer for the joy of living with his delicate flower.

How Rosemary had ever become so proficient in the kitchen when she spent so much time on the range with the men, he couldn't imagine. But the proof was nearly scraped from his plate for a second time.

He realized he had been comparing the two women since he'd arrived home and found his sister-in-law, but how could he not? They looked so much alike, his heart ached—and yet this woman sitting across from him could no more be Rachel than he could.

"More?"

Rosemary's voice pulled him out of his thoughts and he wondered, with surprise, what he'd done to indicate that he'd welcome a bit more of the food. "If it's not too much trouble."

"No trouble at all." She stood, and he handed her his plate. "More coffee?"

He nodded. "Thank you."

When she had filled his cup and plate again, she took her seat once more.

"You're not eating?" he asked, pointing to her plate with his fork.

"My eyes must have been bigger than my stomach." She folded her hands on the table and leveled her gaze with his. "Finn, you said we should discuss my plans."

He could have kicked himself. So that was why she wasn't eating. He'd upset her. "We don't have to talk about it tonight, if you'd rather not. I don't think anyone would start talking if I stay in the barn for a couple of nights. You're kin, after all, and my closest neighbors are good friends."

"We're not blood kin." She sighed. "And people care more than you might think."

He put down his fork and returned her sober gaze. "I know you came all this way expecting to find your sister alive and well and ready to welcome you into our home."

Tears sprang to her eyes, and Finn inwardly chided himself for just coming right out and saying the words like that. He had to remember that as painful as Rachel's death still was to him, for Rosemary, the wounds were only one week old.

Rachel had told him more than once that the bond between the sisters was strong, but only someone who had a twin could possibly understand the depth of their devotion to one another. "It's as though I am only half a person without her sometimes," she'd tried to explain once. "If I'm weak in one area, she's strong." She had grinned and ducked her head. "Like how Rosie is the best cook in the world. Everyone says so. But I'm much better at understanding what a person feels. Sometimes she's not sensitive like I think she should be. She thinks things one way and expects other people to think that way too, and she gets annoyed if they don't. But that doesn't mean she isn't sensitive herself. She cries easily if she's hurting."

And her tears were the last thing he needed right now when he had to say what was on his mind. "So I guess what I'm trying to say," he said, "is that, things being as they are now and all, it would be better if…"

"I know we can't live here together, Finn." A sigh passed her lips—lips so like Rachel's he had to force himself not to be distracted by their fullness. "But I can't abandon Rachel's baby. I won't. Especially when she doesn't seem to be thriving."

"And you feel you need to take care of her?" His ears burned and anger rose quickly inside him.

"I don't know if either of us can fix what's wrong with Sarah, but I don't believe I could leave her. Not now that I've seen her and held her."

Her eyes grew gentle, and Finn held his breath. There was something different about Rosemary.... "Then what do you propose?"

Her face went scarlet. A sense of dread filled his gut before she could even stammer out the words. "M–maybe we sh–should... I mean, for Sarah's sake, do you think we ought to...?"

"Rosemary...," he said with a groan.

"No. Of course you don't want to marry me." Her lips trembled. "I know I'm not Rachel. But, Finn, listen to me. I wouldn't demand anything of you that a wife has rights to. You wouldn't share my bed or even have to share your thoughts with me. I can drive my own wagon and put in a garden. But Sarah..." She paused for breath. "Sarah is my sister's baby, and I have no intention of walking away from her and leaving her without a mother."

"You're not her ma." Finn stood, faster than he'd intended, and the chair fell over with a crash that woke Sarah. She whimpered and then let out a wail. Rosemary stood, but he stayed her with an upraised hand. "I'll get her."

"All right," she murmured, taking her plate and heading to the counter. She poured water from the bucket into the washtub and shaved soap into the water as he quieted the baby and changed her clothes. He cradled her in his arms as he walked back to the table.

Rosemary turned and walked toward him, carrying the coffeepot. Sarah cooed at him and he smiled. As she gave him back

a toothless grin, he lost his breath. "Did you see that?" he asked, glancing up at Rosemary, who had just filled his cup again.

She smiled and nodded. "Her first?"

"Yes." At least it was the first time he'd noticed a smile. Was she feeling better because of the way Rosemary had fixed her milk? He shook off the thought before he let his gratefulness cause him to act rashly. "There, she did it again." His heart bubbled over at the sight.

Rosemary let out a small laugh. "Get used to it." She turned and set the coffeepot back on the stove. "Little girls love their pas."

As she plunged her hands into the soapy water, he frowned. "I know she needs a woman's influence. And I even know Rachel would want it to be you. But I…"

"But you can't bear the thought of another woman calling herself your wife, even if it is a marriage in name only."

He nodded even though her back was to him. "I know it would be sensible to marry up when the preacher comes through, but…" Their neighbors would think it sensible, anyway—for all the reasons his logical nature did. Sarah needed a mother. Rosemary could be a mother to Sarah better than anyone else. He knew she felt his rejection, and he wanted her to understand.

"I understand," she said. "Please, let's stop talking about it." She turned and nodded toward his plate. "Finished?"

Though he'd barely touched the third plate of food, he couldn't have forced a bite down his throat. "Yeah. Sorry. I guess my eyes were also bigger than my stomach."

"The dog'll be glad to get it. What's that mutt's name, by the way?" She combined the leftovers from both plates onto one and walked toward the door. "I forgot to ask Mr. Freeman that night he came."

"Cooper."

"Odd name." She laughed. "Rachel must have come up with it."

He grinned. "She said she read it in one of her dime novels when she was younger and wanted to name either one of her children or a dog Cooper."

"Lucky for Miss Sarah, there, that the dog came along first." She opened the door and stepped outside. "Cooper! Come here, boy!" Laughter exploded from her, jolting Finn. Rachel's laugh had been gentler, more subdued…almost as though she felt she should apologize for laughing in the first place.

"What's funny?" he surprised himself by asking.

"I bent over to give him his food and he licked my nose, the ornery little beast." She walked back inside, carrying the empty plate and wiping her nose with the back of her hand. "He's been trying all week, but I've managed to avoid him. I guess I was distracted this time and he hit his mark."

Unable to resist a chuckle, Finn spoke before he thought. "He knows a pretty girl when he sees one." As soon as the words came out, he wanted them back. And from the indignant look on her face, Rosemary felt the same way.

"I'm sorry." Though it seemed ludicrous to apologize for giving a compliment.

"Don't apologize," she said through tight lips that belied her reassurance. "You weren't seeing me."

The baby began to squirm, searching for food. "She's squirming. Is there enough of the cool milk for her?"

"I filled two of her feeders with the diluted milk and put them in the cold cellar. Would you mind getting one of them?"

"Of course." He stood up and took a step toward the door.

"Are you taking her with you?"

"I planned on it."

"Can you climb the ladder with a crying baby and then back up with her feeder?"

He could—and had—but not without a struggle.

Rosemary raised her eyebrows. "Maybe I could soothe her while you go?"

He relinquished Sarah to Rosemary's outstretched arms. She smiled at the baby. "Did you have a good nap?" she cooed. Turning her back, she walked toward the rocking chair, leaving the rest of the dishes undone.

When he returned, the baby was crying in earnest. "She's ready to eat," Rosemary said, reaching for the feeder.

Finn watched as she deftly maneuvered the tube from the feeder and slid the rubber nipple into Sarah's mouth. Instantly the cries stopped. Glancing about, he wasn't sure what to do now. He knew they hadn't finished their conversation, but the moment felt too intimate with Rosemary rocking Sarah and cradling her while she ate.

"I'll be saying good night now," he said. "Thank you again for the food."

She expelled a weighted breath. "Honestly, Finn. Stop thanking me. I'll have flapjacks and bacon for you at sunup." She met his gaze. "Do you want to say good night to your daughter before you go?"

He reached down and rubbed his fingertips along her silky head. He recognized the signs of contentment as she sighed, the pit in her stomach starting to fill up. An urgent love compelled him, and as though caught in her spell, he bent and pressed a kiss to his daughter's forehead. Without rising up, he pulled back far enough to look at her sweet face.

Then Rosemary's soft breath tickled his ear. Warmth slid up his neck as he realized how close his head was to hers. He stood up quickly without meeting her eyes and headed to the door. He murmured a quick good night and ducked outside.

The chill in the air felt good against his hot skin. He took two steps then stopped to regain his composure and collect his breath. Cooper nudged his hand, and he gave the dog a pat. "Come on, boy," he said. "Let's get some shut-eye. Tomorrow is going to be a trying day."

Cooper whined softly and hung back.

"What's wrong, Coop?"

Inching back to the door, he plopped down across the threshold.

"Good boy," Finn said. "Watch over Sarah." But he had to admit, it wasn't just Sarah Cooper was looking out for. Clearly, this past week, Rosemary had made a friend in the big, floppy dog…something Rachel had never really done. "He's so big, he scares me a little," she had admitted.

Back in the barn, Finn stretched out on the pallet he had made earlier. His mind returned to the awkward moment just before he left the house. It was only natural, he told himself, that he would have been confused in that moment. If Rachel had been feeding the baby and the same opportunity had arisen, he would have kissed the baby and then kissed his wife before standing up. Not that he'd been close to kissing Rosemary. But if he'd turned his head…

A scene like the one with Rosemary would have been so sweet if only he could have shared it with Rachel, but she had never been able to feed the baby. Finn remembered spooning milk into Sarah's mouth, not nearly fast enough for the baby, who fussed her way through every meal. Finally, Rachel had insisted he ride to the general store fifteen miles away and purchase the contraption that fed his daughter now. The baby feeder had a cork and a tube with a rubber piece on the end that would serve as a teat.

Finn never would have left Rachel that day if she hadn't promised him she felt much stronger. Reluctantly, he had moved everything within reaching distance of the bed—including the milk, which he'd set in a bucket of snow to keep fresh as long as possible. Then he'd ridden as fast as his horse could go in the nearly two feet of snow on the ground.

Frank Morehouse, the proprietor of the general store, didn't stock baby feeders, but two years earlier, he'd ordered a dozen of them for a local couple after the woman stopped producing milk. Frank figured the baby was eating solid food now.

Desperate, Finn had ridden the extra seven miles to the couple's homestead and introduced himself. There were four baby feeders left, and he bought them for the cost of the new ones, but he felt they were well worth the price if they put Rachel's mind at ease.

By the time he had returned home, though, she was nearly delirious with fever and Sarah was screaming in her cradle. His Rachel never regained consciousness. She slipped away from him the next night.

He'd gone wild with grief. For two months, he slept when Sarah slept and woke when she did. He took care of the animals and not much else. Shame shot through him once more at the thought of the mess Rosemary had walked into a week ago. He couldn't blame her for being concerned about Sarah.

But that was all in the past. He had left his homestead a broken man who believed exactly what Rosemary believed—that he wasn't capable of caring for his beautiful Sarah. He'd returned determined to do right by the child Rachel had left in his keeping, and by gum, he would not let her down.

He wasn't sure how he would take care of her when he ought to be plowing his fields, but he'd find a way. And he'd do it without a bride of convenience.

* * * * *

The moon was high before Rosemary felt the slightest bit sleepy. How could she fall asleep when she'd made an utter fool of herself by asking a man to marry her? Oh, she was just mortified by her behavior. It was bad enough she'd asked in the first place, but then to make those bold statements—"You won't have to be a real husband."

"Oh!" She groaned and buried her face in the feather pillow. He must think she was some desperate spinster trying to force her way into her dead sister's life. The truth was, she wasn't sure anymore *what* her true motives were. All week she'd been formulating this plan: if Finn had gone for supplies and returned, she would calmly suggest that the most logical thing for them to do would be to marry so they could both be there for Sarah. But somehow when the time came to speak up, she'd gotten all tongue-tied and nervous.

She had never been the sort to beg, and she wouldn't do so now. But somehow she would find a way to make it on her own in this rough Dakota Territory and still stay close to Sarah. Perhaps Finn didn't want to marry her, but she wasn't about to allow him to push her away, either. Not when Rachel's baby girl needed her. And whether he knew it or not, Finn needed her too.

Chapter Seven

....

Rosemary awoke to cold, wet droplets falling on her face in the kind of *drip-drip-drip* fashion that meant only two things: the rain was coming down hard and the roof wasn't holding up. She pulled herself up, ran a hand across Sarah's cradle to assure herself that nothing was falling on the baby, then went to the kitchen for a pot, which she set on the bed where her head had been five minutes ago. The rain pinged into the pot, and Rosemary knew there would be no more sleeping for her tonight.

She glanced at the mantel clock—a gift from Pa on Rachel's wedding day—and noted that it was time to awaken anyway. She needed to gather the ingredients to make flapjacks for breakfast. She wanted to fry bacon as well but didn't like the idea of going outside to the root cellar in the rain, so flapjacks with strawberry preserves would have to do. She had no idea where Rachel had come up with the preserves, but Rosemary had discovered a jar earlier in the root cellar along with the bacon and the rest of the meat.

Still in her dressing gown, she padded to the stove and used the water that remained in the bucket to start the coffee to boiling. Then she gathered the ingredients for flapjacks from the shelf above the stove.

She had noticed the shelves with appreciation the first day she'd arrived. Finn might not have given Rachel a wood home, but at least he'd built her some shelves so she had a way to keep things tidy in the cramped space with the earthen floors.

While the baby slept, Rosemary dressed in her dark green muslin gown. She hadn't brought anything black, even though Pa had died. He'd made her promise she wouldn't wear such a dreary color. She had kept her promise but couldn't bring herself to wear bright colors either, so she had chosen to have the seamstress make deep blue and dark green gowns for her just two weeks prior to Pa's death.

A soft tap at the door made her jump. Mercy, Finn had arrived early for breakfast. "Come in," she called in a soft voice, so as not to awaken the baby. He opened the door and stepped inside.

"Breakfast isn't quite ready," she said.

"I'm not finished with the chores either, but I saw the lamp lit and thought you might want milk for the baby."

"She's still sleeping yet. But she could wake up any time."

"I also remembered you saying something about bacon last night." He set a package on the table. "I didn't figure you'd want to go to the root cellar in the rain just to get this."

The baby began to squirm, saving her from having to stand there awkwardly thinking of how thoughtful he'd been. "Thank you," she was able to say in an offhanded manner as she turned toward the baby. Rosemary picked her up, held her just far enough away so she wouldn't get soaked too, and laid her down on the quilts she had put in the corner to keep dry.

"What happened to the bed?" Finn asked. Then he seemed to

do a quick assessment of the situation. "The roof leaked? The pot is right where the pillows were." He turned to her. "Did you get wet?"

"Not like this," she said, laughing, as she removed the sopping cloth from beneath the baby. She glanced at Finn. "I woke up pretty quick and moved before I could get more than a few drops on my head."

The baby let out a wail that quickly turned into an angry, insistent cry as Rosemary pulled the wet clothes free, dipped a cloth in the washbasin water, and wiped her down. Sarah shivered and her lips trembled as she lay uncovered, kicking her legs at the injustice. Rosemary worked fast to slide the cloth around her and tie it at the navel. Then she slipped a tiny gown over Sarah's head. "Will you hold her for a couple of minutes while I change her bed and then get her milk ready? I know you need to finish your chores, but I hate for her to lie there crying and thinking no one cares."

Reaching for his fussing daughter, Finn nodded. "Of course." He smiled indulgently as she gave a high-pitched squeal.

"She's got a temper, doesn't she?"

"She sure does." Rosemary laughed. Then she cringed at the volume of her laughter. She'd always been one to blurt out a laugh rather than demurely conceal her smile behind her hand, the way Rachel had learned to do from the ladies' magazines and dime novels.

She quickly made up the cradle and tossed the soiled linens into the corner to be cleaned when she did the wash. Five minutes later, she had filled the feeder. "Let me feed her while you start breakfast," Finn said as she reached for the baby.

"Are you sure?" He put out his hand, so she gave him the feeder. "I don't want to keep you from your chores."

"There's not much to do right now. Morning chores are pretty easy. Once I start plowing, there won't be much time for anything but chores and work in the fields. We cleared a hundred acres over the last three years, so if all goes well, there should be a profit come harvesttime."

"Oh, good heavens." Rosemary gathered a sharp breath and pressed her palm to her cheek. "Finn. I completely forgot."

"Forgot what?" He was clearly confused by her sudden change of demeanor. "Are you all right?"

"Of course." She waved him away as she headed for her reticule, which still sat on the trunk just inside the door. Retrieving the bank draft that had been written out to Finn and Rachel, she walked to the rocking chair and held it out to him.

"My hands are occupied. What is it?"

"Rachel's half of the ranch. Papa arranged for its sale weeks before he passed. Rachel and I were both given equal shares, and the sum is quite enough for anything you or Sarah might have need of."

He stared at the draft she still held in front of him, and then he shook his head. "I'm not taking that."

"What do you mean?" Perplexed, she kept the draft before him. He must have misunderstood what she was giving him. "You have to take it. It's Rachel's inheritance."

He shrugged. "Rachel is gone. You should have it."

Without thinking, she dropped to her knees next to the chair so she could force his gaze. "As her husband, not only is this legally yours, but Rachel would want you to take it and use it to make sure Sarah has everything she needs. And that includes your having everything you need to make sure this farm turns a profit. How

many people pull up stakes and never make a go of a homestead?" Her thoughts went to Mr. Freeman. "This inheritance will ensure that you never have to face that decision."

"I already told you, we should make a profit this year come harvest."

"Then use it to build a wood home. Heinrich told me lumber can be shipped in if there aren't enough trees to build a decent home."

He winced, and Rosemary regretted her hasty words. "I'm sorry. I didn't mean it like that."

Why did she always have to say exactly what was on her mind? Even when those words were bound to hurt, she couldn't seem to filter them through reason first.

With his attention focused on feeding Sarah, Finn clearly had no intention of responding to her apology. Kneeling beside the chair felt awkward now, so with as much dignity as she could muster, Rosemary stood and walked to the stove to begin breakfast. Dread nearly overwhelmed her stomach as she realized that this last outburst had almost certainly ruined any chance of Finn's reconsidering her proposal.

* * * * *

Finn swallowed the last of his breakfast, giving a grudging nod of thanks to his sister-in-law. Decent home, she'd said. Decent? He glanced around the soddy. He reckoned it wasn't the sort of house she'd grown up in, but Rachel had understood that this was necessary in the beginning. But the difference between the sisters—Rachel had never behaved as though she felt this home was beneath her.

Still stinging from Rosemary's criticism, he'd found it difficult to stay civil as they ate, but now that the meal was over, he knew he had to speak to her. He gulped down the last of his coffee and stood. "Now that the rain has stopped, I'll patch that hole and then I'll be heading to the general store for supplies. I suppose you won't mind keeping an eye on things here."

Her eyebrows shot up and she looked surprised. "Of course I don't mind. It's what I planned to do anyway. The washing needs attention, and I assumed you would be starting to work in the fields and would need me to tend the baby."

Rosemary Jackson assumed entirely too much, especially when she knew full well that he wanted her gone.

"Before I can start the plowing, I have to take time to stock up on household supplies." Dad-burn…he didn't even know what they needed. He knew that asking her might lead her to believe he was planning some sort of pairing between the two, but he really had no choice. "I don't suppose you could make a list of household goods?"

"I've already started one." She walked to the stove and took down a sheet of paper and the inkwell from the shelf. "I can finish up in a jiffy."

Watching Rosemary move around the house as though she belonged there filled Finn with resentment. He knew his feelings weren't logical or fair, but he couldn't seem to quell them. Especially now, as she took up Rachel's pen. Those were Rachel's private things. No one, not even Finn, ever touched them but her. Watching Rosemary was altogether too much like watching Rachel, and the pain sliced through his heart.

He frowned. "You write with your left hand?" The sight shook him. But in a strange way, the thought that the two weren't exactly alike somehow comforted Finn.

Rosemary nodded. "I know, Rachel wrote with her right. She hated that we didn't write with the same hand." She shrugged. "I liked it." With a sigh, she bit her bottom lip, holding it between her teeth as she stared into nothing.

"She never did that either," he said without thinking.

Her gaze shifted quickly to him. "What?"

"The mouth thing. Rachel didn't bite her bottom lip."

Her eyes grew wide. "I bite my bottom lip?"

Feeling suddenly awkward in her presence, he nodded, knowing it would be even more awkward to ignore the question. "Only when you're thinking about something. You always did."

"Hmm. I didn't know." She shrugged and went back to her list, leaving Finn to look at the top of her head.

He'd been acting the fool, pushing Rosemary away and at the same time looking at her as though she were Rachel. He averted his gaze while she scratched the rest of the items onto Rachel's stationery.

"All right," she said finally. "I think this will do." She walked across the floor to him but hesitated before handing it over. "It's lengthy. Do you...?"

Have enough cash to cover the purchase. That's what she was going to say. "I can afford to take care of my family, Rosemary." He held out his hand, and she tentatively laid the paper on his palm.

"I didn't mean to offend." She breathed out a heavy sigh. "I just can't help but think of Rachel's inheritance and how much it could help."

"In building a proper home for my daughter?" Finn could hear the anger in his tone. He offered no apology. Rosemary was altogether too forward. But she was still family. "Look. I know you believe Rachel would want me to take the inheritance...."

"She would. It's yours, and it's only right that you accept."

Why did she have to go and start a fight just when he was trying to apologize for being testy? "A man has to make his own fortune in this life, Rosemary. Otherwise, what kind of man is he?"

Her blue eyes clouded over, and she crossed her arms over her chest. "A smart man who knows there's no shame in accepting an inheritance. This isn't charity. If it were, I wouldn't be accepting it myself." She lifted her hands, her frustration evident, as though she had given up the pretense of civility. "Mercy's sake, Finn. Even the Good Book says a wise man leaves an inheritance to his children's children. My pa was wise. And so he's left an inheritance. One that Sarah, his grandchild, should benefit from."

"And you're saying I'm not wise enough to provide for my family?"

"You're just being intentionally difficult." She turned her back and walked to the counter. "Rachel would be ashamed."

Her words sliced Finn's heart, the pain burning through him so hot and fierce, it took his breath away.

"Finn." Somehow Rosemary had closed the distance between them, but he had no idea how or when. She reached for his arm, but he jerked it away before her fingers made contact. "I'm sorry!" she said, her voice choked.

He knew she meant it. Knew she regretted saying the cruel words, but now it was too late for her to take them back. Didn't she know that all he had ever wanted was to make Rachel proud? To make her never, ever regret marrying him?

He met her gaze. Tears pooled in her blue eyes. "Finn…"

But he had heard enough of her words. "I always knew you were opinionated and loud and enjoyed making a man feel small, but I never knew you could be deliberately cruel. What you just said, Rosemary—that was plain cruel, and I feel the pain of it down to my gut."

A gasp tore at her throat. "I'm so desperately sorry, Finn. I didn't mean it."

"Then you shouldn't have said it." He reached for the door but turned back before pulling on the door latch. "I don't know if I want someone who can't control her tongue helping me raise my daughter. Rachel would have raised her with kindness and taught her to be kind. I don't want my little Sarah growing up and using her words as weapons. I truly don't believe Rachel would approve."

He slipped his hat on his head and yanked the door open. Somehow Rosemary's stricken expression didn't give him the satisfaction he'd imagined it would. As he walked toward the barn to hitch the team, he could feel her eyes following him.

* * * * *

The team of horses pulled the wagon into Paddington a couple of hours later. He'd spent the ride to town replaying his conversation with Rosemary, his response to her unkind remark. He knew he owed her an apology for the way he had spoken to her, but if the truth were told, he had also meant those words. He didn't care for the way she thoughtlessly blurted out whatever was on her mind, and he didn't want Sarah to grow up learning to do the same. But

Rachel would have found a more tactful way to explain that to Rosemary.

"Whoa," he commanded his horses, as he pulled hard on the reins in front of Morehouse's General Store. He dreaded the conversation he was about to be forced into, after last week's fiasco. Perhaps he wasn't too different from Rosemary after all. He'd certainly treated Mrs. Morehouse horribly by grabbing his child and tearing out of the store without a word of explanation.

Frank Morehouse would demand an apology—at least if he were any sort of real man, he would. And Finn would have to face the woman he'd wronged and explain that his beautiful Rachel was dead. If he'd had any other choice, he would have chosen a different establishment to restock his home, but the general store was the only store in town. He set the brake and wrapped the reins around the lever then climbed from the seat. As he stepped into the store, he pulled the list from his shirt pocket.

Mrs. Morehouse left her patron at the counter and rushed to Finn. She took his hand in hers, and her eyes filled with compassion. "Mr. Tate," she said, her voice fraught with emotion, "Mr. Morehouse and I were extremely saddened to hear of your dear wife's death. Please accept our condolences."

Finn shook his head to gather his thoughts. With a sense of relief that he wouldn't be the one to explain when they asked about Rachel and the baby, Finn handed her the list. "Thank you, ma'am." She frowned and glanced toward the window.

"Mr. Tate! Where on earth is that beautiful baby? Surely you didn't leave her in the wagon."

"No, ma'am."

He lifted his hand to Mr. Morehouse as the proprietor walked into the main room from the back. "Hey there, Finn. The wife and I are sure sorry about that pretty little wife of yours. Heinrich Fischer stopped by yesterday and told us. How's the baby?"

"She's doing well."

Mrs. Morehouse's frown deepened. "But where is she?"

"Rachel's sister is minding her."

Mrs. Morehouse smiled a wide smile, showing a mouth full of crooked teeth. "How nice! And did the sister's husband accompany her?"

"Frieda! Hold your tongue." Mr. Morehouse glared at his wife and jerked his head toward the counter. "Your customer is waiting."

"Of course." Glancing at Finn, she held up the list he'd given her. "I'll take care of this as quickly as possible."

"Thank you, ma'am."

"Mr. Morehouse, does Mrs. Franklin still run that boarding-house at the edge of town?"

The man's gray eyebrows rose, and then he smiled. "I take it your wife's sister did not bring her husband."

Heat warmed Finn's neck. "No, she's not married, so you can see the difficult situation."

"And she has come here to live?"

"Yes, sir. Her pa passed on a few weeks ago and she traveled here expecting to find a home with us, but of course that isn't possible now."

"No, I can see how it isn't."

Mrs. Morehouse finished with her customer, and the middle-aged woman walked toward the door, carrying a package. Finn reached the door first and held it open for her.

The woman rewarded him with a smile. "Thank you."

He tipped his hat then returned to Mr. Morehouse. "I'll head over to the boardinghouse to speak with Mrs. Franklin about a room for Rosemary. I'll come back for my supplies."

"We'll get everything ready for you."

* * * * *

The elderly Mrs. Dorothy Franklin was stern but not overly harsh, as one might expect by the way her brow was creased into a perpetual frown. She bent over a cane as she walked, and her hair was stark white without a hint of gray. She kept it up in a tidy bun and wore black silk every day. At least so he'd heard, and if today were any indication, the rumors were true. Her gown rustled as she slowly took the steps one at a time, her hand tucked inside the crook of his arm. She held on as though for dear life, and Finn was glad he was wearing long sleeves, as he was almost sure her nails would have gouged five tiny holes in his skin.

"I don't cotton to men entering a lady's room." She gave him a pointed look. "Even kin."

"Sounds fair."

"Of course, you may carry her trunk up and leave it just inside, but I shall escort you while Miss Jackson remains properly downstairs."

"Yes, ma'am."

"The rent is due precisely on the first day of each month, and if it is not paid by the fifth, the tenant must leave. No discussion. I am a widow and this is my only income, so I cannot afford charity."

"Of course not, ma'am. You will be paid promptly each month. My sister-in-law recently received a modest inheritance and will not be a problem for you."

Her face brightened as she opened the second door to the right. Inside, the room was furnished modestly but decently, and Finn was sure Rosemary would have no objections. A floral coverlet was spread across the bed, giving a nice feminine touch to the room. In the corner, a rose-painted washbasin and pitcher sat atop a wooden table. A wardrobe graced the far wall, and directly across from the foot of the bed stood a vanity with a mirror and a chair. Everything he knew Rosemary had in her room at the ranch. He knew this fact only because the first few days of their marriage, Rachel and he had stayed in her room waiting for the dressmaker to finish Rachel's gowns. And she had confided that their rooms were decorated much the same.

"I can't abide a young woman who thinks more highly of her looks than she ought," Mrs. Franklin said, "but it never hurts to give an unmarried young woman the opportunity to ensure that her appearance is appropriate to every occasion." She smiled. "They used to tell me I was quite handsome. My George ordered that vanity from New York right after the war."

"You've maintained it beautifully."

"It means a great deal to me. That is why I can't have just anyone occupying this particular room."

"I'm sure you will find Miss Jackson to be just the kind of young woman you are looking for."

She gave him a sharp, discerning look. "Do you intend to call on Miss Jackson?" She stepped aside and motioned for him to step out into the hall ahead of her. "Because I do not allow anything that so much as hints at impropriety. You young folks nowadays… have no morals."

"Mrs. Franklin," Finn said, feeling the need to defend Rosemary's honor, "my sister-in-law is not a woman of loose morals. And while I will, no doubt, call on her as a brother calls on a sister from time to time, no, I am not courting her. My wife has only been dead for a couple of months, and I'm still grieving."

"I see you are a gentleman." She took his arm again as they slowly descended the stairs, taking them one at a time. "If Miss Jackson is all you say, I'm sure she will be the perfect tenant for that room."

When they reached the foyer, Mrs. Franklin let go of his arm. "When may I expect the two of you?"

"Her things are still all packed away, so I imagine we can be here by lunchtime tomorrow."

"I do not serve lunch, Mr. Tate." She pointed to the list of rules on the wall. "Also, the supper meal is served promptly at six each evening, and there is an additional fee of twenty-five cents for anyone who wishes to join us."

"I'm sure that'll be fine." He walked toward the door, relieved to have this particular chore behind him—but dreading the fact that Rosemary would probably pitch a fit.

"I wonder, Mr. Tate…," Mrs. Franklin said, following him with a slow gait. "Why is your sister-in-law not returning to her people?"

"I'm afraid her pa passed on a few weeks ago. She and my wife had made plans for her to come live with us after he passed. He was ill for some time and death was imminent."

"I see." Her soft voice belied the harsh look so much that it was almost jarring. "So the poor dear lost her pa and her sister in short succession."

He nodded. "But, clearly, she can't stay at the homestead. I can't continue to sleep in the barn every night, and people would begin to talk anyway. Her reputation might be sullied, and I can't allow that to happen to Rachel's sister."

The old woman raised an eyebrow. "You could marry her."

Her quick retort jolted Finn. "No, ma'am. I can't."

She shrugged her rounded shoulders. "Suit yourself. I'll look for you tomorrow around noon."

Knowing he'd been summarily dismissed, Finn opened the door and stepped onto the porch feeling more lighthearted than he had in a while at the thought of getting Rosemary out of his hair. But as he left the porch and stepped toward the wagon, a weight settled across his shoulders like a yoke and bore down heavier and heavier, the closer he got to the wagon.

Rosemary might very well refuse to leave. What would he do if his plan failed? He could never insist that she get out. But he couldn't think that way. He'd go crazy if he tried to predict how Rosemary Jackson would react to anything.

Thankfully, Mrs. Morehouse was occupied when he arrived back at the general store to collect his supplies, so he was spared any more advice or questions or, heaven forbid, sympathy. Mr. Morehouse helped him load the wagon before he settled up inside. "We'll see you again soon, I hope."

Finn assured him that they would. He had turned toward the door when Mr. Morehouse stopped him.

"Finn," the man said, placing a hand firmly on Finn's shoulder.

"Yes, sir."

"When was the last time you had a bath?"

Embarrassment shot through him at the personal subject, and he glanced over the storekeeper's shoulder. Mrs. Morehouse turned away from him, her face red, and disappeared into the back room.

"Awhile," Finn admitted.

Mr. Morehouse shoved his glasses up his nose and gave a half smile. He motioned toward a shelf on the far wall of the General Store. "Do yourself a kindness. Get a pair of those trousers over there and one of those already-made shirts and stop at the creek on your way home."

Indignation shot through Finn. His first instinct was to thank Mr. Morehouse for the advice and walk out. Mercy, a grieving man ought to be given the courtesy of a few weeks of wearing a little extra dirt without being humiliated by folks he'd known for years. But the more he thought about it, the more he figured Morehouse was likely right. He looked the man in the eye and nodded. "I'll take a blue shirt and a pair of trousers. I don't suppose you have any soap that doesn't smell like perfume, have you?"

Morehouse laughed. "We don't sell it, but the missus has plenty left from soap making a few weeks ago. I'll go back and cut off a chunk. No charge."

* * * * *

Dreading the upcoming confrontation with Rosemary, Finn headed for the homestead at a much slower pace than he'd set for the trip to town. But he took the Morehouses' advice, and though the air was

cool, he stripped down and scrubbed the dirt from his body and hair. It took awhile to get completely clean, but he had to admit, he felt much better with clean clothes.

He climbed back into the wagon and his gut clenched. First he had to apologize for his unkindness earlier, and then he had to tell Rosemary that she had a room in town and no choice but to go.

Not for the first time, he couldn't help but wonder—what if she refused?

Chapter Eight

....

The house was filled with the delicious scents of apple strudel, fresh bread, and venison stew. If the saying were true that the way to a man's heart was through his stomach, Finn would have no choice but to forgive her when he walked inside.

She still cringed at her thoughtless words. She had prayed and prayed for forgiveness. "Help me to learn to hold my tongue, Lord. Why do I have to say whatever hurtful thing comes to mind just so I can win every argument?"

All day she had worked, cooking and cleaning, in between caring for Sarah. She had rarely taken the time to sit, but the results were more than worth the effort. The wash was still drying on the line outside, but otherwise, the chores were finished, Finn's meal was just about ready to go on the table, and his baby girl was clean and fed and sleeping soundly. He just had to accept her apology when he saw how hard she had worked to make it up to him.

Satisfaction flowed through Rosemary as she stood in the kitchen enjoying her handiwork. "This must be just how You felt at the end of each day of creation, Lord," she said aloud. "And the Lord saw that it was good." She breathed out a slow sigh.

The sound of Cooper barking outside brought a smile to her

lips. Finn must be coming. She walked to the door, twisted the latch, and pulled. A flash of feathers and fur greeted her, and before she could control the situation, she found herself on her backside while the rooster squawked and scratched into the house, followed by Cooper.

"What on earth?" she sputtered, trying to get her bearings. "Coop!" she screamed, jumping to her feet. "You dumb dog!"

Squawks and barks filled the small space, followed by the baby's cries. And then like a tornado that comes suddenly, leaves a path of destruction, and is gone as fast as it came, the rooster and dog sped past her, out the door, and into the barnyard.

Dazed, Rosemary stood at the open door as Coop, tail wagging, flopped to the ground in front of the house, looking satisfied that he'd done his job by shooing the rooster out of the house and back where it belonged.

"Y–you. You're a…" Coop stared at her, obviously waiting for praise. "You—you…bad, bad dog!" She slammed the door. Sarah's cries turned from pathetic to downright mad. Rosemary hurried to the cradle and lifted her. Holding the baby against her shoulder, she bounced her until she quieted. With dread, she heard Cooper bark again and instinctively knew that this time Finn was back.

The baby had settled into her nap once more, so Rosemary carefully laid her in the cradle. Forcing away a sudden rush of tears, she prepared to face Finn, her confidence shaken more than she cared to admit. The house, in perfect order a mere ten minutes ago, now resembled the home of a shameful woman who didn't mind the mess. Chairs were overturned, linens strewn.…

The door opened and Finn stood with his eyebrows raised as

he looked about the room. His expression swept from surprise to annoyance before Rosemary had a chance to explain the mess.

Indignation shot through her. How dare he?

"You should just be glad your supper didn't get knocked off the stove."

"What happened?" He closed the door and hung his hat on a peg sticking out of the wall.

"Ask your dog."

"That would be pretty silly, now, wouldn't it?"

"I opened the door and the rooster came in, for some reason. I think it was to get away from Cooper. But he saw it as a challenge to his authority and shot in here to shoo the bird out. Then he had the audacity to expect me to be proud of him."

A chuckle rumbled in Finn's chest, further igniting Rosemary's ire. How dare he laugh when she had worked her fingers to the bone all day? For him. She grabbed a dishrag and lifted the lid from the stew, stirred the pot, and replaced the lid. Then she opened the oven. Thankfully, the strudel looked perfect. She pulled the pan from the oven and set it on the counter next to the stove.

As anticipated, Finn followed the aroma and stood behind her, staring at the strudel over her shoulder. "What's that?"

He'd obviously stopped somewhere to bathe. Her face bloomed at the very thought, and it didn't help matters that his breath whispered against her neck. Rosemary's stomach dipped. "Apple strudel. Agnes Fischer taught me to make it the week I spent with them before coming here."

"Looks good." To Rosemary's relief, he moved back and she could breathe again.

"Supper will be a couple more hours. Would you like a slice of the strudel with a cup of coffee before you unload the supplies?"

He hesitated then shook his head. "I'd best tend the horses." Reaching down, he righted a chair the dog had knocked over and headed toward the door. When he was gone, Rosemary went about the task of tidying up the linens, once nicely folded but now strewn across the floor. Luckily the cradle hadn't been overturned, but the bed had muddy paw prints on the bare mattress. That much was a mercy, considering she had washed the bedding after the rain came through the dirt roof that morning.

All in all, the mess wasn't as devastating as she had originally thought. And from the conversation she'd just had with Finn, perhaps he had forgiven her for her earlier outburst. There was still the matter of where she would live, but perhaps they would discuss it amicably now that they had argued and forgiven each other.

Sarah awoke again, this time ready to be changed and fed. Rosemary welcomed the chance to sit and rock her niece. Finn found them this way when he came in carrying supplies a few minutes later. The baby's eyes followed her pa as far as they could and then followed him again when he came back into view. He stood over her and she grinned, spilling milk down the side of her cheek.

"She knows who her pa is," Rosemary said, laughing, now that the baby clearly had no more interest in her food. "You may as well go on and take her. I'll start putting away the supplies." She stood and offered the baby to him.

Finn reached out and gathered Sarah close. He sat in the rocking chair. Sarah took his finger as he gazed down at her.

The look on his face made Rosemary ache, forcing her to turn away before the tears fell. How Rachel would have loved watching that moment between her husband and their child.

She turned her attention to the supplies. He had purchased flour, sugar, coffee, oats, baking powder, and the material she had requested to sew Sarah some new gowns. Other than the few items of clothing Agnes had sent, the baby was quickly outgrowing the four that Rachel had obviously sewn during her pregnancy.

"I'll start on these tonight," she said.

"You don't have to do that, Rosemary." Finn didn't look up from the baby. Was it her imagination, or was his neck red, a sign he was uncomfortable? "There are several women who take in sewing to make extra money. Marta Fischer, Agnes's daughter, for one."

"Why would you pay someone to do it? I'm perfectly capable of sewing some gowns for my niece."

Sarah sighed and tightened her fist around his pinky. He lifted it to his lips and pressed a kiss to the soft skin. "Because you won't be here after today."

Rosemary's heartbeat picked up and she stared harder, willing him to look up and face her after that comment.

"What do you mean?"

"I took the liberty of finding you a room in a very nice boarding-house in Paddington."

"You did what?" The nerve—presuming he had the right to send her packing!

"I know you want to be near the baby, and I promise I'll bring her to see you as often as I can. But for now I have to do what is best for all of us."

Rosemary trembled with anger. "I have no intention of being

packed off to a boardinghouse at your whim, Finn Tate. If you don't want me in your home, so be it. But I will make my own decisions as to where I will go."

"Packed off to a boardinghouse at *my* whim? Have you forgotten that you moved in here at *your* whim without giving me a choice? Seems to me it's only fair that I return the favor."

The outburst between the two startled the baby, and she stuck out her bottom lip then screwed up her little face and let out a wail.

While Finn had his hands full with comforting the baby, Rosemary turned on her heel before she gave in to the temptation to tell him exactly what was on her mind. She wanted desperately to slam the door behind her but didn't want to frighten the baby again. Stomping across the yard, Rosemary had no idea where she was going or what she intended to do. She tried to ignore the dog as he wagged his entire body and nudged her thigh.

"Leave me alone, you troublemaker," she said. Then she repented as his ears went back and he let out a little whine. She reached down and scratched the top of his head. "Oh, don't mind me. I'm just the unwanted sister-in-law who's about to be sent away. And clearly I'm feeling sorry for myself."

She paced back and forth in front of the barn then made a heady decision. Before she could risk her reason taking over, she opened the barn and grabbed the dusty sidesaddle Rachel had brought with her from home. If Finn didn't want her, she would leave. The image of Sarah flashed through her mind, and her stomach tightened. How could she ride away like this? But what choice did she have? Finn had made it clear she was not wanted, nor was she allowed to stay. She had no choice but to leave.

She saddled Rachel's horse, Charity. Pa had given Rachel the mare as a wedding present, and Rachel had fallen in love with the horse the moment the two laid eyes on each other. Rosemary led the chestnut mare out of the barn and climbed into the saddle. If Finn didn't want her here, she had little choice but to make her own way.

Fine, she could do that. She certainly wasn't afraid to try. But she had no intention of leaving Rachel's only child to be raised without a woman's guidance. Perhaps Finn had good reason to be concerned about Sarah learning her bold ways. Rosemary knew she should learn to hold her tongue and be more mindful of a child's tendency to imitate the adults in his or her life. And with the Lord's help, she would be more careful. But the one thing she would not do was be bullied by a man who didn't want her and was only trying to get rid of her.

She turned Charity toward the road and nudged her into a trot.

It wasn't difficult to find the Freeman farm. Silas Freeman had described the homestead well. She had no idea whether he had returned from doing the business he'd spoken of. Surely he would have come to Finn and said good-bye if he planned to leave his homestead without proving up. Though she half expected that he'd changed his mind and decided to stay. Goodness, abandoning the homestead after three years of sweat and blood and tears… Even though more than a week had gone by since she had learned of his plan, she still thought that the most foolish thing she'd ever heard.

"Hello!" she called, putting her critical thoughts behind her as she approached. Her unfortunate tendency to show every thought and emotion on her face concerned her as she looked ahead to the conversation she hoped to have with Silas. It would certainly not bode well for her if she called him a fool and offended him.

Chickens squawked inside the coop, and in the barnyard she noted two milk cows. By all accounts, Mr. Freeman seemed to be making an even better go of things than Finn. So why on earth would he allow his wife to drag him away from this place?

"Hello?" she called again, dismounting. She tethered the horse to the railing that stretched across the front porch. The home was made of lumber, another sign that Mr. Freeman must be doing well. By all rights, the house was small…but it was a far cry from a soddy.

As she walked up the three steps to the porch, the door opened. A young woman stood at the threshold with her mouth agape. "Goodness, you're the spitting image, aren't you?"

Rosemary understood the reaction, but understanding didn't keep her from feeling the pain that accompanied the observation. She nodded, holding out her hand. "I'm Rosemary, Rachel's sister."

The woman behaved as though she didn't see Rosemary's extended hand. She still held one palm to her cheek and the other to her extended belly. "Silas told me you two were identical, but I just couldn't picture it." Embarrassed, Rosemary lowered her arm to her side.

Mrs. Freeman's jaw dropped. "Mercy, where are my manners? Please come in, Rosemary. You don't mind my calling you that, do you? I just couldn't even imagine being formal when I feel like I already know you."

"Of course you may call me Rosemary. As a matter of fact, I insist." It was difficult not to be drawn in by the woman's sweet nature and vivacious personality. She was nothing at all like Rosemary had imagined. Because she was insisting on moving to Missouri when her man needed her support right now, Rosemary had assumed that Annie Freeman would be a weak, foolish woman. But the image she had held in her mind certainly didn't match the reality before her now.

"And you should call me Annie." She dimpled as she gave Rosemary a warm smile then turned and led the way to a lovely sitting room. A wooden rocking chair sat next to the fire, and a settee faced the fireplace. The furniture spoke of prosperity. How on earth could the man even contemplate leaving?

As though reading her thoughts, Annie spoke. "You're looking at the nice things?"

"I beg your pardon." Rosemary knew her face must certainly be as red as a rose in bloom. "I didn't mean to be rude."

Waving away the apology, Annie laughed. "Everyone responds this way. My parents are equal parts well-off and overbearing. Sometimes it's easier to allow them to spoil us than to try to explain that we love them but we want to build our own life without the fancy things they had to wait twenty years to enjoy in their own marriage." She sighed. "Try to tell my pa anything, though. He wants his daughter living in a 'proper home.'"

Inwardly, Rosemary squirmed. Had she sounded as pretentious as Annie's parents? Rachel had been proud of her little home. Rosemary knew that from the letters she'd received over the past three years. Rachel had never once mentioned it was made of sod. Rosemary's first opinion was that she had been ashamed to say so, but what if she hadn't mentioned it because she honestly didn't notice? At least not in such a way that would make her unhappy.

Wooden crates lined the floor along the wall at the far end of the room. "Packing crates?"

"Don't mind those," Annie said. "Silas is loading them all in the wagon tonight so we'll be all ready to move out come morning."

Rosemary followed Annie into the kitchen, where more crates were filled with pots and pans and other kitchen items. Rosemary's stomach jumped with excitement. Silas and Annie truly were moving. Perhaps something was finally going right.

"Can I offer you a cup of coffee?" Annie asked. "I'd offer tea, but it's already packed. Silas likes his coffee at each meal, so I left out just enough for supper and for him to have two cups with breakfast in the morning."

"Thank you. That would be wonderful."

Taking a cup from a cabinet across from the stove, Annie poured the coffee and set it on the table. "Supper's cooking," she said. "It's nothing fancy. We killed a chicken to celebrate our last night in this godforsaken territory. I insist that you eat with us. Although I'm sure my fried chicken and bread and beans won't hold a candle to yours. Rachel told me no one cooks as well as you do."

Pleased at the compliment, Rosemary smiled. "I'm afraid my sister was prejudiced."

"Well, that may be true, considering." She smiled over her shoulder. "But Finn isn't one to flatter, and he agreed."

The last person she wanted to discuss was Finn. Rosemary took a sip of the hot liquid then set her cup back on the wood table. "I'm curious, Annie."

"Why we're leaving?"

"Why, yes, to tell you the truth. This place is wonderful."

"Silas became weary of my nagging, I'm afraid. He finally agreed to take me home to Missouri." She smiled as she stirred a pot on the stove. "My baby is due in November. But up here, we can have two feet of snow in one day during the month of November." She stood over the stove, turning the sizzling chicken with a fork. "Silas thinks I'm worrying for nothing, but I just can't help it. What if no one can get here because of the snow? If my time comes and I'm all alone, I know I'll die."

"But your husband will be here to help you."

She shook her head. "He'd be angry if he knew I mentioned it, but Silas can barely watch when one of the animals gives birth. He'd faint dead away if he had to help me."

She put her finger to her lips in silent conspiracy as the door opened and Silas entered. He lifted his hand in greeting. "Miss Jackson," he said. "Mighty nice to see you again. I vow I thought for a minute that Rachel had come for a visit when I saw her horse and saddle."

Rosemary felt the pain of his statement cut deep.

"Miss Jackson is staying to supper," Annie said. "And it's just about ready, so you should go and wash up before taking your seat."

"Yes, ma'am," he said, kissing her cheek. He winked at Rosemary and disappeared into a room off the living area.

Annie turned to her as he left the room. "I'm so sorry he said that. It's just that Rachel rode Charity over here often during those first two years before she discovered she was in the family way."

"I won't pretend it doesn't hurt. I didn't know she was gone until I arrived."

"That must have been a shock." Her tender tone nearly undid Rosemary, but she refused to break down. She needed to be strong and business-minded like her pa had taught her.

She avoided answering by lifting the cup to her lips.

"It's okay," Annie said. "We don't have to talk about it if you'd rather not."

"Thank you, Annie." She held the warm china cup between her palms and glanced up at the mother-to-be as she stood over her stove. "I don't mean to be too bold, but are you sure you want to leave all this?"

Annie set her jaw as though she had made up her mind and had no intention of allowing anyone to talk her out of it. "The home we have in Missouri is even more beautiful. My grandmother passed on last year and left it to us. I'm her only grandchild and Mama and Pa have a big house of their own, so they didn't need it."

Rosemary refrained from asking how that was any different from her parents furnishing this home for her. Was living in her grandmother's house really making their own way?

Annie gave a weighted sigh. "It isn't only that I'm frightened of having my child without help." Returning the cover to the popping skillet, she turned to the table and sat across from Rosemary. "My entire family is in Missouri." A soft smile touched her lips, and Rosemary could well imagine her large, loving family waiting for her to return to them.

Something twinged inside her. Self-pity, she supposed. The only so-called family she had left had pushed her away. Although thrown her away was more like it.

Mr. Freeman came back into the room, looking freshly scrubbed

and wearing a different shirt. He poured himself a cup of coffee and kissed his wife on the cheek.

Annie stood. "Supper will be finished directly," she said.

"Smells good enough to eat, Annie." He winked at Rosemary, and she couldn't resist a smile.

His wife rolled her eyes. "I should say so!"

"I can see why Rachel enjoyed your companionship, Annie. It's too bad you're leaving." She couldn't resist a sigh.

To her surprise, Silas remained at his wife's side. "Anything I can do to help?" he asked, surprising Rosemary even more.

"Goodness," Rosemary broke in before Annie could speak up. "Here I am, sitting idle, while you slave away over that stove. Please, let me help put supper on the table. Just tell me what to do."

"When it rains, it pours. Most days I'd give my right arm for a couple of helpers, and here I am with help but almost all the work is finished." Annie motioned to the shelf along the wall behind the table. "The plates are there." She smiled. "I'm glad I didn't pack them yet."

Rosemary got up and fetched three plates. She set each one on the table—one where she had been sitting, one where Annie's cup sat, and the other at the head of the table, where she assumed Silas would preside over the meal. She glanced around and was about to ask about silverware, when Annie anticipated her question and answered before she could voice it.

"Knives and forks are in the drawer below the shelf," Annie said. She cast a look of regret toward the beautiful, handcrafted cabinet. "I'm surely going to hate leaving that behind tomorrow."

Her words jolted Rosemary, reminding her of why she had come to the Freemans' home. She paused for a moment and turned her gaze to Silas. "Have you spoken to Finn about my suggestion?" Finn hadn't mentioned anything to her about the Freemans pulling up stakes. Not that he would have, but she'd have thought he might connect the idea of the inheritance and adding land to his.

"I did better than that."

"Oh, how so?" Rosemary opened the drawer and removed silverware for the three of them and headed back to the table.

"After you and I talked that night, I paid a visit to the land office and asked about someone leasing the land. The land officer frowned at the idea and said he'd have to research it before he'd know for sure. And of course I'm not waiting around for that. I thought Finn Tate might want to file on the plot, since he's just next door and a person can file for up to 320 acres nowadays if he plants trees on the land."

"Trees? Will they even grow here?"

"I reckon they would if someone moved all the rocks. Besides, they say trees make it rain. It can be mighty dry in this part of Dakota Territory."

That made sense, she supposed. "Did you let Finn know the land office was expecting him after you relinquish the land?"

"I spoke to him earlier this evening when he passed by here on his way home from town."

"And what did he say?"

"That's the curious thing. Finn's not interested, Miss Jackson."

"Call me Rosemary," she said offhandedly as her mind raced one way and then the other. Why would Finn not be interested in this place? Land measured a man's wealth and provided for his family when he was gone. He was the most exasperating man.

"Rosemary?" Annie's voice drew her from her reverie. She heard a clatter and realized she'd dropped a fork on the table.

"Goodness," she said, her cheeks growing hot. "I'm so sorry. I was completely lost in thought."

Silas grinned and righted his fork alongside his plate. "I'd offer you a penny to hear them, but I'm afraid I'd have to give an IOU even for that."

"Don't worry. I'll share them with you for free." She finished setting the table and took her place to the right of where Silas had taken his seat at the head. "Did Finn say why he wasn't interested?"

He stretched back as Annie set a platter of chicken on the table in front of him. He smiled at his wife, and the look of tenderness in his eyes filled Rosemary with longing. No man had ever loved her. Not that she had ever had time for all that silliness. Rachel had been the one given to dreaming and sighing over Lord Byron. Rosemary chided herself inwardly for allowing Silas's affection toward his wife to move her. The only man she'd ever wanted to marry didn't want her. And she'd never even asked him to love her.

That thought could lead to the sad state of self-pity, she knew that.

She leveled her gaze at Silas and placed her palms on the table. Underneath, her foot tapped the air. "What if I file on the land instead of Finn?" Rosemary's heart raced, and her voice shook with nerves and emotion. "Silas, listen to me. I can buy this house from you so you won't lose everything you've put into this place. I know how to run a successful ranch. My pa didn't have a son and I always loved the outdoors. It just seemed natural for me to learn his business. I wouldn't run it into the ground."

"But this is a farm, not a ranch."

"I'll be honest with you, Silas. I could never make a farm go. I'll try my hand at running my own ranch. Like my pa before me." She kept her expression deliberately stoic. "Let's take inventory of everything you've accomplished in the last three years, and I'll give you a fair price for any of the livestock and equipment you feel you need to leave behind. I'm going to have to buy a cow and chickens anyway. I don't even own a horse. I noticed there are several cows, and I assume you aren't planning to take an entire flock of chickens. As I said, I'll give you a fair price. Enough so that you won't go to your people penniless."

"I got to admit, you have a good eye for the way things are, Miss Jackson." Silas drew in a breath and held it then let it out and leveled his gaze at her. "I've tried to sell the livestock, but folks were hard-hit this winter. No one's going to have any cash money for a while. I was going to leave most of it, like you said."

"Well, then. Now you won't have to."

Annie set a bowl of potatoes on the table and then took her seat at the other end of the table, across from Silas. "But we aren't exactly penniless. We have a house and several acres of land in Missouri."

Silas smiled at his wife. "That's true, sweetheart, but without cash money, we won't be able to plant. If we can't plant, we won't have a harvest, and then we can't buy the things we need."

"Oh, that's nothing to worry about. You know Ma and Pa will give us plenty of start-up cash." She folded her hands in front of her. "Will you ask the blessing, husband?"

Rosemary bowed her head respectfully, but she couldn't help the fact that her mind raced far away from the subject of giving thanks for the food. She hoped the Lord would understand.

When Silas said amen, Rosemary waited for the plates to be filled before diving back into the subject. But before she could, Annie regarded her with a thoughtful gaze. "Rosemary, if you want to move in, there will be no one to stop you. The house will just be sitting here, anyway." She lifted a chicken leg to her lips and took a bite. "Why spend money you don't have to spend? Just go to the land office and file a claim tomorrow."

The thought had crossed her mind, but something told her that wasn't the way to do things—and since she'd asked the Lord to give her a solution, she didn't want to go against what she felt was from Him. "I don't feel right about profiting from your hard work, Silas."

Annie swallowed her bite of chicken. "But we're giving it up. It's not ours."

"Annie, Silas, my proposal is solid. I am offering a fair sum for the buildings, whatever livestock you choose to leave, the furnishings, any feed…. And in return, I have peace of mind that the land, with the improvements, plus the house and other buildings, are mine, fair and square."

"Some folks would call you a fool, Miss Jackson," Silas said. "Giving up good money when all you have to do is sign your name to a document and it's yours anyway."

"Folks can call me whatever they want. I'd rather start out with a clear conscience before God than take advantage of good people in a bad situation."

Annie shook her head. "But, goodness, what's a lone woman going to do with a homestead? What sort of man is going to come calling if you've no chaperone? Rachel was worried about you finding a proper match anyway. She so hated this country." Annie's eyes grew wide. "I have a perfect idea. You come to Missouri with us instead. You can buy a little plot of land there. I have two unmarried brothers and a passel of cousins for a pretty girl like you to choose from."

Heat crawled up Rosemary's neck. "I can't leave Rachel's daughter. My sister would have wanted me in her baby's life, even if Finn would rather forget I exist."

The Freemans exchanged an awkward glance.

"I'm sorry," Rosemary said. "I didn't mean to make things tense. I have an unfortunate habit of speaking when I should be silent." Her mind had tripped over Annie's comment that her sister had hated this country. She opened her mouth to ask about it, but their attention was diverted by a knock at the door.

Silas stood. "Who could that be?"

Rosemary had a pretty good idea of who would be standing on the other side of the door when Silas pulled it open.

Chapter Nine

....

There was no excuse for what Rosemary had done, running off like that. Rachel would never have stormed out of the house, saddled her own horse, and ridden off like an outlaw running from a posse. Anger burned through Finn as Silas opened the door.

"Finn!" Silas said, stepping aside. "Come in. What's in the basket? Oh, the baby."

Finn stomped into the room and headed toward the doorway leading into the kitchen.

"What on earth is wrong?" Silas asked.

"I've come to fetch Rosemary."

A gasp sounded from the kitchen. "How dare you presume that you can fetch me?"

"Come and sit down with us," Silas said, a hint of humor in his deep voice. "We've been having an interesting conversation."

Sarah squirmed inside the basket but, thankfully, didn't wake up. "Oh? I can well imagine what she had to say about me." He gave Rosemary a pointed glare.

"About you?" Rosemary's lips twisted into a sneer. "Let me assure you, Finn Tate—you were not the topic of our conversation."

Her words were so forceful, they took him aback. "What,

then? Why did you take the horse and come here, to my neighbor's home?"

"Please, Finn," Annie said, her soft voice beckoning him to the table. "Let me pour you some coffee."

"Thank you, Annie," Finn said. He set the basket on the table and took a seat. Sarah's squirming became a whimper. Rosemary's gaze moved to the basket.

"Go ahead, if you want to," he said.

Without so much as a word of thanks, she stood up and looked inside the basket. "Hi, pretty baby," she cooed. "Did you wake up from your nap? Come here to Aunt Rosie." The baby quieted the instant she heard Rosemary's voice. And when she picked her up, Sarah snuggled against her shoulder and pressed her face into Rosemary's neck in a way she never did with Finn.

Annie set a cup of coffee in front of him, and Silas slid the sugar bowl across the table. "Rosemary came to make me an offer," Silas said. His eyes smiled as he spoke, and Finn had the notion that his friend was mocking him.

"What sort of offer?" Finn narrowed his eyes and turned to Rosemary then back to Silas. "What is going on here?"

"Well," Rosemary said, "at the moment, I'd say what is going on is that your daughter is soaking wet and in need of a change."

Annie reached for Sarah. "Let me take her. I'll get her all fixed up."

"Oh, I forgot to bring her a…" Finn felt like a fool.

"How could you forget to bring her a change?" Rosemary asked, her accusing tone raising Finn's hackles.

"How could you steal a horse and ride off?"

"Steal…?"

Annie interrupted, cooing to Sarah, "It's okay, yes, it is. Mr. Silas has a clean shirt that will do just as well."

"My shirt? Why aren't you using a towel from the kitchen?"

"Don't be ungracious, sir. Princess Sarah is a damsel in distress and in need of your help." Annie grinned at Silas, causing a lump to rise in Finn's throat. He missed the companionship marriage brought.

"Silly woman," Silas said. "Go. My shirt is Princess Sarah's shirt."

The entire exchange lifted the tension.

"All right," Finn said, trying to keep his voice calm as he addressed Rosemary. "Now what sort of offer did you make to Silas?"

She lifted her chin stubbornly. "I offered to do what you chose not to—pay a fair price for anything he wants to leave behind that will help me live on my own here. I intend to file on this land first thing in the morning."

"Well, I'm sure Silas has too much integrity to take advantage of your foolishness. He'd never encourage you to take on such a task alone." He rolled his eyes as he turned to Silas to confirm. "And what is a woman going to do alone on a homestead?"

Silas shrugged. "Women homestead all the time."

"What else would you have me do, Finn? Take in sewing like Marta Fischer?" Rosemary's smile didn't reach her eyes. "I'm sorry, but I'm not that good a seamstress. I'm sure you remember that I spent my time on the ranch with my pa. I have no means to make a living but to own my own land."

Finn gave a short laugh. "You could learn to cook the best food I've ever eaten, but you didn't have time to learn to sew."

"Thank you for the compliment. I didn't say I couldn't sew, just not well enough to make a living at it." She turned to Silas. "Mr. Freeman, my offer is on the table. I could file on a different plot of land, but I want to be near my niece. And if my land is connected to her pa's land, she would have the run of the fields between the two homes."

A hint of respect touched Finn's heart. But he felt sorry for her. She truly believed she would get this place. "Rosemary, I'm sorry, but you can't just take this place over. How will you make it succeed?"

"Really, Finn." Rosemary turned to him. "How can you even ask that? I know business. I ran my pa's ranch for the last two years and practically ran it since I was fifteen. If he hadn't believed that a woman can't be successful without a man, I would be running his ranch right now instead of being removed from my sister's home by her husband who was supposed to love her."

Ignoring the obvious challenge, Finn turned to his friend. "Silas, why are you leaving? You have a prosperous place here."

Rosemary spoke up before Silas could. "Some husbands care enough to keep their wives near their family."

Silas shrugged with a rueful half smile. "She's right. Annie needs to be near her family," he said. "Her grandmother left us a house and land, and she's aching to go home." He shrugged, and then he turned to Rosemary. "Miss Jackson, you have a deal. Thank you for having the integrity to buy me out rather than waiting for me to be gone."

"What?" Shoving to his feet, Finn planted his fists on the table and stared down at Silas. "Why would you do this?"

"Two reasons. One: I need start-up money to plant this year. Otherwise I'll be forced to live on handouts from Annie's family, and I can't do that." He glanced at Rosemary and then back to Finn. "You won't like my second reason. You sure you want to hear it?"

"Yes, I do want to hear it. Help me to understand how you could be my friend for three years and then go against my wishes like this."

Silas leveled his gaze at Finn and took a deep breath before continuing. "You aren't doing right by this woman. You and I both know you should marry her and let her help you raise Sarah. It's what Rachel would want. And it's not just for Rosemary. She's one smart woman and you need her; you're just too stubborn to admit it."

"You don't know what you're talking about."

Rosemary jumped to her feet and commanded the attention despite her slight stature. "Now you two listen here. First of all, Finn, you don't speak for me. I make my own decisions and my own business arrangements. The only choice you have about where I live is whether or not that's with you. And you've already chosen. So you have nothing to say about this arrangement between Silas and me."

Turning immediately to Silas, she gave Finn no chance to respond. "As for you…I'm grateful you've accepted my offer. You may have to hold off traveling for a day so that I may find a bank and draw the funds. And just so we're clear, this is a business arrangement. This is not a consolation prize because you don't believe I've been treated fairly by my sister's husband. Finn is under no obligation to tie me into a marriage of convenience. And the more I've considered it, the less I like the idea anyway. Also, I'd like for you to come with me to the land office just to be sure the land is clear for me to file on. We all know about rumors of corruption. I don't want to take any chances that someone is just waiting to swoop in and snatch up this land."

Finn knew he'd been outvoted, and with a sinking feeling in the pit of his stomach, he realized he'd lost the land he'd hoped to file on himself. It was his own fault, he figured. He should have offered a price the way Rosemary had, but truth be told, he'd used all the cash he'd had left for supplies. He never would have been able to offer Silas the sort of price he deserved. But that didn't mean he didn't feel his friend's betrayal. Rosemary had no business setting up housekeeping on the property next to his. This was nothing more than a ploy to try to take Sarah away from him.

"Well, I reckon there's nothing more for me to say." He glanced about, looking for his daughter, and blinked to find Annie leaning against the wall, cuddling the baby. He'd been so caught up in the current argument, he hadn't noticed her return.

She smiled at him. "Looking for someone?"

"Yes. Thank you for changing her." He reached out as Annie walked across the room. He gently took Sarah and laid her in the basket before turning to Rosemary. "This doesn't change anything. She's mine, and I'll decide how she'll be raised."

Rosemary nodded. "Of course. I'll be by to collect my things in a day or two. May I keep Rachel's horse until then? I'll have to find a wagon and team to purchase."

Finn could almost hear Rachel's voice from the past year. *"Poor Charity. I can't ride her in this condition. It isn't fair to her that she must be imprisoned in that barn day in and day out."*

Knowing what his wife would have him do, Finn relented on this one thing. "The horse and sidesaddle are yours."

She narrowed her gaze. "I don't understand. What do you want in return?"

"I want nothing from you." He shook his head. "Look, Rachel would want you to have her. So she's yours. No catch."

Her full lips parted, and she took in a breath. "Why, thank you, Finn. I–I'm at a loss for words."

"As I said, it's what Rachel would have wanted." He walked toward the door then turned before he reached for it. "Don't bother coming to the house for your things. I'll bring them over first thing in the morning." The sooner he got Rosemary Jackson out of his life, the sooner he could get on with raising Rachel's daughter.

Chapter Ten

....

The morning dawned brisk and clear with puffy white clouds set against a backdrop of glorious blue sky. Rosemary sat alongside Silas on the wagon seat as the wagon dipped and swayed against the ruts caused by the latest snow and muddy travel—according to Silas.

Only after Finn stormed out had she realized she had no place to sleep for the night, nor had she thought to grab her reticule before riding away from Finn's. Of course Annie had assured her that she was more than welcome to sleep in their home and had made up a pallet close to the fireplace in the sitting room for her.

Silas had gone after Finn and returned an hour later with Rosemary's valise filled with the things she'd carried with her on the train, along with her reticule.

Irritation burned her stomach as she realized that Finn had stuffed Rachel's inheritance draft into the bag. If he was truly determined not to accept his share of Pa's ranch, then, Rosemary decided, she would put the money away for Sarah's future. The calendar would turn another century before Sarah grew to womanhood. With the dawning of the twentieth century, who knew the leaps the country might take toward how women were viewed? From where Rosemary sat, Sarah's opportunities seemed endless.

She and Silas rolled into Paddington as the land office was opening. Rosemary had slept little during the night, worrying that someone else might get there first and file on the plot of land. She had trouble holding still until Silas could brake the wagon, jump down, come around to her side, and offer her a hand down.

"Now, there are going to be men inside. They don't have any real business in there. I'd say they're sort of unofficial deputies to make sure no one comes in with a gun and shoots anyone else."

Alarm seized her. "Does that happen?"

"It has." He nodded and took firm hold of her elbow as they approached the door. "But around here, land isn't as scarce nor as wanted. Like I told you last night, it's rocky and we don't get much rain and snow."

"I find that difficult to believe after the blizzard we just experienced."

He nodded, and his mouth tipped. "Trust me. Those are rare occurrences."

Silas opened the door and stepped aside for Rosemary to walk inside first. The sun shining through the front window illuminated the thick layer of dust on everything—the benches, the desk, the shelves, the cabinet....

Four men stood inside the small building, and the odor of unwashed bodies threatened to overwhelm Rosemary's stomach.

The land officer looked up and glanced from Silas to her. He scowled. "Let me guess. You're here to file on Mr. Freeman's land?"

"Yes." Rosemary forced herself to look him in the eyes. "He has just relinquished that portion of land, and I would like to file a claim, please."

The land officer speared Silas with his gaze. "You sure this is what you want to do?"

Silas glanced about. Rosemary watched him. A sense of foreboding slid over her as he shifted from one foot to the other. Was it her imagination, or did Silas seem nervous? He cleared his throat then nodded at the land officer. "I'm sure."

The graying man shook his head and reached into his desk with a sigh. He licked his thumb and yanked out a form. "Fill out this application."

Trying not to show how intimidated she was, Rosemary took the form and looked around for a spot to sit. She hated to sit anywhere in this pigsty. Especially in her barely worn gown. The place needed a good cleaning.

"Allow me, miss."

Looking up, Rosemary found herself staring into a pair of green eyes. The star on the man's chest identified him as the sheriff. His smile lit the room even more than the intrusive rising sun. He shed his coat and laid it gallantly on the bench.

"Why, thank you, sir." She sat down on the coat and watched as he walked to one of the bookshelves behind the desk and pulled down a large ledger book. "You can use this to keep the application steady as you write."

Taking the book, she set it on her lap and smiled. "Thank you, Sheriff."

"You're most welcome."

He crammed his hat on his head and moved toward the door. He glanced back at the land officer. "Try to be more polite to the ladies."

Clearly undaunted, the man grunted and kept to his business.

The sheriff opened the door, and Rosemary stood. "Wait, Sheriff." The book and paper fell from her lap.

The sheriff returned. He knelt down and retrieved the things that had fallen.

Rosemary sputtered her thanks as she took the items and clutched them to her. As he looked down at her, smiling, her stomach fluttered. "What about your coat?"

"You keep it for now. No sense in getting that pretty dress dirty." He tipped his hat. "I'll come back for it."

She watched him as he walked to the door. He lifted a hand in farewell and disappeared into the gleam of light invading the threshold.

Silas leaned down, whispering in her ear, "Don't let that smile of his fool you. Finn's worth ten of that man."

Rosemary's cheeks blazed. Had she been that obvious? She swallowed hard and met his gaze straight on. "Finn isn't an option, and I assure you that I have no interest in anything except filing my claim."

Thirty minutes later, Rosemary walked out of the land office with her shoulders straight and her head high. The sky looked bluer, the air felt fresher, and she couldn't stop smiling.

"You look like you're on top of the world." Silas smiled as he held out his arm.

She grinned and slipped her gloved hand into the crook of his elbow. "I am on top of the world." Laughter bubbled from her. Finally, she had her own plot of land. In her mind's eye, she saw green fields covered with grazing cattle...although she wouldn't be able to raise many head of cattle on 160 acres.

"Silas, is the land on the other side of you taken?"

"Don't you mean on the other side of you?"

Excitement shot through her stomach again. "Yes, on the other side of my land."

His eyes clouded and a frowned creased his brow. "It's taken. And you'll meet him soon enough, so you should hear what I'm going to say and be careful."

"Freeman!"

Silas visibly tensed as a man stomped out of the barbershop next to the land office. "This is the man I was going to tell you about," he said in a low tone that raised Rosemary's curiosity. "He's bad news."

Rosemary stared at the man. She had never seen anyone's face so red with anger before. He still had a towel around his neck, and only half his face was shaved.

"Good morning, Mr. Clayton," Silas said, covering Rosemary's hand with his. "I'd like to introduce you to…"

Ignoring Silas's words, the angry man didn't even glance her way. "I hear you're hightailing it out of here."

"My wife's grandmother passed on and we're moving back to Missouri so she can be with her family. If that's what you call 'hightailing it,' then I reckon we are."

The unpleasant man gave a short laugh. He eyed Rosemary. "This isn't your missus."

"Mr. Clayton, let me introduce Miss Jackson. She's just filed on the land I forfeited."

Rosemary angled a glance at Silas. Was it her imagination, or did he seem a bit too gleeful revealing that fact to the man?

"What do you mean?" The man's face went a darker shade of red.

Rosemary felt compelled to speak up before he went into fits. "It's all fair and square, sir. Just ask the land office. I have my receipt."

"I'm conducting this conversation with Mr. Freeman, miss." His rudeness set Rosemary's teeth on edge. Only then did she notice that the four men who had been standing inside the land office were now perched along their path. Clearly, they worked for Mr. Clayton. So much for them being "sort of deputies," as Silas had claimed.

"Indeed? Well, sir, I was having a perfectly nice conversation of my own with Mr. Freeman before you interrupted in your most inappropriate state of dress." She tucked her hand inside Silas's elbow. "Come, Mr. Freeman. We have business at the bank."

"You don't want to cross me, little miss."

But Rosemary understood bullies like him. From time to time, her pa had come up against landowners who believed themselves to be above everyone else and entitled to unearned respect. As much as she wanted to respect her elders, Rosemary couldn't abide a man of this temperament. "Perhaps it's you who does not want to cross me." She smiled to show him that she wasn't a bit afraid of him, although her legs shook beneath her skirt. "Look straight ahead," she murmured to Silas. "Do not give him the satisfaction of thinking we care whether or not his thugs are following us."

"We meet again, miss." The sheriff seemed to appear from nowhere, but Rosemary realized he had been leaning in the doorway of his office. "Would you permit me to escort you and your friend?"

"Thank you, Sheriff." Rosemary nearly collapsed to the ground with relief. She started to glance over her shoulder, but the sheriff squeezed her elbow. "Don't look back. They're still watching you."

"I'm sorry for all that back there, Miss Jackson." Silas released a shaky breath.

"Oh, don't be. It's not your fault."

"You're much too generous," he said.

The sheriff spoke up. "I agree." Rosemary's elbow was still wrapped in his hand, and she was beginning to get flustered. She fell silent.

When they reached the bank, Rosemary turned to the sheriff. "Thank you, Sheriff... I'm sorry, I don't know your name."

He smiled. "Dennis Mayfield at your service, miss." He turned his gaze toward Silas, and his eyes lost the tender humor of only a few minutes ago. "You should be more careful when you're escorting ladies."

Rosemary felt compelled to defend her friend even against this handsome man who had come to her rescue twice. "But Mr. Clayton accosted us. Silas wasn't at fault."

Sheriff Mayfield nodded. "I apologize if my eyes deceived me. It appeared to me that Mr. Clayton had a bone to pick with your friend." His tone had gone from warm and welcoming to suspicious and maybe even a little angry.

"But that's silly." Rosemary rolled her eyes. "Listen, I was raised on a large cattle ranch. Wealthy men like Mr. Clayton only want one thing: more land. He's just in a temper because I was able to file a claim for the property before he could. And trust me, Silas doesn't need to protect me, and neither did you. I've been dealing with his kind my whole life."

"You're a little bit of a wildfire, aren't you?" The sheriff's eyes lit with something that Rosemary would have labeled interest if she'd had enough vanity to speak of. Rather, she designated the spark in his eye as surprise that a woman would stand up to a man this way.

Besides, she didn't appreciate the word "wild" being used to describe her. That was a little too close to "fast" or "easy."

"No, sir. I'm not wild. But I can see plainly that Mr. Clayton manages things around here. And I, for one, will not be managed. That doesn't make me wild."

"I've offended you, and that wasn't my intention. What I should have said was that it makes you brave."

She felt her cheeks warm. "Brave, I like. Good day, Sheriff Mayfield. Thank you again for your kindness. It was a pleasure to make your acquaintance."

"The pleasure was all mine. I hope to see you again." His eyebrows went up. "Perhaps at the dance next week?"

"Dance?" Rosemary's heart lifted at the thought.

"At City Hall on Friday."

Regret tugged at her heart. "I'm afraid that won't be possible. I live alone and have no one to bring me." A woman might live alone, but she certainly couldn't drive herself to a dance after dark.

"I'd be honored to escort you," Sheriff Mayfield said.

Rosemary's eyes widened as horror shook her to the core. "Sheriff, I assure you, I was not hinting at an invitation. I could no more ride with a man who is not my husband with no chaperone present than I could drive myself. Good day, sir."

She quickly ducked inside the bank.

Silas followed her. "Don't swoon." He grinned. "Looks like Finn best open his eyes soon if he doesn't want to lose the woman who's right in front of his face. Although I still maintain that Finn's worth ten of the sheriff."

"Oh, hush. That was just about the most humiliating experience of my life." She wanted to burst into tears but forced herself to maintain her dignity.

"I'm going to walk down and get the wagon so you don't have to be subjected to those men again."

"I appreciate the thoughtfulness, but I'm not afraid."

He smiled. "Then you're braver than I am. I'll be in the wagon out front when you're finished."

"All right." Rosemary said a quick prayer of protection for him as she watched him go. Then she turned to her own business.

Rosemary's presence in the bank commanded attention— and more respect, she was gratified to note—than she had received from the land officer and the thugs on the street. She wore a stylish gown of dark blue and a small hat she had ordered from New York City a few months before Pa had gotten sick. Pa had always told her that when she visited banks and lawyers, she needed to dress like she knew exactly what she wanted. Otherwise, businessmen would try to take advantage of the fact that she was a woman.

Mr. Lowenstein, the banker, ushered her into his office. He shoved his round spectacles up from the tip of his nose and smiled. "What may I do for you, miss?"

Gathering a breath, Rosemary handed over the two bank drafts to the middle-aged man.

"Now, what have we here?" He spent a few minutes going over the drafts then looked up at her over his spectacles. "I'll need to send a telegram to the bank in Hayes, Kansas, of course. But I see no reason not to open an account for you." He glanced at the second draft and frowned. "This one is made out to a Mrs. Rachel Tate?"

"And her husband, Finn. Rachel was my sister." Rosemary swallowed past the lump in her throat and tried to maintain her composure. She sat ramrod straight in the chair, never allowing her back to touch or her shoulders to slouch. "My pa passed on, and his attorney, Mr. Jacobs, executed the distribution of his will. Unbeknownst to us, my sister, Rachel, died two months before my pa from complications of childbirth."

Mr. Lowenstein removed his spectacles and pinched the bridge of his nose. "I'm sorry for your double loss, Miss Jackson. But upon Mrs. Tate's death, the inheritance must go to her husband. We have only one Tate with an account. Would that be Mr. Finnias Tate?"

"Precisely. And believe me, I want him to have it, but he refuses to accept the money. I am at a loss as to what I can do to convince him." She shrugged. "Would I be allowed to deposit the money into his account without his knowledge?"

"You mean to tell me you truly weren't trying to cash both of these for your own use?" He frowned and leveled his beady gaze at her once more.

"Of course not!" Rosemary's hands shook at the outrageous questioning of her character. She was nothing if not honest. And more often than not, she had been told she was too honest for her own good. She stood and stared down with as much dignity as she possessed. "Perhaps I should take my business to Williston. It might be forty miles, but I'd prefer a good long drive to the insult of being accused of cheating my own flesh and blood. And by that I mean my sister's daughter."

"Oh, there's a child?"

"Well, of course there is. I told you, my sister passed away after giving birth."

"Forgive me, Miss Jackson." He leaned forward and clasped his almost feminine-looking hands on the desk. "I've seen too much treachery to recognize a woman of integrity." He motioned to the chair she had just vacated. "Please, may we begin again?"

Slightly mollified, Rosemary sat back down. "Fine."

"If a child was born to Mrs. Tate and Mr. Tate refuses the inheritance, then, yes, you may set up a trust for the child with the draft once I verify that everything is in order." He held up his left hand. "Not that I believe anything is untoward—it's simply bank policy."

"Of course, Mr. Lowenstein," Rosemary said. "I would expect you to check the validity of the drafts."

"It may be tomorrow before we receive return telegrams. Are you staying in town?"

"I hadn't planned on it, but I suppose I can use the day to conduct other business." She held out her hand.

Mr. Lowenstein stared at her open palm and frowned. "Miss Jackson?"

"The drafts." She gave him her prettiest smile. "I am sure you are as honest as I am, but you'll understand if I take these with me until such time as you verify that I have the right to open the accounts."

His face flushed, and he handed over the slips of paper. "Why, of course. That's only reasonable. Please come back in the morning, and I should have your answer."

Rosemary tucked the drafts into her reticule and stood. She shook Mr. Lowenstein's hand, and he escorted her through the lobby and held open the door as she exited.

Silas hopped down from the wagon where he'd been waiting and walked around to the other side with her while she explained the situation.

He groaned. "Annie's chomping at the bit to leave."

"I'm sorry, Silas. I should have realized that the bank would need to verify a draft of that size." She took his hand as he helped her into the seat. "What would you like to do?"

"That depends on your plans."

"Well, I really must procure a wagon and a team. I also would like to find a local rancher who might sell me a few head of cattle."

"May I make a suggestion?"

"Of course." Anyone who had been so successful at his own homestead in such a harsh part of the country had much wisdom to offer.

"Sheep."

"What do you mean, sheep?"

"Some of the farmers are beginning to raise sheep herds instead of farming. The rocks make it nearly impossible to plow without moving them."

Rosemary shuddered at the very thought of raising sheep. She remembered Pa storming into the house and pacing the floor when a family of sheep farmers took up residence five miles from the ranch. *"Just wait,"* he'd railed. *"Them wooly varmints are gonna tear up all the good grazing land and starve us out of house and home."* She recounted the incident to Silas.

"And did they starve you out of house and home?" He grinned. "You're little, but I'd venture to say you haven't been starved."

Rosemary couldn't help but laugh. "As a matter of fact, within

three years four more sheep ranchers moved into the valley and my pa ended up good friends with every one of them. Although some of the other ranchers tried to declare a range war to bully them out."

Men like Mr. Clayton.

"So, by and large, sheep farmers and cattle ranchers shared the land without any of the animals suffering. Correct?"

"I suppose," Rosemary said. "But that doesn't mean I'm willing to risk everything on them. I wouldn't have the slightest notion how to care for sheep. Or how to get them sheared and the wool to market. I could lose Sarah's future."

"You can always learn about raising sheep. There are plenty of men around here who would oblige you." He shook his head. "Besides, don't you think you should be worrying about your own future? Finn's pretty determined about you not interfering where his daughter is concerned."

"True. But he won't be this stubborn forever."

"You mean you think he'll eventually ask you to marry him?"

"Probably not." Rosemary wasn't sure whether to laugh or be embarrassed at his comment, but Silas was an honest man asking an honest question, and she saw no need to pretend anything other than truth. "He's probably right about marriage. Mercy. Except for the way we look, Rachel and I are—were—very different. He loved her. He couldn't possibly love me. And I wouldn't be happy to live the rest of my life with a man who saw another woman every time he looked at me."

Silas reached down and undid the brake. He flapped the reins, and the horses slowly began to walk down the dusty street. "I think you give yourself too little credit. Finn loved Rachel, no doubt about that. But after ten minutes with you, there's also no doubt that you could be no one but Rosemary Jackson. He doesn't have the two of you confused."

"But Rosemary Jackson isn't the woman he wants."

"Give him time. I think you've done exactly the right thing by taking over the homestead. As you said, he'll eventually come around. Unless you'd rather be courted by someone else." The sheriff stood in front of the barber shop, talking to Clayton's men.

Heat rushed to her cheeks. "I'm not interested in being courted by anyone. And if you're implying I might want the sheriff to come calling, as I've already mentioned, a woman living alone has to take precautions to observe propriety. I could never do anything that might cause Sarah any future embarrassment. You know how scandals, either real or imagined, tend to hang on."

"You are an honorable woman, Miss Jackson." Silas shook his head and she knew he wanted to mention Finn again. She was relieved that he fell silent instead.

Taking in the town of Paddington, Rosemary noted the city hall, the general store, the land office, and the sheriff's office. On the other side of the street stood the bank from which they had just come, the granary, the feed store, and a smithy. She had to admit that for such a primitive culture, compared to Kansas, these hardy Northerners had done pretty well with this town. With the exception of the dingy saloon with a hotel above it.

With a sigh, she addressed Silas's last comment about Finn eventually coming around. "I didn't mean he'll come around to me. I meant, he will eventually realize that he needs my help in raising

Sarah. How will he go to the fields and plow with a baby to care for?"

"How will you run a ranch with a baby?"

"The same way Indian women have always worked and cared for their infants."

"A cradle board?" He grinned as though she had discovered the contraption herself.

"Not exactly, but something similar. Besides, I'm going to hire ranch hands. Especially if I decide to raise sheep."

"So you're considering it?"

She nodded. "I'd like to hear more about the process first."

"If you're truly interested, there's a sheep rancher a couple miles west of here. He's selling out and moving West."

"Sounds like a promising idea. Yes, let's go visit the man."

Expecting Silas to continue out of town, Rosemary frowned when he stopped the wagon in front of a two-story home. "What's this?" she asked.

He set the brake and wrapped the reins, nodding toward the sign out front that proclaimed ROOMS TO LET. "The boardinghouse. I thought you'd want to settle into a room before you went about your business."

Boardinghouse. The very thought raised her ire as it had the day before. Finn had actually thought he could pack her off to this place. And what had he expected she would do with her days? A single woman without a livelihood? Ridiculous. "I suppose it makes the most sense. Besides, I should tell the woman who runs the place that I won't be living here."

She climbed down without waiting for Silas to help. "What do you mean?" he asked.

In as few words as possible she relayed the argument that had preceded her appearance at his dinner table.

Silas tossed back his head and laughed out loud. "I love him like a brother, but that Finn can sure be a fool."

The door opened and an elderly woman stood with her hands planted on her tiny hips.

"Hello, ma'am," Silas said. "The lady would like to rent a room if you have one available."

She leveled her gaze at Silas, her eyes scrutinizing him until Rosemary grew a bit uncomfortable. Clearly she had heard the laughter and drawn the wrong conclusion about the two of them.

"I don't mean to be rude," Rosemary began, "but have you an empty room or not?"

The woman glanced at Rosemary then turned back to Silas, her gaze remaining suspicious. "I've seen you in town before. But not with this woman. I don't rent rooms to riffraff or adulterers. Go on down to the hotel. That man'll rent to anyone."

Indignation shot through Rosemary. "I beg your pardon!" She took another step and glared even though she had never been insolent to an elder in her life. But this was too much. "I am here for a room while I await business with the bank. Furthermore, this gentleman has a wife waiting for him at home, and he is simply offering me a kindness in escorting me to your establishment. I would no more stay in a filthy hotel above a saloon than I would walk across the street unclothed."

The woman frowned but stepped aside. "Land sakes, girl. No need to be vulgar. Come on in. I reckon you'll do."

"Thank you, ma'am." She had to learn to hold her tongue, but her outburst had apparently satisfied the owner of the boardinghouse.

"I'm Mrs. Franklin, and I own this place."

"It's a pleasure to meet you, ma'am."

The woman moved slowly, without solid footing. Rosemary worried she might stumble and stayed close by her side to steady her, if need be. The elderly woman led her into the parlor, waving her to a seat. "Tell me about yourself."

Rosemary took a seat on the settee and folded her hands in her lap. "First of all, I believe my brother-in-law erroneously made arrangements for me to have an indefinite stay in your lovely home."

"Ah, you must be Rosemary Jackson?"

"Yes, ma'am."

"What made him think you needed a room if you don't?" She frowned deeply, which pushed her loose skin around her eyes until Rosemary wondered if she could even see.

While Silas sat a respectable distance away in a wing chair, Rosemary relayed as much of her story as she felt appropriate. "So, you see, I've already filed on Mr. Freeman's homestead and will be moving into the home as soon as Mr. Lowenstein verifies that the bank draft is valid."

"I admire a woman taking matters into her own hands and doing what needs to be done." Mrs. Franklin inched forward and attempted to stand. Silas was at her side, with his hand extended, in an instant. Grabbing her cane with one hand, she sighed, putting her other hand in his. "One day, no matter how much you'd like to see to your own affairs, your age catches up with you and you need more help than you'd like to admit."

They followed her to the stairway just outside the parlor, where she pointed upstairs. "The second door on the right," she said to

Rosemary. "You'll sleep there tonight. It's my best room. I've been saving it for just the right guest. It's a pity you aren't going to stay here permanently." She turned to Silas. "How about you? Do you want a room too?"

"No, ma'am," he said. "I'm going home to my wife, and I'll come back in the morning for Miss Jackson." He hesitated. "That is, after she finishes conducting the rest of her business."

Rosemary and Silas spent the rest of the day purchasing supplies and tending other business. By the time Rosemary made her way back to the boardinghouse around suppertime, she had gone with Silas to meet the sheep farmer and haggled over the price of sheep. She had no idea whether or not she'd made a good bargain. Either way, she walked back into the boardinghouse with her head high, the proud almost-owner of a homestead and the very proud owner of one hundred head of sheep. She hired the young man who had been working for the previous owner, so at the very least, there was someone who knew how to tend sheep.

No matter that the room was beautiful and the feather bed soft and the house quiet, Rosemary barely slept all night. Silas would be back early in the morning, they would take care of business at the bank, and then he and Annie would be on their way to Missouri and she would begin her life as a woman sheep farmer. Pa was likely rolling over in his grave at the thought. But he had chosen not to allow her to run his ranch, so she had made the best decision she could. Raising cattle would have been more taxing and more expensive. And she honestly hadn't known for sure if she could begin a ranch and be successful. But sheep farming, on the other hand, seemed providential.

She daydreamed deep into the night, and by the time the sun rose with the promise of another beautiful day, her thoughts had returned to Finn for what seemed like the hundredth time that night. A soft smile touched her lips. If he hated the thought of her homesteading so close to him, what was Finn going to say when he discovered that not only was she his new neighbor, but his other neighbors were one hundred sheep?

Chapter Eleven
....

By the time she had conducted her business with the banker the following morning and returned to the homestead, the sun had risen high in the sky. With Sarah's inheritance safely tucked away in the bank, Rosemary felt confident in her decision to homestead her own land and raise a herd of sheep. Still, the thought of being alone filled her with uncertainty.

Silas had finished packing up the wagon the night before, and they were all set to leave. "Are you sure you don't want to wait until morning and get a fresh start?"

Silas and Annie shook their heads simultaneously. Annie gathered her for a quick hug and released her. "If we leave now, we can still get in several hours of travel before dark."

Silas shook her hand. "Thank you for everything."

"I only wish you'd let me pay more for the animals. I would have had to purchase them anyway." For some reason, Silas had dropped the price they had agreed upon to half and wouldn't explain why. Rosemary hated to be suspicious of a new friend, but she wondered if perhaps his sudden burst of generosity had to do with the confrontation with Mr. Clayton. There was definitely a situation between the men, a situation Silas had chosen not to share, but Rosemary had a feeling she might have to end whatever problem had started between the two. But that didn't mean she wanted to cheat Silas just because he was most likely feeling guilty. "I would be more than happy to pay the original price."

"With the price you've paid, I will have plenty to buy seeds and a new plow. That's all I need."

But she couldn't feel good about it. "But I feel as though I'm taking advantage of a friend."

He smiled and patted her shoulder. "Don't feel that way. We are grateful that you came along as it was, or we'd have given away everything we didn't want to take."

They had kept one cow, two hens and a rooster, and some of their possessions from inside the house, but otherwise, Silas and Annie truly were starting over in Missouri.

As she watched them amble down the road, she realized with a start that the homestead belonged to her. Or it would in five years after she proved up. And she would definitely finish her time on the land. Slowly she turned and looked at her home. The wood house—made of lumber, not logs—was one of the finest she'd seen in these parts, even though it was small.

She walked slowly to the porch, savoring each step. This was all she'd ever wanted, to live in her own home and run a ranch. She'd always envisioned that to be the ranch where she'd grown up in Kansas, but maybe this was better...putting her finger-prints on her own place. She could never farm on her own—she'd never learned how—and ranching cattle on only 160 acres wouldn't be profitable, but raising sheep made sense. They took

up much, much less grazing land than cattle, and their wool would bring a price every year. In no time the sheep would pay for themselves.

She took the steps to her home one at a time, taking in the smell of wood smoke from that morning's fire. The aroma of fried bacon from lunch still clung to the air. Together they called out to her, "This is home."

She pushed open the door and stood on the threshold. Waiting, she supposed, for an invitation, but mostly she wanted to gather in the sight of her house. Silas and Annie had taken the settee but left the two wooden rocking chairs and a red wing chair. A heavy wooden trunk sat in the corner, filled, she knew, with two quilts and other linens. Annie had waved aside her concern at not taking them along. "My brother makes those trunks. He'll fashion us another, and truly, we have no room in the wagon. My Silas is insisting we travel light to spare the horses."

And the quilts? They looked special. "I have packed the quilt my grandmother made for our wedding and two others. The women in my family have quilting bees all the time." She had laughed then. "Stop worrying so, my new good friend Rosemary Jackson. I left a surprise for you inside the trunk. So after we're gone and you have time, open it up."

Rosemary walked across the wooden floor and dropped to her knees beside the trunk. She lifted the lid and found a note on top.

Dear Rosemary,

Rachel started this quilt as a gift for you. That's why

she rode over here so often. I was teaching her when she discovered her pregnancy. When she died, I finished it for her. Most of the work was done by her own hand.

With love,

Annie

A tender love for her sister washed over Rosemary as she gently lifted the folded quilt from the trunk. She had never understood the differences in quilt patterns when the ladies spoke of them during bazaars and Sunday afternoon dinners at church, but as she spread this one out over the bed in her room off the kitchen, she recognized the silk from their mother's wedding gown. Though Rosemary's heart swelled with love for Rachel and though she appreciated her desire to give her something of their mother that she could keep forever, she couldn't help but wish that Rachel hadn't cut up the gown. Rachel had been able to wear it during her own wedding to Finn. Rosemary had always seen herself wearing Mama's gown too. Now that could never happen.

Had Rachel somehow known she would never marry?

A tear formed in Rosemary's eye and she lay across the quilt, keenly aware that she was alone in her beautiful house. Her joy over finally having her own home somehow seemed a little emptier now. What good was a beautiful house and acres of land if there was no one with whom to share them?

Somehow she drifted off to sleep, for she awoke with a start to find the room growing dim. She couldn't remember the last time she'd slept during the day. Embarrassed, she rose from her bed and walked into the kitchen. The sound of her shoes on the wood floor

resounded through the house. With a sigh, she lit the oil lamp and then the stove for coffee.

She took her Bible from the mantel and sat in the rocking chair to read, keenly aware of every sound inside and outside the house. The crickets were beginning to chirp. The cow lowed in the pen, and she knew she'd have to milk her soon.

The boards groaned from time to time, making her stomach turn. She wished it hadn't been so clear that she'd be staying all alone on the homestead. All the men in the land office knew. She wished now that she had asked her new helper, Rolf, to bring the sheep and start tonight, but they had agreed that tomorrow would be better. After tonight, at least she would have one hand in the bunkhouse. Honestly, she couldn't imagine why Silas had even built a bunkhouse when he'd intended to farm the land, but she couldn't help but be glad he'd done so.

She was just about to go into the kitchen for her coffee and to find something to eat when she heard a noise on the porch. Sucking in a breath, she reached for the Winchester over the fireplace. The noise grew louder, scratching, and...whining?

What on earth?

Walking to the door with the gun in her hand, she grabbed the latch and yanked, hoping for the element of surprise should there be a threat on the other side of the door.

Instead a happy bark greeted her, and in an instant a pair of paws rested on her shoulders, forcing her to take two steps backward to keep her balance.

"Cooper!" she hollered. "Get down."

Her heartbeat picked up. She stepped onto the porch, looking for Finn. But there was no one but the big, floppy dog, nudging her thigh until he nearly knocked her over. "Are you here alone, fella?" she asked, scratching his head. Truth be told, she was thrilled to see him. But she hated the idea that Finn might worry about the dog.

She gave a shrug. "Oh well," she said, walking back inside. "If Finn worries about you, he'll come looking, won't he? In the meantime, you should get to choose where you live. Just like I do." She giggled.

Cooper wagged his tail and licked her hand. "Come on, then," she said. "Let's get something to eat."

Chapter Twelve
....

Plowing the fields gave Finn plenty of time to think, and as much as he hated the thought, he had to admit that Rosemary's absence from the house this past week made it seem emptier and less like a home somehow. Even though he had only shared the home with her for a day, she had forced him back to life and he couldn't get her out of his head. She was a handful, to be sure.

Where Rachel had been compliant and easy to persuade, Rosemary seemed as though she were crafted by God with the sole purpose of getting her back up against sensible solutions. Moving into a boardinghouse, for instance, instead of trying to be a dad-blamed rancher on her own. The boardinghouse would have been sensible, but had she thanked him for going to the trouble of finding her a decent home—the best room in town, as a matter of fact? No, she'd pitched a fit and taken matters into her own hands.

Not to mention the fact that Cooper had also run off last week. Between Rosemary and the dog, Finn's life felt lonelier than he could have imagined. And except for his baby girl, everything seemed to be going wrong.

Wiping the sweat from his forehead, he stopped the horse and slipped off the straps of the plow. He hated the idea of Rosemary homesteading. He wasn't sure why. After all, what did it really matter, as long as she had somewhere to go? Still, the thought that he had made a mistake when he balked against a marriage between them wouldn't stop taunting him.

One thing was certain: the baby was beginning to do a little better with the diluted milk. She still had trouble holding it all down and she seemed small and pale, but she was growing some and didn't seem quite so listless—and she was sleeping better at night, which meant he was sleeping better, as well.

He had set her in her basket and plowed a few feet, gone back to get her, then plowed some more, but he had to admit, the going was slow—too slow—and he was getting further and further behind as the days went by. Rosemary's presence would have helped during plowing.

He lifted the basket and walked several feet beyond the plow then set the sleeping baby down once more. Sarah would be waking soon for food. Since there had been no way to keep the milk from going bad out here in the sun, he would have to take her back to the house and get the cool jar from the cellar. He knew that plowing all the fields this way was almost impossible. He'd prayed for guidance, but the only answer that came back to him was one he already knew he didn't want to pursue. But how on earth would he get the plowing done in time to plant and harvest at the right time?

After two more days of wrestling with the problem, he knew he had no choice but to go to Rosemary, hat in hand, and ask her to keep Sarah each day, sunup to sundown, while he worked in his fields. At the end of the day, he bundled Sarah, hitched the wagon, and made his way the couple of miles down the road.

Cooper's bark greeted him when he arrived, and irritation shot through him. "You dumb dog," he called. "I should have known you'd wind up over here, you traitor."

When he stopped the wagon in front of the house, he smelled freshly baked bread. His mouth began to water, and for the time being he forgot about Cooper. He could kick himself for coming at suppertime, but he had to admit he'd done it at least partly on purpose. What's more, she'd know he'd done it on purpose too.

As he set the brake and wrapped the reins around the lever, his ears picked up strange noises that took him a minute to place. His jaw dropped. Surely that woman hadn't done what he thought she'd done.

Silas had discussed the possibility of joining forces and raising sheep, but Finn had dismissed the idea without giving it any real thought. Apparently Rosemary had a different opinion. Her pa would have taken a switch to her just for entertaining the thought of raising sheep. Still, he couldn't help but shake his head and find humor in the situation. That Rosemary did exactly what she wanted to do.

He jumped from the wagon and grabbed the baby basket from the seat. "Rosemary!" he called. "Rosemary!"

A young man came from the barnyard. "Can I help you?" he asked in a German accent.

"Who are you?" Had Rosemary gone away after all? Finn's stomach tightened. Surely she wouldn't have left without saying goodbye. His stomach sank. After the way he'd treated her, how could he blame her for wanting nothing more to do with him?

"Finn!" The sound of Rosemary's voice weakened his knees as relief filled him. She came from the barn cradling a lamb in her arms. "Isn't he precious? His poor mama didn't make it, so we're trying to get one of the other mamas to adopt him. So far, no one has. I believe we'll have to feed him the same way we've been feeding Sarah." Her eyes sparkled with excitement. "Oh, Finn. When Sarah gets a little older, she is going to love the baby sheep. What if we let her raise one of her own?"

"Rosemary, what are you talking about?"

"Sarah." She handed the lamb to the other man.

"Wait. First things first." Finn walked toward her as she brushed the palms of her hands against her apron. "Who is this man?"

"He's my hired helper, Rolf Georner." She smiled. "He would shake your hand, but as you can see, I just gave him the lamb. Rolf, this is my late sister's husband, Finn. The one I told you about."

Finn bristled at the last comment. She had no business telling other fellas about him.

Rosemary went on. "I imagine you'll be seeing a lot of him from now on, so try not to worry too much about his mean tongue. He's family, after all."

"Ja, Miss Jackson. I vill not vorry about it too much." Rolf grinned at Rosemary then settled a firm gaze on Finn.

A delighted laugh, loud and unrestrained, burst from Rosemary. She patted Rolf's shoulder. "Good! Will you please go back to the mother sheep and try to get one to adopt the poor baby?" She rubbed the lamb's head and nodded to Rolf. The man stood a good three inches taller than Finn. Next to Rolf, Rosemary looked like a child.

Finn stared at her, at a loss for words. She was behaving like a different person. It had only been a few days since she'd moved into the homestead, and she was laughing and cuddling baby lambs and

hiring help? For only an instant, he tried to imagine Rachel in the same situation. The comparison wasn't fair. Rachel hadn't spent her days with her pa riding the range, bossing the men, roping calves, and breaking horses. His memory flashed back to the early days of his acquaintance with Rosemary. He'd forgotten she could do all those things.

Sarah began to fuss and squirm. Rosemary's expression softened. "May I?"

"Of course."

Cooper nudged Rosemary's leg, and she laughed and scratched his head. "Jealous of the baby?"

"I've been wondering where that dog went. Did you steal him?"

She looked at him askance. "Don't be ridiculous. He showed up on my porch and acted like he wanted to stay." She tossed him a challenging grin. "You can have him back if you can get him to stay—without tying him or penning him up."

Finn shook his head. "Keep him. He was never really mine anyway, and Rachel was scared of him. I think he knows he belongs to you."

He held the basket tight as she reached inside and lifted the baby out. "Oh my. You have grown!" She pulled Sarah against her and closed her eyes. The gesture went straight to Finn's chest, and his heartbeat sped up at how much she loved his daughter. Her sister's daughter.

"Supper is almost ready," she said over the baby's head. "Would you like to stay?"

"I'd love to, if you're sure I wouldn't be putting you out." Why was he suddenly nervous around Rosemary, of all people?

He cleared his throat and remembered the latest news from town. "Did you hear about Heinrich Fischer?"

She turned, her brow creased. "No. What?"

Finn followed her inside. "He was trying to unharness the mules from his team last week and got gut-kicked."

"Oh no! That's terrible. I was planning to make a trip to see Agnes next week so I could tell her about the homestead and invite them for Sunday dinner." She held Sarah close and went to the stove to stir a pot. "I hope this is edible. It's venison stew. Silas has a smokehouse full of meat, but I couldn't find onions." She set the spoon back on a small plate next to the stove and readjusted Sarah. Then she looked up at Finn. "How is Heinrich doing?"

Finn hesitated. Clearly she didn't understand what he had been trying to tell her. "He didn't make it, Rose."

A soft gasp left her throat as she lifted the baby's feeder from the basket. "You mean the kick killed him?"

Finn nodded, surprised at how much Fischer's death was affecting her. Her eyes were filled with tears. "Do you want me to take the baby?" he asked.

She shook her head. "Will you go to the root cellar and bring up the milk? She's getting fussy. I think she's hungry."

"Of course. I'll be back." He took a couple of steps toward the front door, but Rosemary called him back.

"Silas built the root cellar directly under the kitchen so Annie wouldn't have to go outside to bring in vegetables and the like." She sniffled, and Finn saw that she still had tears trailing down her cheeks. He reached into his pocket and pulled out a handkerchief. Luckily it was fresh.

"Thank you, Finn," she said around a gulp. "How are Agnes and the children holding up?"

He was ashamed to admit that he hadn't been to see them. He hadn't known about it in time to attend the funeral, and he had been too busy trying to plow a few crooked feet a day to even think about the widow and her children. "I'm sorry, Rosemary. I don't know how she's doing."

"I'll have to ride over there tomorrow. I haven't seen them since Heinrich brought me to your homestead. H–he was with me when I f–found…"

Rachel's grave. Finn drew a halting breath. "It's okay. I understand."

She wiped at her face clumsily, while trying to hold Sarah with one hand.

"Here, give her to me while you compose yourself. I can feed her."

Rosemary nodded and left through the door off the kitchen. Apparently she'd taken the room that Silas and Annie had shared, which made sense. The only other place was the loft over the living room. All in all, Silas had built a nice home that would have been comfortable for a family.

Guilt niggled at him. A woman shouldn't homestead alone, eat alone…sleep alone. Again he wondered if perhaps he had made the wrong decision.

Sarah's wail pulled him back to the task at hand. "All right, sweetheart. Let's go get you some milk."

By the time he came back up to the kitchen, Rosemary had composed herself and was slicing bread. "Let's see," she said, the tears held at bay as she began to organize her thoughts out loud. "I'll take them whatever stew we don't eat tonight, and I made three loaves of bread, so of course I'll take one of those. No, I'd best take two. There are five children."

She grew silent, and he glanced up from filling the baby's feeder. Her eyes rested on Sarah with a troubled frown.

"What?" he asked.

"Finn, do you think Sarah looks healthy?"

He screwed the lid back on the jar of milk and handed it to her. "Now, Rosemary, don't go borrowing trouble. Just because someone died doesn't mean Sarah will."

"Of course it doesn't mean that. I'm not a ninny. It's just that her cheeks aren't red and healthy like the Fischer children's were. I was just thinking maybe we could get the doc to take a look at her."

"Doc Richards said to bring her to him if she doesn't hold down the diluted milk. But she's been doing pretty well with it, and you have to admit, she's bigger." He took a seat in one of the kitchen chairs and settled the tube along his arm so it didn't get twisted while he slid the rubber nipple into Sarah's hungry mouth.

"She's growing some," she nodded. "You're right. And I'm thankful she's holding down the milk."

Finn stared down at the baby. Come to think of it, she did still look a little pale. "If it'll set your mind at ease, I'll take Sarah there one evening this week."

"It would. Thank you." She went back to calculating. "I have strudel, but why on earth would I take strudel to them? Agnes makes it to melt in your mouth. Mine is only so-so. You should take it home with you when you leave tonight. It'll make a good breakfast before the plowing tomorrow. Oh, I know! I baked a cake yesterday for Rolf's birthday. There is over half left. I'll take that." A relieved smile touched her lips.

"Do you want me to drive you in the wagon?" Finn heard himself asking.

Rosemary seemed just as surprised at his question as he was. "Don't you need to plow?"

"Well, I won't be able to with Sarah anyway."

"I can take Sarah with me to the Fischers' while you work in your field. I don't mind."

"She won't be too much for you to care for, with the wagon and food?"

"No. Not at all."

"Thank you, Rosemary," he said, hearing the relief in his voice. "I desperately need a full day to work."

"I'd be happy to keep her." She smiled at the baby. "I'll keep her every day while you work the fields, if you need me to. I–is that why you came?"

He nodded. "I know I should have come sooner to give you my best wishes on the homestead." The truth was, he still felt that a woman shouldn't try to run a homestead alone. Even Rosemary. At some point she would need help, and there would be no one here to take some of the burden.

"Well, you know I'll keep her so you can work in the fields."

"I'd appreciate it." He met her gaze. "I've been trying to do this alone, and I can't. I owe you an apology for treating you so badly."

She smiled. "Yes, you do. But I forgive you."

"There is no good excuse for the way I acted."

"Yes, there is." She set a bowl of stew in front of him and a spoon next to it. "It's called grief."

As she turned to go back to the stove, Finn reached out and took her hand. She whipped back around. "What is it?" she asked.

"Rosemary. I've reconsidered what we discussed that day at my house."

"Which topic?" Her eyes narrowed as she studied his face.

He drew in a deep breath and expelled it. "Do you still want to get married?"

"Yes, I do."

Finn blinked in surprise at her frank and quick response. "Okay then, when the preacher comes through, we can say our vows— or we can make a trip to Williston, but we can't do that in one day, so we'd need a chaperone."

"Finn, wait a minute." Rosemary sent him a tender smile and shook her head. "You've misunderstood me. I want to get married when the right man comes along. Finn, you're a good man or Rachel wouldn't have loved you so devotedly. But I don't want to marry someone who will always be looking for traits that remind him of his first wife."

"I wouldn't be doing that."

"Really?" She sat in the chair catty-corner from him. "How many times since you arrived have you compared me to Rachel, either favorably or unfavorably?"

"None. Well, yes, a few times. But it's hard not to when you look exactly like her."

"I know, Finn. How could you not compare us? Especially when you loved her and you don't love me." She stood and walked to the stove, filling her own bowl. She set the slices of bread on a plate before carrying both dishes to the table. "The thing is, I don't want to fall in love with you—as I will surely do if we marry—and be jealous of my sister's memory because you can't help loving her."

"That's not what would happen," Finn protested weakly, sounding unconvincing even to himself. He couldn't imagine Rosemary loving him. She was independent and wanted things her own way. Most likely, they'd fight all the time. But at least Sarah would have a mother.

But Rosemary wasn't finished with the reasons why she wouldn't marry him. "I don't want to be a poor substitute for you to pour your grief into, Finn. When I marry, I want to be my husband's first choice." She smiled and her face softened, stealing his breath. She looked so much like Rachel. "For now, I want to help with Sarah. And if you remarry, I hope you'll allow me to stay in Sarah's life as dear old Aunt Rosemary."

"Of course. You'll always be her aunt, no matter what."

"Good. That's all I want." She looked down at the baby. "I think she's sleeping. Do you want me to put her in the basket so you can eat?"

"I'd appreciate it." He gently pulled the nipple from Sarah's mouth and set the feeder on the table. Rosemary lifted her from his arms and Finn's stomach dipped at her nearness. He shoved aside the feeling. After all, it had been awhile since he'd held a woman. And she looked exactly like his wife. That's all there was to it.

Still, when Rolf walked into the kitchen a few minutes later without being invited then grabbed a bowl and sat across from him, he didn't have to analyze anything to recognize jealousy when it slammed him in the gut.

Chapter Thirteen

....

Rosemary's heart felt as though an anvil had fallen on it. She couldn't imagine what Agnes and the children were going through. And what would Agnes do to make a living without her husband? At least the land belonged to them. Agnes had told her they'd proved up just a few months ago. That had to be a relief.

Baby Sarah started fussing just a couple of minutes from the Fischers', so Rosemary did her best to calm her without stopping to feed her. When she grew close enough to see the house, there were three wagons in front and men were carrying belongings from the house. Agnes wept but didn't try to stop them. Were she and the children moving away?

Rosemary yanked hard on the reins and the horses stopped. She lifted Sarah from the basket, and immediately her wails ceased. The baby was getting a little spoiled, but Rosemary couldn't help that right now.

Agnes looked up and held out her arms when she spied Rosemary.

"Oh, Agnes, I'm so sorry. I would have been here sooner, but I just learned about Heinrich yesterday."

"It is sad. So sad," she said. "Your Rachel. My Heinrich." She looked at Sarah and frowned. "This is Rachel's baby?"

Rosemary smiled and relinquished the baby to Agnes's open arms. "This baby does not look healthy. She is so small, and her skin and eyes…they do not shine." She focused her gaze on Rosemary. "What has the wet nurse been eating? She is not making good milk for Rachel's baby."

"There is no wet nurse, Agnes. We have to feed her milk from the cow through a feeder Finn bought when Rachel was too ill to have any milk of her own." She glanced about as the men continued to come and go. "Agnes, are you moving away from here? Did you sell your land?"

She shook her head as Marta joined them. She placed her arm around her mother. "It is good to see you again, Fräulein Jackson."

"Thank you, Marta. What is happening?"

"My papa."

Agnes snapped her head around and gave Marta a fierce stare. "Do not say bad things about your papa. Heinrich was very goot man and this vicked bank man haf swindled him."

"What happened?" Rosemary still couldn't make sense of the half sentences and poor English, which appeared to be worse when Agnes was upset.

"Tell her, Marta," Agnes said.

"Papa…"

"Vas swindled by the vicked bank man." Agnes waved her hanky toward Marta with one hand while she held Sarah with the other. "Tell her, Marta."

"Mama, I will try to tell her. Please do not be so upset."

Rosemary reached out and touched Marta's arm. "Tell me."

"Papa's plow broke, as it had many times. It was old and very much repaired. The last time, Papa said we must have a new one for planting this season, so after harvest when it appeared we did not make enough to buy seed and food and shoes and materials for clothing, Papa went to the bank to ask for money."

"For a loan?" Rosemary asked, her stomach sinking at the implication of what was coming.

Marta gave a sad nod.

"So I guess what you're saying is that your papa mortgaged the homestead."

"Yes, Fräulein Jackson." Marta's eyes were troubled and shone with unshed tears. "And now these men are taking our things, and they tell us we must leave our land as well."

Rosemary slipped her arm around Agnes's shoulders and the woman sank against her. "I'm so sorry."

Agnes sniffed. "Thank you, Rosemary."

Rosemary realized Sarah hadn't whimpered once since going into Agnes's arms. She opened her mouth to say as much then realized the baby was covered with Agnes's shawl the way Rosemary had seen Agnes cover Gerta when she was nursing. "Agnes! What are you doing?"

"Rachel's baby is not healthy. Cow milk is for cow babies."

"You mean calves, Mama," Marta said.

"Yes, calves."

Rosemary looked from one to the other. "But what about Gerta?"

"Gerta is big enough for cow milk now." She smiled. "It is time to vean her. For now, I have milk for both."

"Listen, do you really believe Sarah looks pale and pasty because she isn't getting the right food?"

"Of course. There is no question."

In Rosemary's mind, there was no question that Agnes would have to come to the homestead, or Rosemary would have to look for a wet nurse. She had prayed for God to help her find a way to make the baby healthy. Perhaps in this time of grief, God had chosen a way to help them all.

"Agnes, where do you intend to go after today?"

"They say ve cannot stay in our home. Vicked bank man."

Impatience pricked her, then guilt. After all, the woman was losing her home—of course she would be upset. Still, an idea was forming in Rosemary's mind, and there was no reason to wait. "Yes, they are taking your home. There is nothing we can do about that. But where will you go?"

"It is getting varmer." She shrugged. "Ve vill sleep under the stars."

"No, you won't."

Agnes frowned and Rosemary hurried to explain. "Will you come with me and be Sarah's nurse? If you don't want to continue after she's healthy and growing better, we'll look into another method of feeding her."

A look of utter horror crossed Agnes's florid features. "I cannot leave my children, Rosemary." She glanced down at Elsa, who clung to her skirts and peeked shyly at Rosemary.

"Oh, Agnes," Rosemary laughed, "of course not. I have a solution for us all, if everyone will just listen and cooperate." And she wasn't positive Finn would, although he had no choice about Agnes

feeding Sarah. Rosemary wouldn't give him the option of turning her away.

Curiosity gleamed in Agnes's eyes. "Vat do you suggest?"

"The two older boys are big enough to work in the fields, yes?"

Agnes straightened her shoulders. "Of course. Strong like grown man." Pride was evident in her tone. "Heinrich taught them vell."

Rosemary nodded, relief flowing through her. "Finn is in desperate need of help on his farm. The baby has him so far behind, he hasn't gotten any plowing done. If he could get plowing and planting done together, he won't miss the peak growing season."

Excitement built and she knew it flowed through her words. She loved when Providence seemed to be working on her behalf. "The boys can stay in the bunkhouse with my worker, Rolf, and go to Finn's each morning. Your job would be to take care of Sarah—and Elsa and Gerta, of course—and help with meals." Rosemary finished up with a great sense of satisfaction. The plan couldn't have been more perfect.

"And what should I do, Fräulein?"

Rosemary turned to Marta. "What do you know about sheep?"

Marta's eyes sparkled. "I know much about them. Before coming here, Papa worked for a family who had sheep. We all learned to care for them."

"Perfect. Then you will help Rolf with my sheep."

"Agnes, you and Gerta may take my room, and I will sleep in the loft with Marta and Elsa. As long as they stay on their own side of the room." She winked at Elsa, and the little girl buried her face in her mother's skirt. "I do not want their ice-cold feet in my back again."

A question seemed to lurk in Agnes's eyes.

Rosemary smiled. "You're wondering why I have a separate home?"

"Ja," she answered softly. "I vas expecting to hear of your marriage to Herr Tate."

"Finn didn't want me to stay, so I took over the homestead next to his when the Freemans left to go back to Missouri."

"Finn Tate is a foolish man." Agnes scowled.

"I agree." Rosemary shrugged. "But he was probably right about the marriage. However, we will need to convince him that Sarah must stay at our house. And that won't be easy."

"When he sees his baby girl getting better, he vill not be so stubborn."

"Let's hope so."

Without a kind word to the widow or her children, the men who had been sent to take the furnishings climbed into the wagons and left. Rosemary glared after them. At least they hadn't locked the door to keep her out.

"Let's go see if there's anything left to salvage," she suggested. Her mind went back to just three weeks ago when she had stayed with this family. Their lively laughter and deep faith and warm openness had caused her to love them. And now they were out without anywhere to go. It wasn't right. But their circumstances proved how easily fortunes could turn in this harsh land. The thought made her even more determined to keep her land safe for Sarah.

The satiated baby lay content and drowsy on Agnes's shoulder as they walked inside and Marta rounded up the rest of the children. Agnes's perfectly cozy home had been reduced to a bare

room with tattered blankets and strewn clothing. There were a few books from which the children did lessons, but the men hadn't left much else. Even Agnes's pots and pans and dishes were gone.

Elsa leaned against her ma's arm. "Will we perish now, Mama?"

Her words jolted Rosemary. That she could say them so calmly broke her heart.

"We vill not perish." Agnes smiled down at Elsa. "Ve vill go to Fräulein Jackson's home to help her cook and clean and take care of the baby." She handed Sarah down to the eight-year-old. "You must learn to help Mama take care of her."

Elsa smiled. "I like her. She is a good baby. Like Gerta."

Agnes reached out and took Rosemary's hand. "You are God's angel to me. You haf saved my children."

Rosemary squeezed the work-worn hand. She looked at Elsa holding Sarah and could have sworn the baby's color was already getting better. "And you are saving mine."

Chapter Fourteen
....

Finn fought the moisture threatening his eyes as he drove his wagon filled with the cradle and all Sarah's gowns and diapers to Rosemary's homestead. He knew it was the best solution for now. He'd be a fool not to accept the offer.

The baby had slept with Mrs. Fischer last night, but he had promised to bring over the cradle after he finished in the fields today. And so even though his heart ached at the thought of being without his baby, he was keeping his word in order to get her healthy.

All in all, Finn knew Mrs. Fischer's presence was a gift, and she couldn't very well stay at his homestead with her children. But knowing this was for the best and feeling good about his daughter living at Rosemary's homestead were two different things.

He wanted to blame Rosemary—to say this was exactly what she'd wanted all along, to take Sarah away from him. But he knew that wasn't fair. He also knew he should be feeling a deep sense of gratitude not only for the woman willing to feed his daughter, but to Rosemary for having the forethought to organize everyone's position.

Having the two boys to help in the fields would more than halve his workload and put him back on the right track to harvest the fields when the rest of the farmers went to harvest. The relief nearly overwhelmed him, just knowing he'd be able to start buying lumber again for his new house.

He pulled his wagon to a stop and expelled a weighted breath. As he climbed down from the seat, the door to the house opened. Rosemary stood on the porch holding Sarah around the waist, facing outward toward him. Coop, of course, sat at her side, watching over his mistress and the baby. "Look, Sarah," Rosemary said, "there's your pa. Say 'Hi, Pa.'"

Finn couldn't resist a smile. Of course Sarah was months away from saying anything resembling "Pa," but the thought of how it would feel when she finally did say it already filled him with such joy, he could barely contain it within the boundaries of his chest. And that shoved out some of the ache.

"We're teaching her to say 'Pa' first. I figure there's not much chance she'll say 'Auntie Rosie' first, so I can be generous. We might let her say 'Coop' next, since he loves her so much." Rosemary laughed. Then she sobered and softened her voice. "How are you doing with all this?"

He shrugged. "It's like losing Rachel all over again."

"Oh, Finn." Her voice trembled. "I'm so sorry it has to be this way for now. You mentioned that the doctor said it only has to be for a few months, and then she'll be strong enough to start trying soft foods from the table."

Rosemary sounded sincere, but then, she was the one who had Sarah day and night, while he had her during supper and for a little bit in the evenings while at Rosemary's. Would his little girl forget that she belonged to him?

Stepping aside, Rosemary allowed him to precede her into the house with the cradle. "Where do you want it?" he asked.

She pointed to the bedroom. "Agnes is sleeping in there."

Finn turned to her. "Where are you sleeping?"

Ducking her head, she blushed and cleared her throat. "I'm going to sleep in the loft with Marta and Elsa."

Agnes let out a sound of outrage. "You do not ask a young lady vhere she sleeps. This is not proper, and you have no right." She glared at him. "You are fool not to marry this Rosemary, so you have no right to ask things vich are not proper."

"Agnes, please." Rosemary's face glowed, and Finn gave her a pointed look. Clearly, she had told Agnes only part of the story. She hadn't bothered sharing the fact that he had been willing, in the end, to marry her and she had chosen to wait for true love.

"Vell, he should not ask vhere you sleep. That is all."

Finn couldn't resist the half smile playing at the corners of his lips. "I suppose you're right." He carried the cradle across the room to the door. "May I enter your room, Mrs. Fischer? I'd like to put my daughter's cradle next to the bed so she has a place to sleep."

"Of course, Herr Tate." She moved aside, and her tone softened. "You vill be staying for supper, ja?"

"Yes, he's staying for supper," Rosemary said, clearly over the embarrassment. "Won't you, Finn?"

He captured her gaze and noticed for the first time that a spray of freckles dotted her cheeks. "I'd be happy to."

Laughter filled the evening, with the lively Fischer children, Rolf's exuberant voice, and Rosemary's stories of growing up on the ranch.

It wasn't until he was driving home, much later than he'd planned to stay, that Finn realized he *hadn't* spent most of his time making comparisons between the two sisters. As a matter of fact, he hadn't seen anyone this evening but Rosemary.

* * * * *

"Miss Jackson." Marta rushed inside, her breath coming in short bursts and deep gulps.

"Marta, for mercy's sake." Rosemary set aside the pair of Afonso's trousers she was mending and stood. "Did you run all the way from the back fields?"

The girl nodded. "He's here again."

"Mr. Clayton?"

She bobbed her head, swallowing hard to catch her breath.

"Where are the boys?"

"They are still helping Mr. Tate in his fields," Marta said.

"Elsa?"

"I don't know, Rosemary."

Agnes walked into the room. "Elsa is in the cellar, fetching kraut for supper."

"Is Coop down there with her?"

Agnes nodded. "He does not let her go alone."

"Good. Keep him locked down there so he doesn't go after Clayton or his men. I don't want him shot. Sarah is down for her nap?"

"Yes, Sarah is sleeping." Agnes looked from Marta to Rosemary and back to her daughter. "Marta, vhy are you breathing so heavy?" Agnes frowned. "Vhy are you talking of that evil man? Vat is happening?"

Still struggling to catch her breath, Marta answered, "Mr. Clayton is almost here, again. Rolf and I saw him riding through the fields."

The girl must have run like the wind to beat them here on foot.

Mr. Clayton had paid two visits to the homestead over the past month, each time to complain about Rosemary's sheep—though she knew full well that not one of them had left her property. She had told him as much both times. She knew it infuriated him that she refused to show fear around him.

Rosemary turned her gaze to Agnes and met her troubled eyes. Not for the first time, Agnes offered her opinion. "Perhaps you must sell the sheep and make a farm instead."

Rosemary shook her head. "It isn't about sheep or farming. This is about greed." She walked across the room and took the Winchester from its place over the mantel. "Mr. Clayton won't be satisfied until I leave this land the way Silas did."

She loaded the rifle and headed for the door. "Stay inside with your mother and help her watch over Elsa and Gerta and the baby," she instructed Marta. "If it looks like something might happen, run out the back way and get Mr. Tate." She glanced at Agnes. "But only if your mother says you may go."

Fear shone in Marta's enormous blue eyes, but she swallowed hard and nodded.

Rosemary opened the door and stepped onto the porch.

Predictably, Mr. Clayton had traveled with his four stinking henchmen. They flanked him on either side, leering at her in a manner that made her feel unclothed. "That's far enough." She rested the rifle in an easy grip on her arms, keeping the weapon turned away from human flesh. "What do you want, Clayton?"

Mr. Clayton stared down at her from his horse. His cold, hard eyes sent a shiver down her spine, but she refused to give the satisfaction of letting him see her fear.

"I've come to make you an offer."

"In that case, I'm sorry you've wasted your time." She smiled. "Good day."

She backed toward the door, keeping her senses attuned to the men wearing guns.

"My dear girl," Mr. Clayton said, "I said I have come to make you an offer."

Fixing her stance, she nodded. "I understand, sir. But an offer has to be of mutual benefit for any reasonable person to accept." She lifted her eyebrow. "And you have nothing I want."

"Hear me out. You might be surprised." He smiled without warmth. "And truly, if I don't want to go, how will you force me to? So you may as well listen."

The men around him chuckled, and she felt her knees go weak. But she knew she had to stay strong. If she didn't protect herself and her possessions, who would?

"All right, then." Rosemary hated the feeling of helplessness, weakness. "Say what you came to say."

"Aren't you going to ask me in?" He moved as though he might dismount.

"No. And truly, sir, perhaps I cannot force you to leave, but I can keep you from coming inside. And I'd be within my legal right to use whatever means I have, as a matter of fact." She fingered the

rifle to make her point. "You might as well stay on your horse. You won't be here long."

"Very well, little miss." His expression darkened to a scowl. "I've tried to reason with you about the sheep. I've tried to buy you out fair and square. But your stubbornness has forced me to disclose the truth behind my insistence that you go."

A smile tipped Rosemary's lips. "I see. You want to be honest?"

"That's right." His tone had grown hard and lowered in pitch as his anger built. "The land you are on is rightfully mine. I consider you little more than a squatter, and I intend to have the acres you've laid claim to for those stupid creatures with wool."

Rosemary shook her head and took another step back toward the door. "You may think you are entitled to any land you choose, Mr. Clayton, but I have a receipt that says otherwise when it comes to my acreage. I have no intention of failing to prove up like Silas did."

"You don't understand." He gestured toward the house, the barn, the bunkhouse. "I bought all this."

He was lying, of course. He had to be, because she had paid Silas a fair price for the buildings. She thought back to Silas's insistence that she pay him only a portion of the amount they had agreed upon, and a sick feeling of dread threatened her stomach. Had Silas taken a purchase price from Mr. Clayton as well as from her?

No, it couldn't be. Clayton had to be lying. But something in his eyes made her wonder. And suddenly she wasn't so sure. "You can't buy land that someone else has filed a claim on." She narrowed her gaze. "The government wouldn't do that."

"Don't misunderstand. I'm not saying I bought the land from the government. Although I suppose I should have, instead of trusting that weasel of a man, Silas Freeman. I paid him to file on the land, and I put up the buildings you are enjoying."

"What are you getting at?" Not that she believed anything the likes of Bart Clayton said.

"Your friend Silas Freeman took me up on my offer and then went back on our agreement."

"I don't know what sort of offer you're referring to," she said, trying not to believe that Silas had double-crossed this man and then left her to manage the repercussions of his duplicity. "One thing you should know about me, Mr. Clayton, is that I don't like innuendos and half-truths. So get to the point, or get off my land."

"Has anyone ever told you that you have a sharp tongue?"

"More than once." She gripped the rifle, ready to swing it around and protect her home if necessary. But she prayed the rancher and his men only intended to threaten her. "What so-called offer did you make Silas that he accepted and then went back on?"

"This claim was never supposed to be his and his little wife's."

Rosemary kept a steady gaze on him. "Indeed?"

"Do not believe this man's lies." Agnes stood at the threshold. "He vill say vhatever he must to steal your home."

She was right, of course. The man had cattle, and cattle needed pastures in which to graze. She knew cattle. And that's why she had chosen sheep. Silas hadn't had to say much to convince her that she would do better with the woolly creatures, despite her inexperience. She could readily admit that she would never be as well-off as a man like Clayton and most likely never as prosperous as her pa had been. But she would do well enough. And she was glad she'd bought the sheep.

"I've come to appeal to your sense of fairness, miss, and to offer you twice what you paid for the sheep, for you to simply give up the claim like Silas did and leave. A girl like you could marry anyone you want. You don't need to make yourself so unappealing to possible prospects by trying to homestead." He winked at her and motioned to his own men. "Any one of these men would snatch you up in a jiffy, if you weren't trying to behave like a man."

Only one of the men, the youngest of the group by the looks of him, averted his gaze and expelled what appeared to be a frustrated breath. Was he frustrated with Mr. Clayton? Rosemary eyed him further. Mr. Clayton obviously mistook her curiosity for interest. "I can see you've taken a shine to Luke here." He reached out and clapped the young man on the shoulder. "Luke, you'd be honored to court the little lady, wouldn't you? If she moved off this land and stopped trying to be a man?"

"I r–reckon so, sir." He blushed to the hairline of his orange-red hair.

This was getting too ridiculous. "Let's not discuss my marital status or my likelihood of getting a husband, Mr. Clayton. And as for Luke here—I wouldn't allow any man who has the bad judgment to work for you to come anywhere near me."

"Now, little miss, think about what you're saying."

Rosemary lifted her hand to silence Mr. Clayton. "I don't know if what you say about Silas is true or not." Rosemary couldn't help but think back to the confrontation in town when Silas had accompanied her to the land office. Looking back, it seemed as though Mr. Clayton might be telling a version of the truth, anyway. "But even if it were true, the agreement you had with him has nothing to do with me and my land or my sheep herd. My pa ran a thriving cattle ranch in Kansas and I helped him do so, and I understand that you need more land than you have for the size of herd you own, but that has nothing to do with me, either. My advice to you, sir, is to stop being so greedy and make sure you have enough grazing land to support the cattle you already own before you bring any more up here from Texas."

"I don't think you understand my position." He shifted in his saddle, and Rosemary tightened her grip on the rifle.

"That's where you're wrong." Rosemary kept her senses alert to the movements of the men with him, but her gaze remained steady on his. Now wasn't the time to be distracted...or to show fear. It was time Mr. Clayton learn just who he was dealing with. "I've known men like you my whole life. Men who believe they can have whatever they want, just for the taking. Well, Mr. Clayton, you're not getting my land."

"We'll see about that." He nudged his horse, and it moved closer to the porch. "Don't underestimate me, little miss."

"And don't underestimate me." Her heart beat so hard in her chest, she had to fight the urge to press her fist against it to slow down the pounding. "I'll burn every building and set fire to the fields before I give you even one acre for your cattle."

His face grew red with rage, and he turned his horse without another word. He rode off at breakneck speed, with two men flanking each side.

"Oh, Rosemary," Agnes said, sliding an arm about her shoulders. "You are so very brave, but I am afraid you haf made an enemy."

"He was already my enemy." She stepped inside and closed the

door. "Now he's just no longer going to hide behind a friendly smile. I'd rather have the honesty." She set the rifle back in its spot over the fireplace. "Don't worry, Agnes. I can take care of Clayton."

Agnes blocked her path as she started to head into the kitchen. Her fists were planted on her generous hips. "You tell me do not vorry?"

Rosemary's eyebrows rose at the anger in Agnes's voice. "Agnes," she said, "what have I done to offend you?"

"Do not tell me not to vorry. You are family to me. Like a sister. I vill not allow this man to bring you harm." Her eyes blazed with fierce loyalty. "You only *think* you are strong alone. But you are not as strong as that man with all his men. So ve vill stand together, you and I and the children. He vill not vin."

Her vehemence surprised Rosemary. She'd been taking care of herself for so long that the thought of someone else wanting to help keep her safe seemed out of place. And though she wasn't sure Agnes could actually do anything to protect her should any real harm threaten, it meant more than she ever would have thought possible that someone wanted to try.

Chapter Fifteen
....

Finn stopped the horses and pulled his handkerchief from his pocket. Removing his hat, he wiped the sweat from his brow then shoved the handkerchief back into his pocket. Movement in the distance caught his eye and he tensed, ready to head for his wagon to get his rifle in case it was an animal. But as he took another look, he realized it was a person walking through the field directly from Rosemary's homestead.

When the figure waved, he noted the feminine shape, the curves of the person, as she came nearer, and he recognized Rosemary. He frowned. Why wasn't she riding Charity? Dropping the straps from the plow, he walked toward her. Then fear that something had happened to Sarah prompted him to break into a run. She began to run toward him, and when they closed the distance, he could see she was crying. He grabbed her by the arms. "What? What happened?"

"Nothing. I just…"

"What do you mean, nothing? What's wrong? Where's Sarah?"

Her blue eyes widened and she shook her head. "Finn, she's fine. Sarah's with Agnes."

Relief rendered him weak. "Why are you crying then?" His voice sounded gruff, and he inwardly chided himself when she drew back from him.

She frowned and took a shuddering breath. "Nothing. It's... I'm sorry I frightened you. I should have thought before I started over here. I'll leave."

Rosemary turned on her heel and started to walk away. Indignation swelled his chest. She had nearly scared the life out of him and now she wanted to forget she had done it and just go back to her homestead, leaving him to wonder what had upset her so? Just because he hadn't spoken to her like a beau reciting poetry? He stomped after her, reached forward, and took her arm. She turned to him, shaking him loose, but didn't move to leave until he had his say. Tears were flowing down her cheeks again.

"I'm sorry I was so gruff with you. But I want to know why you're upset." He reached into his pocket and grabbed his handkerchief. She glanced at it and wrinkled her nose.

"Oh, sorry." He shoved it back into his pocket and reached out. Cupping her cheeks, he wiped away her tears with his thumbs. "What happened? If it has nothing to do with Sarah, then why did you come to me?"

Her eyes filled with tears again. "I don't know for sure why I came here."

"Start from the beginning," he said, keeping his voice soft so she wouldn't get defensive. "Tell me everything."

"Bart Clayton came by again."

"Clayton? What did he want?" And what did she mean by "again"?

"The same thing he's wanted for the last three weeks, Finn."

"Are you saying that Bart Clayton has been threatening you?" Finn dropped his hands from her face and slid his hand through his

hair. "Why am I the last to know everything? My daughter is living at your house. If you're being threatened, I have a right to know, Rosemary."

"Well, he never really made threats until today, Finn."

"Tell me exactly what happened. What did he say?"

For the next few minutes, Rosemary shared the most recent conversation she'd had with Clayton. Finn clenched his fists as he pictured the tiny young woman defending herself against five grown men. Fear and admiration vied for first place in his emotions. He couldn't help but try to imagine Rachel in a similar situation, and his mind refused to even allow it. Rachel would never have stood her ground alone with a rifle, protecting the women inside.

But Rosemary...this maddening woman had fierce bravery. It was a bit misplaced, perhaps, but how could one not find such an indomitable spirit admirable?

"At first," she said, "he pretended his objection to my having the land was because of the sheep, which I understood, coming from a ranching community." She rolled her eyes. "You know how things were when the sheep farmers first started coming into the area with their sheep. But eventually things smoothed out, and most of the ranchers, including my pa, came around. Within a couple of years, they shared the land fine. I originally thought that's what would happen with Bart Clayton. But after his first visit to the homestead, I realized that he's not concerned about sheep. He wants my land."

"And today he stopped all pretense, huh?"

She nodded. "I won't give him the land, of course. But I'm not sure how far he might go to win this fight."

Finn didn't know either, but Clayton wasn't the sort to make idle threats. If he wanted Rosemary's land, he would do whatever he had to in order to get what he wanted. There weren't too many men who would challenge him, and he could only think of one woman. "Rosemary, there's another way."

Her eyes lifted with hope. "You have an idea?"

Swallowing hard, he nodded and stared into her eyes, willing her to read his question.

When she realized what he meant, her expression hardened. "No."

Irritation shot through him. "You're being awfully all-fired stubborn for someone who came to me for help."

"You're mistaken." She lifted her chin. "I didn't come to you for help. I came to you for support because you're the only family I have left. Clearly, it was a mistake."

Her last words stung. Perhaps she didn't want his help, but hadn't he shown her support? "Fine. But I'm not leaving my daughter in danger."

She swung around, her eyes blazing as she glared at him. "Sarah is in no danger as long as she is under my roof. I'll keep her safe."

"But what if you aren't safe, Rose?" He reached out and took her arm again. "Why do you think you have to pretend to be so strong?"

"I don't think I have to pretend, Finn." A sigh escaped her lips, beckoning him, and he had to force himself not to bend down and press his mouth to hers. She covered his hand. "I'm strong because it's who I am. You want me to marry you to join our property and cause Clayton to stop threatening me. And that might help, but I don't want to get married out of fear or necessity. Not to mention the fact that I have a right to that land. Me. On my own. And that man shouldn't be able to run me off just because he made a bad deal—an illegal deal—with Silas and lost out."

"If that's even true," Finn said. "I find it difficult to believe that Silas would be involved with Clayton."

She shrugged and dropped her hand from his. "I don't know what I believe. You weren't there that day in Paddington when Clayton came at Silas. From the exchange I heard, the story could just as easily be true as false."

Finn frowned. Rosemary always had to see things differently than he did. "If it's true, it means my good friend swindled Clayton. Can you honestly see Silas Freeman being that bold? Clayton would put a bullet through his head."

"Maybe. But probably not. Especially after the words they had in the middle of town. If he turned up dead, the law would go after Clayton."

That made sense. Rosemary was too smart for her own good... but that just might be her undoing. "Just promise me you'll be careful. Don't go to town alone or even just with the children. Make sure Agnes is with you—or Rolf or me." He smiled. "Yes, even me. You can come to me for help. It doesn't make you weak."

Her cheeks bloomed, and she looked away. "Actually, I do want you to come with me to town. Friday night."

"Friday night? Why?"

"Rolf has asked Marta to accompany him to the monthly dance at City Hall, but of course they can't go those many miles alone. It'll be dark when the dance is over. And it would seem strange for me to go without someone else to come along and even out the number."

"I see. So you're saying it would be odd for you to go without a male escort."

"Would you mind terribly?"

He thought about teasing her and forcing her to pout the way Rachel would have if she'd wanted to go to a dance and he'd said no, but Rosemary wasn't her sister. Rosemary was straightforward and no-nonsense. If he told her no, she'd just take them herself without asking twice. And although it took him by surprise, the thought of going to the dance with her appealed to him. "I'd be happy to escort you."

Her face brightened. "Thank you, Finn. When you come to dinner tonight, I'll cut your hair for you. By the way, you look much more handsome since you've begun shaving again." She looked over her shoulder toward her homestead. "I'd best go. I went out for a walk and sort of ended up here. I didn't tell Agnes where I was going, so she's likely afraid that Clayton has done me harm." She frowned, glancing past him, across his field. "Finn, where are Heinrich Jr. and Afonso? Shouldn't they be helping you?"

"I have them in the back field using Silas's plow. I figure we can get the fields ready much faster if we plow two at once."

"Will you be ready to plant soon?"

He nodded. "I'll start on Monday." Excitement fluttered inside him as he thought about the new crops he had planned. "I'm going to plant late beets in this field."

"Beets?" Rosemary's brow furrowed. "What are they?"

"They're a red vegetable. Almost like a fruit. There's a demand for them in the East, and I intend to meet some of that demand. I'm planting turnips and cabbages, as well. And it's time to plant strawberries. I've lost some of the growing season, but most of the root vegetables will still grow, and there is already hay growing in the fields we planted last year."

"Agnes will be happy about the cabbages. You know how she loves her kraut. Though I'm not sure it agrees with Sarah's little tummy."

Alarm seized Finn. "Is she sick again?"

Rosemary laughed. "No, Finn. She's growing like a weed. Every day, it seems, she fills out more and more. I just mean, some things that Agnes eats appear to affect her."

"Oh." Finn frowned. "You mean it goes into…"

"Yes, like when the cows get into the onions, it makes their milk bitter." She cleared her throat and ducked her head the way she did when she was embarrassed. "Anyway, I'd best get back."

"I'll see you later, then."

He watched her go, and his hand went to his stubbled jaw as he remembered her compliment. So Rosemary thought he was handsome when he was clean-shaven? Rachel had always liked his beard.

He scowled and turned toward the plow. He had to stop comparing the two. Even if he stood them side by side, he would be able to see the differences between them. There weren't too many differences in their looks—other than the freckles on Rosemary's cheeks from the sun that Rachel never would have allowed to touch her skin. Although he had to admit, the freckles were becoming and he couldn't understand why Rachel had been so against getting them.

Shaking off the images of the two women, he lifted the reins and flapped them at the horse. The fact was, he hadn't been able to save Rachel, and now Rosemary was in danger as well. A different sort of danger, perhaps, but the fact that she refused to marry him was frustrating. He couldn't imagine how else to keep her safe. Clayton would have no choice but to stop harassing her if she had a husband.

Finn expelled a weighted breath. How on earth could he keep Rosemary safe if she refused to believe that she needed anyone to take care of her?

＊ ＊ ＊ ＊ ＊

Rosemary set the chair in the middle of the kitchen and instructed Finn to sit down. The children milled around, watching with amusement as she first wrapped a towel around his shoulders and then grabbed the shears from her sewing kit. Coop prowled around the kitchen too, interested and worried.

"Have you ever done this before?" Finn asked.

Rosemary rolled her eyes. "Don't be such a baby," she said. "Who do you think cut my pa's hair?"

He turned in the chair and stared up at her, one dark eyebrow arched. "I happen to know for a fact that Owen Armstrong at the barbershop cut your pa's hair every other week."

Caught, Rosemary scowled and, putting her fingers at the top of his head, twisted him back around. "Okay, fine, I didn't cut Pa's hair. That doesn't mean I don't know how to cut yours."

"Rosemary, so help me, you'd better not do this wrong."

"Good heavens, Finn," she said with more levity than she felt. "You're not setting a very good example for the children."

"Is that so?" he asked. "I'm not the one who just lied in front of them."

The boys laughed aloud, and Marta's lips quivered into a tiny smile.

Agnes looked up from her book. "Out. All of you. Boys, go check on the cows and chickens and then go to bed."

"Yes, Ma," Heinrich said, though his tone belied the ready obedience. Clearly, given his choice, he'd have stayed.

Afonso was not quite so subtle. "But I want to watch Finn get his hair cut."

Agnes gasped. "Are you now a grown man the age of Mr. Tate? Do you not show him the respect he deserves?"

Rosemary frowned, unsure at first what had riled Agnes, until Afonso hung his head. "Sorry, Ma. I meant I want to watch Mr. Tate get his hair cut."

"That is very much better." Agnes swatted her younger son on the behind. "And no, you may not stay and watch. Fräulein Jackson is scared enough without you making her more so."

"Scared!" Rosemary glared at Agnes over Finn's head. "Who says I'm scared?"

She reached forward and ran the comb through Finn's thick, wavy hair that had grown so long, it now hung past his collar. He shivered when she took a lock between her fingers.

"Admit it," he said, his tone quiet, almost intimate.

"Admit what?" She slowly placed the shears around the lock of hair and squeezed the handle together.

"That you've never done this before."

"Oh, for mercy's sake. Fine. I've never cut anyone's hair before, Finn." She walked around the chair until she stood in front of him. She bent and looked him in the eyes. "But I have never attempted anything that I didn't succeed in doing."

Once the words left her mouth, she realized how vain she

sounded. She was just about to apologize when Finn took her wrist and pulled her even closer—so close, in fact, that she had to adjust her footing to keep from dropping into his lap. His breath fluffed the tendrils of hair that always sprang free by evening.

"You're right," he said. "Until now, everything you've tried has worked in your favor. But don't make this the one thing you can't do. Not when you're experimenting on me."

He smiled, and his eyes slanted just a little as they moved over her face. He held her there, so close that she could feel the warmth of his skin, and she nodded and smiled back. "Have a little faith," she whispered. She pulled back.

Twenty minutes later, she stared at the pile of hair on the floor and knew Finn was never going to forgive her. "Are you finished yet?" he asked, his impatience a vast contrast to the closeness they'd shared moments before.

"Agnes," she called, her voice trembling a little.

"What?" Finn reached up to touch his hair, but she slapped his hand away.

"Just wait. You're acting like a child."

"Agnes!" She had gone to feed Sarah a half hour ago. She should have been finished by now.

The woman came out of her room seconds later, her frown turning into a look of surprise as her gaze fell on Finn. Rosemary groaned inwardly. There was no mistaking the amusement combined with compassion in her expression.

"I knew it!" Finn hopped up from the chair. "Where's your mirror?"

"Sit down, Mr. Tate," Agnes ordered. "Do not vorry. Your hair vill be fine. I haf much experience cutting hair."

"I don't mean to be rude, but someone else told me the same thing just a little while ago."

Agnes let out a chuckle and held out her hand for the shears. "Rosemary has discovered something at vich she is not competent."

Rosemary's cheeks burned. "I'm sorry, Finn. It didn't seem like it would be that difficult."

His face softened. "Agnes is fixing whatever mess you've made."

Bristling at his choice of words, Rosemary huffed. "I wouldn't exactly call it a mess. It was my first time. I'll do better next time."

He gave a short laugh. "I'm not letting you cut my hair ever again, and the good Lord help those sheep when it's time to shear them."

Agnes chuckled and Rosemary shot her a look. "I am sorry, Rosemary," she said, grinning. Under her expert hand, the misshapen, uneven hair was beginning to look nice. A little shorter than she ever remembered Finn wearing his hair, but presentable.

Her own incompetence to complete this task stung Rosemary.

"You know," Finn said, as though reading her mind, "pride goeth before a fall."

Her eyes went big, and her jaw dropped. "Are you saying you not only think I'm incapable of doing this one task correctly, but I'm also prideful?"

He met her gaze straight on and nodded. "Yep. That's exactly what I'm saying." His voice rose in pitch as he mimicked her. " 'I can do anything I set my mind to.' "

"Well then," Rosemary said as anger clenched her midsection, "I can do without your company on Friday night."

His eyes glittered, hard as stone. "That's fine by me. I didn't want to go anyway."

"Fine. I didn't really want you to go."

"Okay then." He sniffed. "I generally prefer to do the asking anyhow. If you ever expect to find a husband, maybe you should learn to wait until you're asked."

"Oh!" Rosemary's anger boiled over. "I seem to remember twice being asked for more than a dance!" She knew that her voice had risen and Agnes stared at her in shock, but she didn't care one bit. "How many times are you going to ask me to marry you when you know I'd sooner marry a big fat frog than be stuck with the likes of you for the rest of my life?"

"Maybe that's your best bet. At least a frog doesn't have hair for you to butcher. You can wager I'll never ask you again." He jumped up and yanked the towel from his shoulders. Stomping across the room, he grabbed his hat and turned at the door. "Thank you for fixing me, Mrs. Fischer."

"It isn't quite finished, Mr. Tate," she said. Her voice was barely audible.

"It's okay," he said. "I'll tidy it up later."

He yanked open the door and stepped outside. "Rose, quick!" he hollered. "Start bringing buckets of water."

The panic in his voice sent her running to the porch, and as she looked across the yard, she understood the urgency.

"The barn!" she screamed. Flames shot up from the top of the building. "Barney!" She hopped from the porch and ran for the barn. The lamb without a mother still slept in a pen alone until he was weaned. Tears came quickly and ran down her cheeks. Just as she reached the barn, strong arms caught her and pulled her back. She found herself pressed back against a rock-hard chest. Finn's arms

encircled her, and he practically carried her away from the burning building. There was no use in trying to save the barn. Even as Agnes and Marta shot from the house with buckets filled with water, Finn waved them away. "We'll keep an eye on it," he said. "But there's no wind. I think it'll burn without spreading to the other buildings."

Agnes raced forward and tossed her bucket of water on the fire then ran back to the house. "Marta, come! Ve must save Rosemary's barn."

"There's no point, Mrs. Fischer," Finn called. "We can't stop it from taking the barn. It's too far gone."

Rosemary shuddered through her tears. She turned to Finn. "Go check on the boys in the bunkhouse."

"We're here." Rolf and the two Fischer boys walked toward them.

"Rose, look," Finn said softly, pointing at the boys.

Rosemary let out a cry of joy at the sight of Afonso carrying the lamb in his arms. "Barney! Afonso, you wonderful boy. You saved him."

He nodded.

"Tell her." Heinrich nudged him. "Now is the time to tell the truth."

"What truth?" Rosemary asked.

"Barney has been sleeping next to me in the bunkhouse." He looked at the ground. "I am sorry, Fräulein Jackson."

"Sorry?" Rosemary laughed despite the burning building. She ruffled the boy's hair. "All you had to do was ask. I wouldn't have cared if you kept Barney with you at night, as long as your mother didn't mind. As a matter of fact, he's yours."

Afonso grinned broadly. "Truly?"

"Truly." She reached out and ran a hand over the woolly baby. "You saved his life. If you hadn't taken him as a pet, Barney would be inside that barn right now." She glanced at the fire and fresh pain sliced through her heart. She was only thankful the horses were out to pasture when the fire started.

Afonso's eyes lit with pride and Agnes stepped up and slipped her arm around him. "You did goot to save the baby sheep, but you must ask permission from now on, ja?"

"Yes, Mama," he said, sobering.

Finn looked at the boy. "Did you leave the lamp burning in the barn when you took Barney from his pen?"

The boy's eyes went wide. "No, Mr. Tate. I did not use a light at all. I did not want anyone to see me go inside, so I would not be caught getting Barney."

"And there was no lamp at all when you went in there just twenty minutes ago?"

He shook his head. "No, sir."

Though neither Rosemary nor Finn said anything as they watched the barn burn, Rosemary could see from the anger burning in Finn's eyes that he believed the fire was deliberately set.

The barn continued to burn, and by morning there was nothing left but smoldering debris. Finn hadn't gone home but instead stayed on the porch, watching the fire to make sure it didn't spark another blaze. Thankfully, it didn't.

After a sleepless night, Rosemary brought Finn a cup of coffee on the porch. He sat back against the wall, a quilt wrapped around him. Rosemary dropped to the porch beside him and hugged her knees to her chest.

Neither of them stated the obvious until the final board fell with a *crack*. Finn turned to her. "You know it was Clayton."

She nodded. "Most likely."

"I'm going to see him today."

Rosemary shook her head. "No. This isn't your fight, Finn. It's mine. If anyone is going to go see him, it'll be me."

Anger ignited in his eyes and he stood, letting the quilt drop. He set the coffee on the rail and shoved his hat on his head. Reaching down, he took her arm and lifted her to him. He stared into her eyes, inches from her face. "One of these days you're going to realize that you need someone to help you, Rose."

He cupped her neck and pulled her close, pressing his lips to hers. Before she could react by either kissing him back or slapping his face, he'd dropped his hand and pulled away. "If you get this wrong with Clayton, it won't be the same as messing up a haircut. Be very sure you know what you're doing."

Chapter Sixteen

....

Three days later, Finn still had no idea why on earth he'd kissed Rosemary, especially after she'd told him—for all intents and purposes—that she didn't need him.

It was just that she was so small, so frail-looking. He couldn't help it. He wanted to take care of her. Everything in him wanted her to stop being so stubborn and just give in to marrying him. For mercy's sake, she was the one who'd first brought up the subject. Why couldn't she see the wisdom of joining their lives, their property? But he'd told her he wasn't going to ask again, and that was a promise he intended to keep.

At least she had given in and agreed that they should not disappoint Marta about the dance. The barn fire wasn't Marta's fault, and the girl had been through enough lately. She should not be denied the dance.

Rolf and Marta rode in the back of the wagon, along with the basket of food the four of them would share as a picnic dinner on the way to Paddington.

The breeze was cool but not cold, although they had come prepared with blankets in case the weather turned cold later, as it was likely to do even now, in early summer when the days were nice and warm.

The tension between each couple was palpable—the two young folk because they had never been together in a courting situation, and Finn and Rosemary because of the kiss they still hadn't discussed.

Finn glanced at Rosemary out of the corner of his eye. She sat demurely, her hands in her lap. The sun fell across her cheeks, illuminating her face. While he was feeling the tension, he wondered now, as he glanced at her, if she felt it too. She seemed at peace.

As if sensing his perusal, she turned to him. Her eyes widened. "Is something wrong?" she asked.

"No. I just wondered if you're still angry with me."

"Angry? When was I angry?"

"What happened on the porch?" Finn couldn't help but be a little stung that she didn't even remember.

He was about to enlighten her when her face registered understanding. "Oh. You mean because of the kiss?"

"Yes."

"At first I wanted to be angry." Her face had grown pink, and he was gratified to know that she at least thought about the moment.

"What changed your mind?"

"Rachel." She smiled and gave a little sigh.

"Rachel? I don't understand how she had anything to do with it."

"She told me once that you tend to act rashly in situations where you don't know how to fix a problem." A shrug lifted her shoulders. "I thought about it and realized that's what happened. You were trying to make me feel better, and it seemed like a kiss would make me forget the barn."

Her explanation was ridiculous, of course. Rachel's words were true, but the kiss wasn't to make her feel better. Or had it been? Maybe it had been to make himself feel better instead.

"Well," he said, "I'm glad you're not offended."

"I'm not." She pointed to a creek in the grove of trees just ahead. "Is that a good place to stop and eat? We'll be in Paddington in an hour, and the dance won't start for two."

"I reckon it's as good a place as any."

Relieved to have gotten the discussion of the kiss behind them, Finn enjoyed the sausages, sauerkraut, and strudel Agnes had packed. Stretching out his legs, he leaned back on the quilt and rested on his elbow.

Rolf and Marta took a walk along the creek, staying properly in sight.

Finn knew that the easy silence he and Rosemary had shared in the wagon would grow uncomfortable if it continued in this setting. He was also aware that anything personal would be awkward, so he decided to raise the subject that was most likely foremost on her mind anyway.

"What will you do about the barn?"

She turned to him, her neck long and soft as she looked down. "I'll have to pay workers to build another one, I suppose."

"As soon as planting is finished, I can help."

She nodded, her eyes serious. "I had hoped you would consider overseeing things. I don't have any experience when it comes to building."

He had to admit, he enjoyed the idea that she had thought of him. "Do you want me to find the workers for you?"

"It would probably be for the best." She began packing up the leftovers and sliding them into the basket. Finn enjoyed the steady, capable way her hands moved. There was no hesitation, just gentle confidence…the same way she seemed to approach every task, with the exception of hair cutting. He grinned in spite of himself.

"What's funny?" Rosemary asked.

Heat crawled up his neck, but he saw no reason to lie. After all, they were entering into a friendship now. Why shouldn't they laugh about the haircut?

"I was just thinking that you are good at everything."

Her eyes lit and she looked pleased.

He leaned over and tucked a strand of silky hair behind her ear. "Except for cutting hair."

In a flash, anger replaced the smile and she scowled at him. "What a time to bring that up! I'll always remember that haircut as the night my barn burned to the ground."

Finn couldn't help it; he laughed out loud. "Admit it," he said. "You're just upset because you did a poor job."

She glared at him and shrugged, standing to her feet. She looked down at him. "Think whatever you wish."

"I will." He stood and brushed off his trousers.

"Will you call them back?" she asked, nodding toward Rolf and Marta. "It's probably time to go. We don't want to be late."

Personally, Finn couldn't care less if they were late. If it were up to him, he'd stay here, resting alone in the sun with Rosemary, for as long as they could. The best part of the entire adventure was the long drive and the picnic dinner. Dances made Finn uncomfortable, and he typically didn't enjoy being in the company of so many people. But he did as Rosemary asked. "Rolf, Marta, we're leaving."

Bending, he grabbed the basket.

"Thank you," Rosemary said. Her voice still sounded offended

as she pulled the blanket from the ground. She shook off the grass and leaves and folded the quilt. Together, they walked back to the wagon. Finn deposited the items in the back of the wagon and held out his hand. Rosemary slid her fingers inside his palm and allowed him to help her into the seat.

She breathed out a soft sigh as he climbed in next to her and they waited for Marta and Rolf.

"Everything okay?" he asked.

"Yes. I was just thinking how nice it's been so far, getting away from the homestead." She gave him a sharp look. "Not that I don't love the homestead."

"I know you do." Finn couldn't resist a smile. If anyone knew how much she loved that place, he did.

"It's just very peaceful out here in the quiet."

"It's been nice." Finn unwrapped the reins from the brake. "I almost hate to go to the dance."

Laughter bubbled from her. "I agree. I've been dreading it, to be honest. If Marta hadn't wanted so desperately to accept Rolf's invitation, I never would have thought twice about going."

Rolf and Marta reached the wagon before Finn could respond.

Marta held up a flower. "Look! The wild roses are blooming. I will put this in your hair."

"Wild roses." Rosemary's face lit up. "Rachel told me about those. She said..."A pretty blush stole across her cheeks. "Never mind."

Finn didn't press, but he had a pretty good idea of what was on her mind, because the same thought had occurred to him: Rachel had always compared Rosemary to the wild rose. *"Look at it, Finn. It's full of beauty and grace and yet it refuses to be contained."* She had spread her arms to take in the wide expanse of flowering bushes. *"Just like my Rose."*

* * * * *

Rosemary slid into Finn's arms as he helped her down from the wagon. He smelled of fresh air and soap, and her mind flew back to the kiss they had shared—or, rather, that he had given her without allowing her the opportunity to decide whether or not to kiss him back.

The air had grown crisp as twilight descended upon the little town of Paddington. From the congested street lined with wagons, it appeared as if the entire township had arrived for the dance. Glancing up at Finn, whose warm hands still spanned her waist, she couldn't keep the worry from her voice. "Do you think Mr. Clayton is going to be here?" *And his men.*

"There's a pretty good chance he will be. He and the mayor are friends." He stepped out of the way as Rolf escorted Marta past them toward City Hall.

Rosemary didn't understand, and her face must have shown it. Finn motioned toward the building. "Clayton paid to have this built. And the mayor looks the other way when Clayton has *dealings.*"

Rosemary's stomach squeezed at his emphasis on the last word.

"So he might look the other way if Mr. Clayton tries to steal my land from me."

Finn smiled and held her elbow as he guided her toward the door. "If it were that easy, most of us wouldn't have homesteads around here. Clayton would own the whole territory."

"That's probably true." She shrugged. "Perhaps he'll refrain from confrontation. It is a party, after all."

"I wouldn't count on it." He smiled again as he reached forward and opened the door. "But don't let it ruin your night."

She'd been thinking about the fire and had finally realized that he had ordered her barn to be set on fire because she had threatened to burn all the buildings and fields. This must have been his way of showing her that he would have the land with or without the buildings. One way or another he intended to win, and he'd used her own threat against her.

The music was already playing, and couples were beginning to wander onto the dance floor, Rolf and Marta among them. Untying her cape, Rosemary slid the covering from her shoulder. "I'll hang it up for you," Finn said.

"Thank you."

As he moved away through the crowd of others who had also just arrived, Rosemary glanced furtively around the room, half expecting Mr. Clayton to jump out at her. Instead, she spotted Mrs. Franklin sitting in a wooden chair along the wall just to her right. The elderly proprietor of the boardinghouse smiled and lifted her wrinkled hand, motioning her over.

Rosemary walked the short distance. "Well, look at you," Rosemary said. "You look awfully pretty tonight."

Mrs. Franklin waved away the compliment. "Honey, I haven't been pretty in forty years." She squinted at Rosemary. "But you're looking pretty. Even have a wild rose in your hair. Did your young beau give you that?"

"I don't have a beau. We're here as chaperones for that young couple." She pointed to Marta and Rolf.

Mrs. Franklin glanced at the dance floor then back to Rosemary with a knowing smile. "At any rate, the rose is becoming." Rosemary felt a blush creep across her face. She reached up and plucked the bloom Marta had slid into her chignon. "I forgot it was there."

Mrs. Franklin scowled. "Should have left it be. I said it was becoming." She glanced toward the refreshment table, where Finn was standing. "I had a feeling the two of you would end up courting."

Rosemary opened her mouth to say, "We're not"—but the elderly woman gave her no opportunity. The benefit of age, she supposed. One could do and say just about anything without folks being too offended. Mrs. Franklin tapped her cane on the floor in time with the music. "I hear you bought out Mr. Lyle's sheep herd."

"Yes, ma'am." Bracing herself for a scolding, Rosemary stiffened her back.

"Good for you." She nodded. "Even if you and Mr. Tate get yourselves married, a woman needs to have something of her own."

"We're not getting married."

"There you are." Finn's voice startled Rosemary. She spun around and barely avoided the cup he carried. "Whoa," he said. "I brought you some apple cider, and I'd rather not wear it."

She took the drink with a muttered apology.

"I don't suppose you brought one of those for me?" Mrs. Franklin said.

"As a matter of fact," Finn said, "I was about to ask Miss Jackson for a dance, so you can have mine." He winked at the elderly lady. "I haven't sipped out of it." He turned to Rosemary, the hesitation in his eyes belying the confidence in his tone. "Would you care to dance?"

Rosemary took his hand, setting her cider on the table next to Mrs. Franklin. "Let's do."

At the first touch of his hand in hers, Rosemary felt a rush of warmth in her belly. When he took her into his arms, it was all she could do not to close her eyes and feel the moment as he began to lead her in a waltz. "Rolf and Marta seem to be getting on well," he observed, nodding to the couple not far from them on the dance floor.

"Yes."

He peered closer at her. "You don't seem pleased."

"It's not that Rolf isn't a fine young man, but he's a few years older than she is."

"No more than three or four, I'd say. What's wrong with that?"

"There's nothing wrong with it. It's just that he's obviously looking for a wife."

"And you have objections to Marta being that choice?" Finn's gaze slipped to the young couple then back to Rosemary.

Rosemary shrugged and looked up into Finn's brown eyes. "I would never presume to object. It isn't my place to do so. It's just that, given Marta's circumstances, I'm concerned that she might accept a proposal out of obligation. You see?"

"She could do worse, Rose." Finn turned her around the dance floor, smoothly and with a grace that surprised her. "Not everyone has the fortitude to run a sheep ranch."

Rosemary's defenses went up at his sarcasm. "I'm not suggesting she should. I'm not even saying they wouldn't eventually be a good match. But she's only fifteen—sixteen in a couple of weeks. She's much too young."

"Sixteen?" Finn's eyebrows rose. Rosemary could feel his annoyance and surmised his implication. He had started courting Rachel when she was just sixteen, and she was barely seventeen when they married.

Rosemary had been opposed to Rachel's marriage as well and had begged her to wait just one more year. She looked up at him and read the anger in his face, but she saw no reason to lie. "It's how I feel, Finn."

Why did every encounter with him have to end in someone getting angry? She was about to try to toss him an olive branch when Mr. Clayton tapped him on the shoulder.

"May I have this dance?" he asked.

Finn tensed and his eyes glittered cold as ice. "You have a lot of nerve coming over here."

"Indeed? Are you going to refuse me the honor of a dance with your lady?" Clayton's tone rang with challenge, and Rosemary believed he almost hoped Finn would refuse—or that she would—so that he could show the town how poorly they treated him.

Rosemary considered the situation, though her stomach roiled at the very thought of this man touching her. If she humiliated him in public, she would be declaring an all-out war with Clayton and his men. And in a dirty war, he would win.

Clearly, Finn hadn't taken the time to consider the situation. "Crawl back into your hole, Clayton," Finn said. "You're not getting near her."

Rosemary patted his shoulder. "It's all right, Finn. I'd be more than happy to dance with Mr. Clayton."

"Forget it."

She smiled, though anger flashed through her at Finn's assumption that he had the right to tell her what she could and couldn't do. Wordlessly she stared at him until he relinquished her and stomped away.

Clayton wrapped one hand around her waist and took her other in his hand. Rosemary was glad she wore gloves. The thought of being forced to actually touch him with her bare skin turned her stomach.

"That look on your face is most unflattering to me, little miss."

She smiled for the onlookers. "Be glad I'm not losing my dinner all over your suit."

Rather than the anger she'd expected, he gave a boisterous laugh, drawing attention to them. "I find your honesty refreshing, my dear."

"Indeed? I'm surprised you even recognize honesty when you see it."

The humor faded from his eyes. "And how are things on my property, Miss Jackson?"

"I wouldn't know. I've never been on your property."

"The sheep are well? No mishaps?"

If she'd had any doubts as to who had ordered the barn fire, his last question certainly would have removed them. But she refused to play into his game. She shook her head. "Nothing."

His eyebrows rose. "No mishaps at all? Where is that honesty we were just admiring so?"

"Sir, there have been no mishaps on my property."

"I must have gotten the wrong information, then. I was told there had been." His eyes dared her to deny it, but again Rosemary refused to give in.

"None, sir. You must have been misinformed. We have most definitely not had a mishap."

"You're telling me your barn did not catch on fire."

"No, it did not."

"You are lying, young lady."

The music stopped as the dance ended. She glared at him. "No, sir. I never lie. There were no mishaps. Mishaps are accidents. My barn did not catch fire; it was deliberately set on fire by you or one of your men. But you don't scare me, Mr. Clayton. And you can't have my land."

She spun on her heel and walked off the dance floor. Finn met her halfway, intercepting Mr. Clayton, who had followed with anger blazing in his eyes. Finn leveled his gaze at the older man. "Leave her alone, Clayton."

So far, the other guests of the mayor's dance hadn't noticed the tension. Rosemary had continued smiling during their conversation and hadn't left him until the dance was over. "Surely you don't want to make a scene, Mr. Clayton," she said.

He glanced about as the music picked up for the next dance. "This is far from over, my dear."

"I didn't think otherwise."

He glided away, and she turned to Finn, her heartbeat slowing to normal. "Thank you."

His eyebrows lifted. "You're not angry that I interfered?"

"Everyone needs someone by their side sometimes, Finn." She smiled. "I'm not foolish enough to think otherwise."

Chapter Seventeen

....

The late July sun beat down on Finn and his workers as they labored to finish rebuilding Rosemary's barn. He'd been to a lot of barn raisings before he moved to the Dakotas, where the communities had pulled together, making a day of it...but that hadn't been the case with this barn. The community was too spread out, and Rosemary hadn't been homesteading long enough to make many friends. And she'd certainly made just the opposite with Clayton. They had already been working for a week, and Finn anticipated at least one more, perhaps two. But at least the timber framing had been done, although he'd had to hire out as far as Williston to find men who weren't afraid to cross Clayton.

The heavy beams were now raised, and they were beginning to nail on the boards for the roof. He climbed down from the ladder and pulled his handkerchief from his pocket. Wiping the sweat from his face and neck, Finn looked over their handiwork and had to admit that the barn was coming along nicely. The six Germans he'd found to work for him were strong, hard-working, and barely took a break. He knew they were uncomfortable at first over Rosemary's insistence that they take their breakfast and supper meals in the house. There wasn't enough room around the kitchen table, but the bunkhouse had a table as well, and instead of having to haul food out to the bunkhouse, she had enlisted Rolf and Peter to carry it into the house. It made for a crowded living room.

"After all," she had explained when Finn voiced his uncertainty, "these men are away from their families, trying to make ends meet. The least we can do is feed them properly. It's only for a couple of weeks."

Agnes had objected to her two young sons sleeping in a bunkhouse with men she didn't know, and Afonso and Heinrich objected to the humiliation of sleeping in the house with the women. So Finn had taken pity on the lads and offered them a place to sleep in his soddy. In return, they managed his fields for him and made sure the sprouts weren't wilted or being stolen by various insects or prairie dogs.

"I thought you might be thirsty."

Finn turned at the sound of Rosemary's voice. She wore a cotton dress of light blue, the first time he'd seen her in anything other than dark colors since she'd arrived. "You look awfully pretty," he said.

She blushed and handed him the bucket of cool water with a cup. "Thank you. These were in my crates you brought from Williston. I have no idea how long they were at the post office before you went, but I'm so glad they finally shipped from Kansas. I've been debating with myself about whether I should cast off the dark clothing and allow myself cooler attire."

"I'm glad to see which side of the debate won out." He couldn't help but think how the blue in her dress made her blue eyes seem two shades darker. Her beauty took his breath at times. But then, with Rachel it had been the same. Lately he'd spent most of his time confused and lonely.

Finn drained the cup in a few gulps. "Thank you. I guess was thirstier than I thought."

"I thought the men might need something to drink too. They work so hard in this hot sun." She frowned. "They should take more breaks before someone winds up ill."

She shielded her eyes with her hand across her forehead and stared up at the new barn's wooden frame already standing as tall as the old barn. "It's going up much faster than I believed it would," she said. "How is Peter working out?"

Before making the trip to Williston, Finn had hired Rolf's brother Peter and his uncle Ian to begin removing debris and cleaning up the site where the old barn sat. After he returned, he'd kept them both on to make the building of the barn go that much faster.

"Good. He works hard." As did Ian. But there was something about Ian that didn't quite sit well with Finn. He'd kept a close eye on the man over the past week since he'd been back from Williston with the others, but so far, his concerns had seemed unfounded.

Rosemary watched the men work. She nodded toward Peter, who was pounding a board onto one of the walls. "I noticed last night at supper that Marta seems to have switched affections from Rolf to Peter. Is that causing any problems?"

"Between the brothers?" Finn shook his head. "Not that I'm aware of."

"Did you even know there might be bad feelings between them over a girl?" Rosemary laughed and gave his arm a playful shove.

"Never mind. I can tell by the look on your face that you have no idea what I'm talking about."

"Sorry." He gave her a sheepish grin. "I reckon I'm oblivious to young love."

"You'd best get unoblivious before Sarah grows up, or you'll be in trouble. She's going to be a beauty when she's Marta's age."

"Lucky for us both we'll have you to keep me aware of any young men who show an interest in her."

Her expression went from teasing to pensive and she expelled a weighted breath. "What do you think will happen with Mr. Clayton?" She shook her head. "What if the violence escalates and these people I'm responsible for truly are in danger?"

"I don't know." He wanted to pull her to him and comfort her, reassure her. But to do so would confuse the relationship between them even more. Some days they argued like the worst of enemies, only to make up the following day—like the haircut incident.

Rachel had never fought with him, so Rosemary's volatile temperament and her need to defend herself still took him aback even after three months. Other times they laughed and chatted like old friends, finishing each other's sentences and anticipating each other's needs—as she had with the water just now.

He hadn't asked her to marry him again, though he still believed that would solve her problem with Clayton. She knew he believed marriage to be her best solution as well as his concerning Sarah, but so far she wasn't inclined to change her mind. And he'd already asked her twice. He wasn't going to ask her again. A man had his pride.

He knew there were two things keeping her from agreeing to marry him when the preacher came, which should be any time

now. First, she didn't want to be his replacement for Rachel. He had grown to know her enough that he understood it now and respected her decision. While he still couldn't honestly say to her, "Rosemary, I love you," and mean it in the romantic sense of the word, the two had become closer than friends since the town dance last month. At least to his way of thinking.

She now took his arm automatically when they walked together. And there had been times when they sat on the porch together and she had laid her head on his shoulder. But whether he loved her was only part of the reason she wasn't willing to stand before the preacher. She wanted to beat Clayton. Finn wasn't sure why it meant so much to her, but she simply wasn't willing to marry him and let him add his name to hers on the claim, making it that much harder for Clayton to try to take away the land.

"Well," Rosemary said, "I'd best get back inside. The meals are more than Agnes can manage alone these days."

"It'll be good to get the barn finished and have things return to normal?"

She nodded, but her eyes clouded over. Was it worry? "Everything okay?" Finn asked.

"Agnes."

Alarm seized him. "Is something wrong with her?"

Rosemary shrugged. "I'm not sure. She's been ill lately, and if I can be so bold, I don't think Sarah is getting the milk she was before. She seems to be wanting to be fed more times in the day. It's wearing Agnes out and frustrating the baby."

"Have you discussed it with Agnes?" Just hearing that there might be a problem sent his mind spinning back to the days before

Agnes came to live with Rosemary and saved his daughter. Had it just been two months ago that Sarah was too thin and pale? He hadn't even realized how malnourished she'd appeared until she began to thrive under Agnes's care.

"She tells me not to 'vorry,' " she said. "I just don't know." Her gaze moved past him. "Someone's coming."

Finn heard hoofbeats and followed her gaze. His stomach clenched as he recognized the black suit and sturdy build of the approaching rider. "It's the circuit preacher," he said.

Rosemary's face crimsoned at the news. "I'd best go tell Agnes to set another place for supper. Will you please welcome him and invite him to join us? He's more than welcome to stay in the bunk-house with the men."

Without awaiting his response, she bolted toward the house. Finn barely contained a grin. Rosemary had grown up in a town that had always had a preacher. When a person died, the preacher immediately said words. When someone wanted to marry, they planned the wedding and the preacher performed the ceremony. But even though progress and modern ways were moving from the cities to places like Hayes, Kansas, here in North Dakota life remained much the same as it had been for pioneers thirty years before. There was no church and no permanent preacher. Reverend Bishop rode his circuit through this country and sometimes only made it once a year.

From the way Rosemary had fled to the house, Finn knew she was every bit aware that she had a decision to make. If she had any inclination to marry him this year, she had less than a week to say so. The preacher would provide comfort for those in mourning, he

would preach a revival in City Hall, and he would marry anyone within a thirty-mile radius who wanted to get married. And then he'd be gone.

* * * * *

Rosemary knew Agnes and Marta were watching her all through the meal. Gracious, she had already given her answer to Finn and there was no need for anyone to think that she might decide otherwise. She repeated this to herself over and over, though her heart refused to believe it. She deftly avoided all eye contact—or contact of any other sort—all evening while the reverend shared stories of his travels with the entire group.

Of course she wanted to marry Finn. She had admitted to herself, if to no one else, that she had fallen in love. But that didn't fix the problem that Finn didn't love her. She knew he cared about her as a man cares for a friend. She also knew that he would be a good and faithful husband and would likely give her children of her own. But his heart would always be looking for Rachel. He would hold her at night and she would believe he was pretending to hold her sister, and she would never be able to bear the pain she would feel.

Feeling Finn's eyes on her, and Agnes's and Marta's, her chest began to tighten and her breath came in short bursts. She stood suddenly and knocked over her glass. "I'm so sorry," she gasped out. "Please excuse me."

She maneuvered her way through the kitchen, into the living room, and past the workers. "Excuse me," she said as she bumped against someone. She burst through the door and started to run. She heard Finn calling her name, but she didn't stop. Instead, she picked up her pace and headed for the fields. Her favorite pasture had a tiny creek, more a watering hole for the sheep, but she loved sitting on the grass with her shoes off, letting the water run across her feet. Only she had never gone out there in the dark. And as she ran, she lost her bearings. How could she have been so stupid as to run out without a lantern?

She had run too far from the house to see the lights.

"Rosemary!" Finn's voice filled her with both dread and relief. As much as she hated the idea of a confrontation, the idea never crossed her mind not to call out to him. "I'm here, Finn. I can't see where I am."

"Keep talking. I'm coming. Do you see my lantern?"

"Yes. I'm over here."

Within a couple of minutes, he reached her. He dismounted and walked his horse to her. "What were you thinking?" His voice held no accusation or anger.

She released a shaky breath and tried to push her loose hair from her face. "I wasn't thinking at all, obviously. I just needed to leave the house. Everyone was staring and expecting us to announce a wedding, and it was just too much."

"I take it you haven't changed your mind?" There was no mistaking the disappointment in his tone. Rosemary couldn't help but wish the disappointment stemmed from Finn's love for her and not simply his need to provide Sarah with a mother.

Rosemary opened her mouth to apologize once again, but he quieted her with an upraised hand. "But," he said.

"But?"

He smiled and said, "Yes. But."

Rosemary laughed. "You're disappointed that the sight of the preacher didn't send me rushing to the altar, but…" Already Rosemary's pulse was beginning to return to normal as his calm reaction soothed her.

"Right." He hung the lantern on the fence post, turned to her, and, taking both her hands in his, said, "*But* I am still glad to have you in my life and in Sarah's life. Even if you're 'Auntie' instead of 'Ma.' "

Though she wished her heart could soar at his sincere words, it nearly broke instead. He had to know that she was waiting for him to say, "I love you, Rosemary," and she would marry him in an instant. They could merge the homesteads and begin to build a life that was only theirs. But that was more than she knew she should hope for.

"Thank you, Finn," she said softly, refusing to give in to the tears. If he simply couldn't love her, then she too would be happy to be in his life as "auntie" to Sarah.

Chapter Eighteen
....

Sunday morning dawned as bright as any Lord's Day should, as far as Rosemary was concerned. Of course, they had left the house before dawn to reach Paddington before service, and just now, the sun peeking over the horizon painted a coppery sky with hints of pink as the sun rose higher with each passing minute. The beauty of the moments as they came reminded Rosemary that a hand bigger than hers was guiding her life. And as the wagon rolled forward, she became lost in silent praise, preparing her starving heart for the day ahead.

She hadn't attended a service since leaving Kansas almost four months earlier, and she was more than ready to sit beside still waters and feed on God's Word. Rosemary drove the wagon carrying Agnes and the children while Finn rode his horse next to them and his men rolled along in his wagon. The day would be long, with two services and a picnic beside the lake. The boys were ready for baseball, footraces, and the planned bonfire. They hadn't had much time to organize the day, but the residents of Paddington were accustomed to the preacher's unannounced visits and the necessity of quick planning.

If the air of excitement running through their group was any indication,today promised to be a fun day. Emotions were running high, and the children couldn't contain their laughter.

Only Agnes seemed out of sorts. Rosemary turned to her on the seat. "Is something troubling you?"

Agnes shook her head. "Oh no. I am not troubled." She smiled and drew the baby closer.

One thing Rosemary had learned since Agnes moved into the house was that the woman wouldn't complain. The closest she had ever seen her come to complaining was the day she lost her homestead. Rosemary cut a glance from the corners of her eye. "There!" she said. "I saw you wince."

"Vince? Vat is that?"

"You frowned like you're in pain...or angry."

She scowled. "I am not."

"Mama!" Elsa called from the back of the wagon, clearly upset. At the same time, little Gerta let up a howl.

Agnes closed her eyes, took in a breath, and then turned to her children. "Vat is it, Elsa?"

"Gerta will not get off my dress. She is getting it creased."

"Gerta, precious," Agnes said, "come, sit with Mama and Fräulein Jackson."

The little girl stood and toddled forward, climbed over the seat with Afonso's help, and sat between Rosemary and Agnes. Agnes held Sarah with one arm and slipped her other around Gerta. The conversation was over for now, Rosemary knew, but she had every intention of returning to it later. Agnes wasn't well or she was angry. Whichever the case, Rosemary intended to discover the cause and try her best to set things right for her friend.

They reached city hall, where the church services were going to be held. Today the building held very little fanfare, nothing like the

night of the dance. Today there were no banners and no tables with bowls of cider and sugar cookies. Only benches and a roughly hewn pulpit that were most likely brought out only once or twice a year when the preacher visited.

Mrs. Franklin arrived at nearly the same time with a middle-aged man at her side.

"Good morning, Mrs. Franklin," Rosemary said, smiling at the elderly woman in her black silks and lace. The man stared at Rosemary, his eyes steady and curious.

Mrs. Franklin nudged him. "Stop staring, Dr. Richards."

"I beg your pardon, miss." He shook his head. "I'm afraid I haven't seen a pair of identical twins before. It is truly remarkable, isn't it? I knew your sister. I'm sorry I couldn't do more for her."

Rosemary shook his hand. "Please don't apologize for something you had no control over. I'm Rosemary Jackson. I'm so looking forward to the service today." She offered Mrs. Franklin her arm as they entered through the open double doors.

The elderly woman handed Rosemary her cane and slid her hand through the proffered elbow. She gave a snort. "The preacher is nothing but a bag of wind. Hardly worth the Lord's time for any of us to attend, but we do anyway because to a starving man even a bug can seem like a feast."

Hiram Richards chortled at the woman's assessment, and Rosemary hid her own smile. "Now, Mrs. Franklin," the doctor said, "that's uncharitable of you. Besides, we're not listening to Reverend Myers. You were visiting the East the last time the preacher came. This is a new, younger man, Reverend Bishop."

"Younger." Mrs. Franklin heaved a sigh. "The whole world is

going to young folks. Pretty soon there won't be any place at all for someone my age." She glanced at the doctor. "Or you either, my boy. You're not so young anymore."

Rosemary smiled at the doctor over Mrs. Franklin's white head. "Where would you care to sit, ma'am?"

Mrs. Franklin scanned the seats and chose a row toward the back. "In case I have to get up to use the necessary. This fellow might be a windbag too, for all I know."

Rosemary's cheeks warmed as the doctor chuckled loud and heartily. A pair of dowagers on the front row turned and shot him a frown. After all, church should be somber, Rosemary supposed.

After getting Mrs. Franklin settled in, the doctor took a seat next to her. After setting the cane on the back of the bench in front on them, Rosemary realized she was standing alone next to the row of seats, looking conspicuous. "Well, young woman," Mrs. Franklin said, "are you planning to sit or stand during service?"

Spying Agnes, Finn, and the children speaking with the reverend, she nodded toward Mrs. Franklin and the doctor. "If the two of you will excuse me, I'd best go and join my family." She caught Mrs. Franklin's eye and thought she detected a hint of displeasure that she wouldn't be sitting with the elderly woman. "May I find you afterward during the picnic?"

Shrugging her silk-laden shoulders, Mrs. Franklin stared straight ahead. "I certainly am not your mother. You may do as you like."

The doctor winked at her. "I, for one, would be thrilled to hear all about what it was like to grow up as a twin. I'll be looking for you if you do not come to us."

Gratitude flowed through her like the rush of water through a pump. "Thank you, Doctor. I'll see you later."

As she approached Agnes, she grew more concerned than ever. Her pale skin and pain-filled eyes meant she was ill. Rosemary moved discreetly to her side. "Agnes," she said in her ear, "you are not well. It's plain as day in your eyes. I think we ought to ask the doctor to take a look at you."

Agnes handed over the baby but shook her head. "No, Rose. You must not pull the doctor avay from the service, please." She motioned toward the back door. Rosemary followed her finger and saw Marta and Rolf. His hand encircled the girl's arm, and she looked distressed. The next instant, they disappeared outside.

"What on earth?"

"He is very much vanting for Marta to marry with him today while the preacher is in town."

"But that's ridiculous. She's much too young. Besides, they hardly know each other." She leaned in and lowered her voice. "And doesn't Marta have more affection for Peter these days?"

"I am afraid so." She slowly lowered herself onto the bench and reached for Sarah.

Rosemary shook her head. "I'll take care of her. Why do you say you're afraid so about Marta and Peter?"

"She should not trifle with the affections of one and then the other. It is not kind."

Trifle seemed a strong word for a young girl losing interest in one boy and becoming much more interested in another. It happened all the time without too much heartache. "I'll go after them and make sure Marta gets in for service. I see the reverend making his way to the front."

Finn raised his eyebrow in question as he walked toward their bench. "Where are you going?" he asked. "Service is about to begin."

"Ask Agnes," she said. "I'll be right back. Here, take Sarah."

Rosemary slipped through the back door and spied the pair almost instantly. Rolf still had a tight grip on the girl's arm, and Marta winced with pain.

As if sensing Rosemary's gaze, Rolf glanced her way and then began walking toward the lake that ran behind the town on that side of the street. Rosemary quickly closed the distance. "I will be taking her inside to her mother now, Rolf. Let her go."

"You shall not." Rolf's knuckles whitened as he tightened his grip on Marta's arm. Marta winced and Rolf practically dragged her away from Rosemary.

Indignation shot through Rosemary, and she stomped forward. "Rolf! Come back here."

He turned, anger flashing in his blue eyes, his hand still firmly clasped around Marta's arm.

"I said, let her go—immediately." She kept her voice low but firm, leaving no room for misunderstanding. She meant what she said.

But Rolf shook his head. "Marta vill be my wife. She vill not disobey me in this manner." He sneered at Rosemary. "She vill behave as a voman should. Not like you, Fräulein. You haf poisoned her mind to me."

Taken aback by the anger and contempt in his eyes, Rosemary pressed her hand to her stomach and gasped. In the months he had worked for her, she had never witnessed this sort of behavior from him. The only reason she could think of for his possessive attitude was jealousy. Didn't he know that Marta preferred his younger brother? Where was Peter, anyway?

Rosemary knew she couldn't allow him to intimidate her this way. He had no right to force Marta to do anything she didn't choose to do. "Rolf, I must insist that you unhand Marta now." She met Marta's panicked gaze. "Marta, do you plan to marry Rolf?"

The girl's lips trembled. "Mama says I must marry soon so that I am taken care of."

Anger flashed through her at the thought of Agnes saying that to the girl. She supposed it had to do with Agnes's own situation. But she should know that Marta was welcome at the homestead for as long as she wanted to stay.

"And she thinks Rolf is going to be the one to take care of you?" Rosemary glared at the young man, for the first time not liking him at all.

Rolf sneered, but his expression remained proud and confident. "I take goot care of her vhen ve are married."

"That won't be for a long time, if at all." Rosemary couldn't believe they were even having this conversation. "And as long as you're on my property, you'll not treat Marta in this manner. Turn her loose immediately, or you will find yourself without a job and banned from ever setting foot on my land again. Try to see Marta then."

Slowly, one finger at a time, he turned her loose. Marta rubbed the spot on her arm. He silently warned her with his eyes then said, "The preacher will not be here after the meeting. Peter vill not marry you. He is too young and too stupid to take care of a voman."

Marta jerked her head at his words. "Peter is not stupid. He is... very...smart and...wonderful. Don't you say those things about him."

Rolf shook with anger, and his hands balled into fists. Rosemary stepped in quickly. "Don't even consider laying a hand on this child."

Rolf stared hard at Marta. "Ve shall speak after vhile."

He stomped away from the meeting, but Rosemary wasn't as concerned about his soul as she was with Marta's well-being. The girl melted against her and Rosemary held her while she cried. When she finally pulled back, Rosemary removed her lace handkerchief from the sleeve of her dark green gown and handed it to the girl.

"Has he treated you that way before, Marta?"

She averted her gaze, but not before Rosemary noticed her beautiful blue eyes filling with tears. "It's okay. You don't have to answer. Do you want to marry him? If he's this rough with you now, in front of me, how will he treat you when the two of you are alone?"

Marta shuddered. "I do not know, Rosemary."

"What is it that you want to do?"

Her eyes took on a dreamy look. "I would like to go to school and get a certificate to teach school. Peter says he would also like to be a teacher, but his papa says he must work to help the family."

Delight filled Rosemary's heart, and she couldn't help letting out a big laugh. "You want to be a teacher?"

Mistaking her laughter for mockery, Marta ducked her head. "But I am marrying Rolf, of course."

"No, you're not, you silly girl. If you want to go to school, you certainly must go to school."

"It is not possible."

"Of course it is." Rosemary winked at her. "Anything is possible. You just have to believe. It is even possible for you to marry Peter if you want to, if the two of you care for each other. I wouldn't suggest

it for today, of course. But, honey, you are not beholding to Rolf. And you are welcome to stay with me for as long as you want. Don't get married because you feel there is no choice."

"As you didn't, Rosemary?" The girl's eyes shone with admiration, and it was clear to Rosemary that Rolf resented her for the influence she wielded, unwitting or not.

Slipping her arm across Marta's shoulders, she led her toward the building. "My situation is a little more complicated. Mr. Tate was in too much pain to consider a marriage to me when I first arrived or I would likely be his wife now, or at the very least be planning my wedding for today."

"He did not wish to marry you?" She shook her head. "But he loves you so much. Even Mama says so."

The girl's words were like rain on a parched land. "Your mama said that?"

"It is so plain in the way he smiles at you and listens to the things you say as though they were sent from angels' lips."

"Gracious. Angels' lips." She chuckled. "We must be speaking of two different Mr. Tates."

Marta giggled as they reached the door. "No, ma'am. There is only one Mr. Tate."

She was certainly right about that. As they tiptoed into the hall, the congregation was standing for prayer. Finn turned, and as his eyes found her, he smiled, motioning to the seat next to him on the bench.

Shoulder to shoulder, they shared a hymn book. As loudly as her heart sang, Rosemary was surprised her voice didn't overpower the congregation around her.

Chapter Nineteen

....

Finn kept a sharp eye on Clayton during the service, so much so that he had trouble staying focused on the preaching. He had no intention of allowing him to waylay Rosemary again like he had at the dance.

The parts of the message he heard he liked, and he sure hoped Clayton was paying more attention than he was. The topic appeared to be "love your neighbor as you love yourself" and included the command to not covet your neighbor's land," or something like that. Anyway, it seemed to be directed at Clayton, and Finn sure hoped the man had ears to hear.

The sermon went on for over an hour and a half. The temperature inside the building began to rise, and the baby grew fussy. Agnes reached for her and stood slowly, grabbing the bench in front of her for support, as though she were losing her footing. He reached for her. Rosemary leaned over. "Go with her, Finn. She won't admit it, but she's not feeling well."

The reverend's voice rose in volume to draw the congregation's attention back to himself as Finn escorted Agnes and the baby out the front door. Thankfully, a breeze wafted over the little town, bringing relief from the stifling air inside. "Let's go and sit next to the lake, where you can be comfortable, Agnes," he said.

"You cannot sit vhile I feed the baby." She sighed as though her strength was gone. "It is indecent."

"I know. I'll just help you over there and get you settled, and then I'll wait for you to finish, okay?"

"Ja, okay."

Finn would have given just about anything to take off his shoes and slip his bare feet into the cool water of the lake. He hadn't worn these shoes since the last time the preacher came through, two months before Christmas. This past winter had been too harsh to allow the circuit preachers to make the rounds as often as usual. The tightness of his shoes was a testament to the fact that they were rarely used. His feet were in for a long day.

He walked away from the lake to give Agnes her privacy and leaned against the side of City Hall, realizing he had never seen the town so deserted. Of course, the only Sundays he'd come were meeting days, and no one would have been out and about on those days, for the most part. Which is probably why movement behind the sheriff's office caught his eye. He shifted so he could see who the men were. It was Rolf and two of Clayton's henchmen. Indignation welled up. Were they bullying him over his position as one of Rosemary's men?

He shoved away from the wall and was about to go to the young man's aid when he stopped short. One of the men laughed and clapped Rolf on the shoulder. The other handed him something that Rolf shoved into his pocket. Finn slid behind the next building, where he could watch without being discovered. Rolf walked away, head held high and unafraid. The two men went into the sheriff's office through the back door.

Shaking inside, Finn tried to piece together what he'd just seen. It didn't make sense that Rolf might be a traitor to Rosemary. She had been good to the boy and his family. If he had to bet on who was behind the barn fire, if indeed it was one of Rosemary's men, he would have bet on Ian, Rolf's uncle. The man was a good worker, but Finn didn't like the way he eyed Rosemary. Leered was more like it. And he had chosen to stay in the bunkhouse today rather than come to church.

What if both men were working for Clayton? Had he bought them off? If so, what did that say about Peter?

Finn didn't like the idea that Ian had remained on the home-stead. He glanced at his horse, tethered to the hitching post in front of the city hall. On horseback, without the wagons to accompany him, it wouldn't take him long to ride out there, check things out, and ride back to escort the ladies and children home.

But he dismissed the idea. The day was shaping up to be a hot one, and without any proof, he couldn't do that to his horse. Besides, surely Ian wouldn't be foolish enough to sabotage anything when everyone knew he was the only person on the property. He'd be fingered and convicted before he could defend himself.

No, he was going to stay in town and keep an eye on Clayton and his men and, most of all, make sure Rosemary and Sarah were protected. A man like Bart Clayton wasn't above creating a little havoc on the Lord's Day.

* * * * *

The service finally let out after two and a half long hours of sweating in the seats as the sun beat down on the roof, making the temperature inside feel like an oven. Rosemary gathered up Agnes's children while holding a sleeping Gerta in her arms. The child's angelic face rested on her shoulder, and Rosemary ached for one of her own. She smiled at Mrs. Franklin, who had slept through the last hour and a half of the sermon.

"Land sakes," the elderly woman said, not bothering to keep her volume down. "We got us another windbag of a preacher."

"Mrs. Franklin!" Rosemary said. "Don't be unkind."

"Me? He's the one who kept us in this hot room like the three men in the fiery furnace. A man of God oughta have more compassion."

Rosemary couldn't help but glance around the room. Shock spread through her when she found the preacher, who was too close not to have heard and was laughing under his breath as he wiped perspiration from his face and neck. He met her gaze before she could look away, and Rosemary knew he'd heard the old woman— but, true to his message, he'd chosen to love her as he loved himself and laughed instead of being offended. She smiled at the preacher and made a note to invite him to share their lunch.

She spotted Finn walking toward them by himself. "Marta?" she said softly. "Will you please take Gerta while I go and find your mama?"

Finn reached them. "Finally over, huh?"

"Finally," Afonso said, yanking on his tie.

"Finn, honestly. Don't be a bad example."

Obviously unaffected by her scolding, he grinned.

Rosemary turned to Marta. "Please take the children to the wagon and wait for me to come back. We'll find a nice cool spot by the lake for lunch."

"Agnes already has us a spot," Finn said. "Don't tell anyone, but we cheated and got lunch set out early. There was no sense coming back in after Agnes fed the baby."

Though she gave him a scolding glance, Rosemary almost envied the two of them that extra hour away from the heat.

The doctor and Mrs. Franklin walked near them, presumably heading for the doctor's buggy. Was he taking her home? Mrs. Franklin might have complained about the heat, but Rosemary had a feeling she would prefer to continue with the festivities rather than go to her house alone while the rest of the town lunched and played games.

"Mrs. Franklin," Rosemary called just as the doctor was about to help her into the buggy. "Will you come and have lunch with us? Finn can bring out a chair for you from the hall so you don't have to sit on the ground."

The elderly woman's face lit up. "If you're sure there's room."

"Of course there's room. You can meet Agnes and the rest of the children."

"I don't want to be any trouble, now," she said, taking Finn's proffered arm.

"Trouble? I'll be surrounded by the most beautiful women of every age at this shindig." He grinned, turning on that Finn-charm Rosemary had first spied back in Kansas...the charm that still had the ability to make her heart race.

Mrs. Franklin cackled and nudged him with her elbow. "I still think you and that one ought to be speaking to the preacher today."

"That one" could only mean her, Rosemary knew. Her face grew warm under the scrutiny, and she didn't even bother to look at them.

They found Agnes seated on the blanket, leaning against a tree with a beautiful view of the lake and the grandstand, where musicians were beginning to tune up their banjos and guitars. In the large open space beyond the grandstand, the older boys and men were setting up bases for baseball, and off to the side, sack races were already underway.

Rosemary couldn't help but be surprised that no one objected to such fanfare on the Lord's Day. She said as much to Mrs. Franklin.

"Oh," the woman said with a dismissive wave, "no one's working, so what's wrong with a little bit of merriment?"

"No one has ever given you trouble about it?"

"Only one preacher, and we told him not to come back if he didn't like it."

"And did he return?" she asked.

The old woman's eyes sparkled with a merriment of her own. "He liked the generous offerings." Mrs. Franklin looked at Agnes. "You're the woman who got snookered out of her land?"

Agnes lifted her eyebrows in surprise. "You haf heard of such?"

"The bank's been having a field day since Clayton bought up the lion's share. I'd lay odds he snatched up your property at pennies on the dollar."

Indignation shot through Rosemary. "Is he trying to be the only human being left in these parts? If he pushes everyone out, there'll be no one left but the cows."

"Some people are only fit to associate with animals," Mrs. Franklin said.

Agnes nodded. "He is one bad fella, that Mr. Clayton. I do not haf no respect for him."

"You're not alone, Mrs. Fischer."

"Please, call me Agnes." Agnes reached up and pressed the woman's wrinkled hand. "Ve shall be goot friends, Frau Franklin."

"Oh, well, then call me Dottie."

Rosemary started at the woman's first name. "Mrs. Franklin, I had no idea your name was Dottie. That's a very fun name."

"Land sakes, girl, if it brings you such pleasure, you can call me Dottie too."

The boys wolfed down their food and ran off to play ball. Finn turned to Rosemary. "Do you want to help me carry the baskets back to the wagon?"

"Certainly."

Finn stood as she gathered the food left on the blankets and slipped it into the baskets. He reached down and offered her a hand up then took both baskets. "What are you doing?" she asked. "You didn't really want my help?"

He shook his head. "Not really, just your company."

"Oh."

"I thought you might like to take a walk down the shore, away from the crowd a bit."

"I'd love to, but I hate to leave Agnes and Mrs. Franklin—Dottie, that is—with the children."

"Marta's there to help. I think they'll be fine."

"I don't know," she said. "Agnes hasn't been feeling well all day."

His eyebrows rose. "She seems fine."

Admittedly, Agnes had been showing a bit more color, but that could have been the result of the heat flushing her skin or the sun burning it. Finn must not have noticed the number of times Agnes had excused herself and walked toward the privy, and of course Rosemary would rather die than mention such a thing. Come to think of it, though, Agnes had seemed happier and more like herself during the past hour. "All right, Finn. A walk down the shore would be nice."

"Good."

They didn't have to go too far before they were clear of the crowd. Most of the townsfolk were enjoying their lunches and listening to the music beginning to play from the grandstand. The sounds of games and laughter filled the town, and it was difficult not to love the atmosphere such joy brought.

She didn't object when Finn snatched up her hand and held it as they walked. She told him about the incident between Rolf and Marta before service. "And the truth is, Marta would have married him for Agnes's sake," she said. "Some days I think I know Agnes as I know myself. Other days I wonder how on earth she can believe certain things."

"Certain things like a girl should get married and let a man take care of her?"

Rosemary blushed. "Certain things like a girl of fifteen should have the opportunity to go to school and become a teacher like Marta wishes to. And for your information, Peter also wants to go to school and become a teacher."

She couldn't resist sending him a triumphant grin. "So you see? Those two are perfect for one another. And Peter isn't pushing her to get married today, for mercy's sake."

"Like I'm pushing you?"

"No. I mean the way Rolf is pushing Marta. As a matter of fact, we should probably try to keep an eye on Marta today. I don't want Rolf cornering her alone again and bullying her into doing something she doesn't want to do."

"I will. But I'm more concerned with keeping an eye on you so that Clayton or his men don't try to bully you."

She gave him a dismissive wave. "He doesn't scare me." Rosemary hoped she sounded braver than she felt.

Before she had time to think, Finn caught her wrist mid-wave and gently spun her to face him. His hand wasn't tight on her wrist, and he did nothing sudden that would frighten her—but when his eyes caught hers, she knew he was angry.

"Wh–what do you think you're doing?" she asked.

"You should be afraid of Clayton, Rosemary." He pulled her closer until she could feel his breath fluffing the ever-present loose tendrils about her face. "Clayton has no scruples. He threw a woman and her children out. If you hadn't taken Agnes in, where would she have gone? What would she have done? I'll tell you. She would have ended up in a city somewhere, and she and all her children, including little Elsa, would be working in some hot factory, half starving and living in God-knows-what."

Rosemary drew in a quick breath. "Or she would have entered into marriage with a man who didn't love her just so she had someone to care for her and her children."

She pulled her fingers from his and turned to face the river. The sun glistened off the ripples, and a soft breeze fanned her face.

"You're comparing the idea of Agnes marrying a complete stranger to your marrying me?"

Something in Finn's tone, more than the words he spoke, caused

Rosemary to turn to him. A muscle in his jaw twitched and his eyes narrowed dangerously, at least enough to make Rosemary relent just a bit.

"Maybe it isn't exactly the same, but…"

He reached over and buried his fingers deep in her thick tresses until the pins popped from her hair and it tumbled down her back. He cupped the back of her head.

"What do you think you're doing?" she whispered, unable to find her voice.

"I'm going to kiss you unless you tell me to stop."

Rosemary's brain screamed, *Stop! You know I'm not the one you want.* But she couldn't force the words from her throat. His other arm curled around her waist, his palm flat against the small of her back, drawing her closer still, until Rosemary could feel his breath against her cheek. He trailed kisses along her jawline. He pulled back and kissed her forehead. A sigh escaped her lips, and Finn drew a sharp breath. In the next instant, she felt his lips, warm and soft, against hers. Rosemary matched him kiss for kiss and prayed she was the only woman he held in that moment. She protested when he pulled back, and he tightened his arm around her waist and kissed her again until she could hardly breathe. Only then did he pull back and stare into her eyes, deeply and earnestly, the fire still burning as he fought for his own breath. "Her marrying a stranger is nothing like me marrying you. Admit it."

If only she could be sure of what he felt, that he wasn't staring into her eyes and remembering Rachel or kissing her lips and holding her sister. But she took too long to answer and Finn dropped his arms, shaking his head. Despite her lack of breath, lack of experience, and suspicion that she wasn't the only woman Finn had been kissing in his heart, she desperately resented the loneliness she felt when he released her.

Her hands trembled as she reached back and realized that her hair had fallen and all the pins must be on the ground. She stooped and searched the gravelly bank.

"What are you looking for?" Finn asked.

She expelled a heavy breath. "My hair pins, obviously. Thanks to you, my hair is all over the place and I have no way to put it up. The pins are nowhere."

"Rachel used to put hers up without pins. Just tuck it."

Stabbing pain nearly doubled her over. His words were so casual and thoughtless. "Rachel had more talent when it came to primping. She didn't work on the ranch. All she had to do was read and play with her hair. I never learned how. That's why it never stays put."

Finn's eyes darkened. Fine, let him get defensive about Rachel. If anyone understood unconditional and never-ending love of her twin, it was Rosemary.

"Did it bother you that Rachel didn't help work the ranch?"

"Just let it go, Finn."

"I don't want to." He moved in front of her again and tipped her chin to look at him. "I wonder if you're still bitter that you did all the work while she was the one who got married and had a child."

"And died? No, I'm not bitter that I'm alive." Then she could have bitten her tongue in half for saying those words. Guilt filled her, and fresh pain over the loss of Rachel sliced into her.

"That was cruel."

Quick tears burned her eyes. "You're right. And I'm sorry. But it was also cruel for you to kiss me like that to try to make me love you a–and marry you today when you still love her. It was just plain mean, Finn, and you know it." She placed her hands on her hips and shook her head. "It's not that I begrudge her your love. I miss her too, Finn. So much that it steals my breath sometimes. When I look at Sarah nursing with Agnes, I want to scream how unfair it is that Rachel isn't here with us, raising her baby next to you inside her little sod house that she absolutely adored." She paused a moment and regained her composure. "But I saw you first in that way. Rachel didn't know, and I didn't fight for you. And if I wasn't willing to fight for you when she was alive and could fight back, why would I try to gain your love now?"

"That's… I had no idea you had any interest in me at all."

"Of course you didn't. Why would you? Now you know just how truly laughable I was." She gave a short laugh to prove the point. "And I'm even more so because I gave myself to those kisses and allowed you to hold me and make my mouth look kissed for everyone at the picnic to see and criticize. And I don't even care." She stepped back just as she read his intention in his eyes. He was about to take her into his arms again. "It's too late. I have enough self-respect that, even though I still want your arms around me and I still want you kissing me until I can't think and can't breathe, I know how ridiculous I am."

"Why do you say you're ridiculous?" Finn stepped closer again, this time closing the gap. He took her hands in his. "Rosemary, look at me."

She didn't have the strength it would take to resist, so she angled her head and met his gaze.

"Why do you say you're ridiculous because you want me to be close to you? It's what I want too. If you're ridiculous, so am I."

"I don't want to discuss it anymore." She had to get away. "You can't marry Rachel twice this way." A sob caught in Rosemary's throat. "Let me go."

"Have it your way, Rosemary." He paused then dropped her hands. "I reckon we should get back to the picnic."

"Yes, I think we should."

They remained silent as they walked back to the group. Finn escorted her to Agnes and Mrs. Franklin and mumbled something about going to play ball with the other men.

"Vhy is Herr Tate angry?" Agnes asked.

"I don't know."

"Hogwash." Dottie Franklin sniffed. "Something happened while you two went walking down the way, hand in hand."

"For mercy's sake," Rosemary said, scowling.

"Marta," Agnes said, "please go and bring Mama some of that lemonade. I am very thirsty."

"Yes, Mama." She rose from the blanket and walked toward the booth that was giving out lemonade.

"You tell me." Agnes peered at Rosemary's face, and her gaze rested on her mouth. "You haf been kissing?"

"How could you possibly know?"

She pointed to Rosemary's mouth. "There is a shine to your face that vas not there this morning. Does this mean you vill marry Herr Tate?"

" 'Course it does," Dottie said. "Those two belong together."

Rosemary shook her head. "Finn wants my sister back, and that can't happen. I can't pretend to be my dead sister just because we both want her back so badly. And if you want to know the truth, Agnes, I don't want to stand in another woman's shadow for the rest of my life. I want a man of my own."

"Really? Does it matter whether he has hair?"

Rosemary spun around and found herself facing a broad chest covered with a white button-down shirt. Lifting her chin, she looked up into the face of a handsome man with laughing green eyes and a beautiful smile to match. He held out his hand. "I trust you remember me? Dennis Mayfield."

"Of course I remember you." She accepted his proffered hand, her cheeks burning. "I apologize that you had to witness my little show of temper, Sheriff Mayfield."

"Don't be. It's rare to find a woman who speaks her mind. And I've seen you do that twice now." He still held her hand but didn't seem a bit embarrassed that it had been too long for propriety. "I don't like guessing games. I like knowing exactly where I stand."

Dottie gave a *humph* that left no room for doubt as to her opinion of the conversation.

Rosemary felt the impropriety of this conversation down to her core, but after those few moments by the creek with Finn, she suddenly didn't care. "Mr. Mayfield, you can be sure I prefer to know exactly where I stand as well."

A shadow fell across their still-clasped hands, and Rosemary knew it belonged to Finn. "Right now, Miss Jackson," he said with a sharp edge to his voice that made her shudder, "you're standing in the middle of a picnic holding hands with a stranger."

Chapter Twenty

....

Didn't the fact that she had accepted his kisses and kissed him back mean anything to Rosemary? Finn glared as Rosemary sat on the other end of the blanket with the interloper who had swooped in. He especially hated the way the other women were taking on so over the new sheriff—except for Dottie, who had excused herself and requested an escort back to her home.

He supposed the lady was exhausted after a full day. The afternoon service had begun at three, and now at six o'clock it had finally ended and the festivities were starting up again. Sheriff Mayfield had not attended the service but had shown right back up once the music began. Finn bristled at the way Rosemary smiled and laughed. The man was bald, for mercy's sake. Yet Agnes, Marta, and even little Elsa couldn't get enough of his stories. Stories—ha. *Lies* was more like it.

And where was Agnes, anyway? Shouldn't she be chaperoning over there on the blanket? Even Marta and Peter were sitting together. Marta's face had lit up when Peter arrived and stated that Rolf had offered to take his place with the sheep, since Marta clearly preferred Peter to Rolf. Unmarried couples on a blanket at night? They definitely needed a chaperone.

"Herr Tate?" The sound of Agnes's strained voice caught his attention, and he turned to find her holding a drowsy Sarah against her shoulder. There was no doubt that the baby had flourished under Agnes's care and nourishment. For that reason, he would forever be in her debt.

"Are you as bothered by that sheriff as I am?" he asked. "Something isn't right about him."

Her smile seemed forced. "It is only because you are jealous."

"Jealous?" He gave a short laugh. "I'm not jealous." At the sound of his voice, Sarah perked up. She leaned over for him to take her.

"It would be goot if you take."

Reaching out for Sarah, Finn peered closely at Agnes. In the lantern light near the booths where they stood, her eyes seemed dull and her face pale. "Are you ill, Agnes?"

She gave a rueful smile. "I haf ate too much. I vill be fine."

"I don't think so." He took her arm. "Let me take you to the wagon. You can lie down in the back."

"Ja, I do that, Herr Tate."

He settled Agnes in the wagon and went back to find someone to help Agnes. She needed Marta or Rosemary. She didn't need to be alone when she was so ill. Finally, the glow of a lantern illuminated Marta and Peter walking hand in hand around the corner of a building. When he reached them, he hesitated, as their shadow showed the couple embracing. He cleared his throat, and Marta gave a little gasp. "Marta? It's Finn. I need to speak with you."

Marta's chin was lowered, and she refused to look up as she stepped into the light. Peter followed, looking every bit as guilty.

"Marta, your mother is not feeling well."

The girl jerked her head up. "Mama is ill?"

He nodded. "I helped her to Rosemary's wagon. She's lying down in the back. I thought maybe she shouldn't be alone."

"Of course." She turned to Peter. "I will see you back at home. I cannot dance when Mama is ill."

"You must go be with her." He took her hand, despite Finn's presence, and lifted it to his lips. "I will see you tomorrow."

She nodded and sped away.

Finn raised his eyebrows at the lad. "What are your intentions toward her?"

Peter leveled a gaze at Finn, unflinching under his scrutiny. "I will marry her after we are both finished with school."

"I thought you couldn't go to school."

He shrugged. "I will. Also I will work for Papa and Mama."

"What about Rolf? He has his heart set on marrying Marta."

Peter scowled. "Rolf is unkind to her. He does not love her. And Marta doesn't love him."

"But Rolf is your brother. Don't you feel guilty about taking his girl?"

Peter gave him a solemn look as he considered the question, but then he shook his head. "I do not feel guilty. I love Marta and she loves me. There is no reason we should not be together."

"I agree." But something about the whole thing gnawed at Finn. Rolf wasn't the kind of young man to step aside for anyone, even his brother. Finn remembered seeing him earlier that morning and wanted to warn Peter to be careful, to not accept that Rolf would simply hand Marta over because she was in love with Peter. But he didn't want to step into a situation he wasn't invited into. Instead, he changed the subject. "You going back to the field tonight to take over for Rolf?"

Peter shook his head. "My brother will keep watch this night."

"Alone?" Peter might not be aware of the rules, but Rosemary wanted two of them watching together. Considering Bart Clayton and his threats, Finn believed her orders to be sound. "Miss Jackson has made it pretty clear that she doesn't want just one of you watching overnight."

Peter shook his head. "Ian did not want to come into town as I did."

Ian. He'd forgotten about Rolf's uncle. Again a hint of suspicion clenched his stomach. He wasn't quite sure why he felt it so strongly, but he knew something wasn't right. He had every intention of speaking to Rolf in the morning, without alarming Rosemary. Perhaps he could resolve the issue before it got out of hand. At the very least, he needed to assure himself that Rolf wasn't working for Clayton.

Sarah grew restless against Finn's shoulder. He patted her back and she settled down, but only for a minute before she began to whimper again. He wondered when Agnes had last fed her. As much as he hated to leave his position, where he had a good view of Rosemary and Sheriff Mayfield, he had to know.

He heard the moans before he reached the wagon and could tell Agnes was in a bad way.

Relief washed over Marta's face when she saw him standing there. "Mama is very sick. I believe she should see a doctor."

"No, Marta." Agnes spoke up with such a thin voice that Finn immediately handed the baby to Marta.

"I'll be back as soon as I find Doc Richards."

"No, Herr Finn. I have no money to pay him."

He patted her shin. "We'll work it out, Agnes."

It turned out, the doctor was one of the fiddlers at the grand-stand. But as much as Finn hated to draw attention, he couldn't let Agnes writhe in pain just for the sake of entertainment.

He walked up to the grandstand in front of the doctor and got his attention.

The other two fiddlers frowned but kept playing while the doc-tor bent down. "What wrong?"

"The woman who takes care of my baby has a terrible pain in her stomach. She's lying down in the wagon, and it seems like it's getting worse."

"Meet me at my office," he said. "I'll be right there."

"They aren't letting any more wagons back through town until the grandstand is taken down," Finn said. "She won't be able to walk that far."

"Finn?" He turned at the sound of Rosemary's voice. "What's wrong?"

His stomach clenched at the sight of the sheriff towering over her shoulder. "It's Agnes. She's having terrible pain in her stomach." He glared at the sheriff. "Can you make yourself useful and escort the wagon through town to the doctor's office?"

"Be happy to."

Rosemary touched his arm. "Thank you, Sheriff."

"My pleasure."

Finn swallowed a growl at the way the Sheriff Mayfield smiled at her. He looked like a bald pirate. He intended to speak with the mayor to find out if this Dennis Mayfield had been thoroughly investigated before they blindly swore him in and handed him a star-shaped key to the city of Paddington.

"The wagon is this way." Finn forced a civil tone, though being civil was the last thing he wanted to do.

"I'll meet you at the edge of town," the sheriff said. "I'll need to go to the livery and grab my horse."

"She doesn't have time for you to do that."

Giving an amiable nod, the sheriff followed Finn. "I can escort you on foot just as easily as on horseback, I suppose. If anyone objects, I'll explain that there's a woman in pain in the back of the wagon."

As much as Finn hated to admit it, Sheriff Mayfield was an agreeable sort of fella. But those were the ones who generally turned out to be the biggest liars and cheats.

He reached the wagon a moment later and glanced at Rosemary.

She nodded. "I'll tell Agnes what we're doing." She turned to her friend. "Agnes, it's Rosemary. Finn is taking you to the doctor."

Finn helped Rosemary and Marta into the back of the wagon then climbed into the front seat. He flapped the reins and the horses moved forward. Agnes groaned as the wagon swayed.

* * * * *

Rosemary held tightly to Agnes's ice-cold hand. "Hang on, my friend," Rosemary said. "We'll have you to Dr. Richards's office in no time. Agnes gave her hand a weak squeeze.

"Rosemary," Marta said, her lips trembling as she tried to

comfort Sarah, "Mama says her baby has gone to heaven and that is why she is in so much pain."

"What do you mean?"

"She only knew a baby was coming a week ago, maybe two."

"Oh, Agnes," Rosemary said, her eyes filling with tears. She pressed Agnes's hand to her lips and kissed the dear work-roughened hands. "I'm so desperately sorry."

There was no answer, and she realized Agnes had fainted. She had been miscarrying her own baby all day while nursing Sarah? Why hadn't she told them? Rosemary felt the weight of guilt and sorrow deep inside her as she held her friend's limp hand.

The wagon stopped and Finn hopped into the wagon bed. He gently stooped and slipped his arms under Agnes's back. He lifted her with a grunt then frowned as her arm flopped out.

"She's fainted," Rosemary said. "Sh–she lost Heinrich's last baby." Her voice broke, and she let the tears fall. The loss had to be doubly painful knowing that the last of Heinrich's children would never walk this earth.

Rosemary turned to Marta. "Go find the other children and bring them here to the doctor's office. They shouldn't be on their own this late."

Sheriff Mayfield held out his arms for Agnes. "Hand the woman out to me. It will minimize having to jostle her too much if she's hemorrhaging."

Finn gave a curt nod and gently lowered her into the sheriff's arms.

Once inside the office, the doctor hurried the sheriff into the exam room. Then Mayfield joined Finn and Rosemary in the waiting area. Within a few minutes, the doctor called Rosemary into his office. He confirmed that Agnes had indeed miscarried and that she had been three months along at least, so the bleeding was extensive. "We'll try to stop the worst of it. But if she is still hemorrhaging to this degree in the next half hour, I will have no choice but to perform surgery to stop it."

Rosemary stared at the doctor. "What surgery?"

"I'll have to remove her uterus."

"What do you mean? Remove..."

"She'll no longer bear children, but if all goes well and there are no complications, she'll live to raise the ones she already has. And Miss Jackson, trust me, the alternative is not good. If we do nothing, she'll bleed to death in an hour."

"I understand. You have to do it, then."

He stared intently into her eyes. "I have a request for you that will not be easy."

"Of course. Anything you need me to do." Rosemary swallowed hard.

"I need you to get Mrs. Fischer completely undressed. Be sure her stomach is clean. I have lye soap next to the washtub, which I have already filled with water for you. When she is clean, I'll have you take the sprayer next to the bed and spray it over the bed, the floor, and the table next to the bed. But don't spray her. It's carbolic acid, and we use it to kill germs that can make her very ill. Hopefully that will keep her wound from becoming infected.

"While you do these things, I'll be placing my instruments in the carbolic-acid solution to disinfect them, as well." He patted her on the arm. "Now, you know everything you need to know. Go in there, please, and get started. I'll go speak with her daughter and

Finn, and I'll be right there."

"D–doctor. What if she stops bleeding on her own?"

He shook his head. "It isn't likely, and it's best we get prepared for the surgery. But don't worry. I've done this procedure before."

"And did the woman…"

"Live?" He nodded. "I'm happy to say she did. As do most of my surgical patients since I've adopted Joseph Lister's philosophy about unclean, unsterile environment and instruments causing infection. Some of my colleagues are not so ready to accept something they can't see without a microscope." He seemed to be talking to himself now, but he came quickly back to the present. "There now, run along and undress her. You may cover her with a sheet when she is ready."

Dread filled Rosemary as she entered the room. Agnes remained unconscious the entire time Rosemary attended her. Her cheeks burned as she realized the doctor had set a pan under Agnes. She did as she was instructed, including spraying the room.

The doctor entered just as she completed the task. He inspected the pan underneath her hips, and sadness filled his eyes. "Yes, she is losing too much blood still. I'm afraid I have no choice but to proceed with the surgery."

"M–may I leave now, Doctor?"

His head shot up. "You may not, young lady. I have no nurse here. I need someone to help."

"B–but I'm not a nurse."

"You'll be fine. She'll need someone to monitor the ether that will keep her asleep. And don't mind the phenol. We have to breathe it to keep ourselves sterilized during the operation. It's abrasive and will likely irritate your nose and throat, but the effects are mild and will go away by tomorrow."

As if in a dream, Rosemary stood near Agnes's head as the doctor performed the operation. Somehow she obeyed his commands, and when the operation was over, she rushed outside, dropped to her knees, and lost a day's worth of food.

She heard the door open but couldn't turn around. Her body shook with the horror of what she had witnessed. "I'm so proud of you, Rosemary," Finn said. "The doctor told me you helped with the surgery. I don't think I could have done that."

Rosemary turned and buried her face in his chest. His arms encircled her with none of the passion of the morning, only tenderness. He stroked her hair and held her as she wept.

"I just kept thinking about Rachel," she cried. "I know it wasn't the same thing, but I just kept seeing her lying there on that table. It was horrible."

The door opened again, and this time Rosemary glanced up. The doctor handed Finn a jar of some sort of powder and a baby feeder like the one they had used before Agnes came to live at the homestead. "This is a replacement for mother's milk," the doctor said, his voice weary. "I made some inquiries after I saw your baby a couple of months ago, and it seems this is having success. Fewer babies are experiencing the sort of difficulties associated with feeding them cow's milk. Agnes won't be able to feed the baby for a while, and she may dry up in the meantime, so I suggest using this formula."

"How will she eat this?" Finn asked the same question Rosemary had been asking inwardly. How was this powdery substance going to feed Sarah?

"Mix it with six ounces of warm water. But not too warm. We

don't want to burn her. Then put it in the feeder like milk."

"Thank you, Doctor," Finn said.

"I suggest getting all those children to a bed somewhere. They're worn out. I'm sure Dottie will be happy to have you all." He glanced at Finn. "Marta is a little girl. Go get your baby from her. She has enough to worry about with her mother ill like this. I imagine she'll assume the responsibility of her brothers and sisters while Agnes is indisposed. She doesn't need your baby too."

Finn's face fell, and Rosemary's heart went out to him. "Finn, please go inside and get the children, and we can go." She turned to the doctor. "Will Agnes sleep all night?" She couldn't bear the thought that her friend might awaken and not understand why she was in a strange place and in pain.

He nodded. "I've got her pretty heavily sedated. Otherwise the pain will be difficult to manage. I'll put a cot in her room so I can monitor her," he said as though reading her thoughts. "There's no need for you to stay here. You would be more useful taking her children to the boardinghouse and asking Dottie for a room or two."

Rosemary nodded. "I think that's a good idea. Thank you for everything, Doctor. I'll settle the bill when I come back tomorrow."

"Let's just take one step at a time. Now go on and get those children out of my waiting room and into bed."

Finn returned with Gerta in his arms, followed by Marta, carrying Sarah, and Elsa between the two boys, holding their hands. Finn turned to the doctor. "Gerta was too heavy for Marta, so I had no choice but to leave Sarah with her." The children looked weary, somber, and worried.

Rosemary wanted to gather them all into her arms and reassure them that their mother would be just fine. Instead, she took the sleeping baby from Marta. Sarah's tear-stained face nearly broke her heart. Rosemary still held the feeder and the jar of powder. She knew the baby was hungry. As Finn got the children into the wagon, Rosemary suddenly remembered what had happened in that wagon. "Finn. We can't put them back there."

He turned and placed his fingers to his lips. "Your sheriff came out and cleaned it up."

Rosemary opened her mouth to deny that the sheriff was "hers," but she had to admit, she had enjoyed his company. After this afternoon's fiasco with Finn, Sheriff Mayfield's attention had soothed her wounded pride. Not to mention, the man was handsome and could clearly be counted on in a crisis.

Rosemary went to the door alone when they arrived at the boardinghouse. There was no need to unload all the children if Dottie didn't have rooms or simply didn't want to offer rooms for children. But after a quick explanation, the elderly woman glanced out at the wagon. "For mercy's sake, don't leave those children out there. Get them in here so we can put them to bed."

Rosemary motioned toward the wagon, and Finn and the children climbed down and came into the house. Finn held Sarah closely, as well as the feeder. The baby's cries had grown louder during the ride over, and now she was so upset, there would be no consoling her without feeding her. Finn said, "May I heat some water to feed Sarah a powder the doctor gave me to try?"

Dottie looked at the powder with skepticism, but she nodded and pointed toward the kitchen. "Be my guest."

Then she turned to Rosemary. "Come along upstairs." She

escorted the girls to the room Rosemary had occupied the night before she purchased her sheep. She pointed to the wall in the hallway. "You two gentleman, kindly wait right there. We'll get you fixed up directly." Dottie then walked to the wardrobe and pointed to the top shelf. "There are plenty of quilts to make the children pallets."

Marta laid the sleeping Gerta on the bed. She and Rosemary worked together to make a thick pallet large enough for the three girls, including Marta, to share. "I'll keep Sarah with me in the big bed," Rosemary said. "You go ahead and lay down and try to sleep." She put her arms around Marta and gave her a quick hug. "Don't worry about your mama. The doctor said he's done this surgery before with success. Trust the Lord to pull her through this ordeal."

Marta nodded. "Will we see her tomorrow?"

"Of course we will."

After kissing Elsa and Gerta good night, Rosemary accompanied Dottie to the next room, the boys trailing behind. "It's not as pretty, but it'll do for a couple of boys." She ruffled Afonso's unruly red hair. He rewarded her with a sleepy smile. "You boys climb into bed. You're too sleepy to wash, I can see. But tomorrow you have to wash your hands and even behind your ears or no breakfast."

Heinrich Jr. and Afonso grinned. "Yes, ma'am," they chorused.

Rosemary couldn't resist pressing a kiss to each messy head before shooing them off to bed. "Good night, boys."

Dottie and Rosemary walked slowly down the stairs, Dottie holding tightly to the railing.

"I hear it rumored you've got Bart Clayton's dander up," Dottie said.

Word got around fast in a town the size of Paddington. But

Rosemary didn't really mind. She loved her sheep, and she wasn't about to let him scare her off. "Yes, ma'am."

"You look out for that Bart Clayton. He's one dangerous man, and word is, he's not happy about you bringing sheep in."

"Well, I don't much care what he thinks, and you and I both know it's not the sheep that bother him. He wants my land, and he doesn't like the fact that I'm not cowering to him."

Dottie nodded. "You're likely right about that."

Rosemary gave a heavy sigh. "The truth is, I've raised cattle back in Kansas with my pa. Sheep are much easier to raise. They consume less food by a large margin. If I were a cowman, I'd be more concerned about the other cattle ranchers taking up all the grazing land."

"You're one smart young woman, Miss Jackson." She nodded toward Finn as they approached the kitchen. "Don't be too smart for your own good and let that one slip away."

Rosemary sat with Finn in the kitchen while he fed Sarah. Dottie kept her distance, claiming she had knitting to do in the sitting room. After a few minutes of draining the feeder, Sarah had kept the baby formula down and slept peacefully.

"It's late, and I have to check my fields in the morning," Finn said.

Rosemary reached for the baby. "Of course. I never expected you to stay in town. We'll be fine."

She walked him to the door, Sarah cuddling against her shoulder. Finn hesitated before opening the door. "Rosemary, I'm sorry for earlier."

Averting her gaze, she nodded. "I forgive you, Finn." A rush of

boldness suddenly overcame her, and she looked up. "I'm not sorry."

His eyebrows rose. "About the…"

"Kiss. Right. I'm not sorry for that." She stepped back, afraid he might take her words as an invitation. "I kissed you because I wanted to, Finn. The only regret I have is not knowing if you were kissing me because you wanted to or because you wanted to kiss the image of Rachel."

He released a heavy breath, leaned forward before she could protest, and pressed his lips to hers so fast she barely felt the kiss. "This much I can promise you, Rosemary Jackson. That one was for you."

Chapter Twenty-One

....

A sense of unease filled Finn as he headed for his fields the next morning. His horse seemed antsy as well. Finn kept a close watch for wild animals, though morning wasn't a typical time for predators to be after horses.

He heard them before he saw them—the soft bleating of sheep. What on earth? The sight of his field stunned him. The tender shoots of hay had been pulled up by the woolly beasts, the dirt turned up by two hundred pairs of hooves.... Horror filled him and he rushed forward on his horse, Cooper on his heels, barking with abandon as though the creatures were there for his amusement.

In the months since Rosemary had purchased the animals, Finn had purposely kept Coop away from the sheep because he wasn't sure if he would try to harm them. But now he couldn't care less. Let the enormous dog slaughter the whole herd.

It just didn't make any sense how the sheep could have even gotten into his field. But there was no fence, and only the one field between his property and hers. Rosemary hadn't wanted a fence. *"As long as the boys keep them herded away from your fields, we'll never have a problem. You'll see. I don't want a fence between us."*

And now a whole field of tender new hay was ruined because of her arrogance.

Coop's low, menacing growls and barks began to clear the field at last. The sheep turned, and as they were scampering away, Peter and Ian raced toward Finn. "Mr. Tate!" Peter called. "We had no idea this happened."

"Why didn't you two know?" Finn growled, his jaw set as his anger built. "Weren't you supposed to keep them all night?"

"When I got back from town, Rolf chose to stay in the fields and not sleep," Peter said. "He told me to go."

"So Rolf is the one who let these sheep ruin my field?"

For the second time in three days, Finn had an uneasy feeling about Rolf. It wouldn't have surprised him if the jilted young man had set the sheep loose on purpose rather than keeping them herded in Rosemary fields. He recalled again the scene between Rolf and Clayton's men.

He glared at Ian and Peter. "Why didn't one of you stay with Rolf? There is never supposed to be less than two of you out here with the sheep at a time."

Peter shrugged and stared at his boots. "I apologize, Mr. Tate."

"That doesn't tell me why you left Rolf alone at night when you know that doing so is expressly against Miss Jackson's orders for this place. If the two of you can't start obeying orders, I'm going to recommend that she let you go. And Rolf."

"Mr. Tate," Peter said, still refusing to meet Finn's gaze, "I am sorry for not staying when I was told to do so, but my brother ordered me to go, and because he has been so angry with me over Marta, I went. I didn't want to anger him further."

Finn scowled. "All right." He looked at Ian. "Is that what you say happened also?"

Peter jerked his head up and frowned. "I am not a liar, sir."

"I don't suppose you are, but I still need to know whether your uncle heard the same thing you did."

Ian's face grew red as Finn stared at him. "Well?"

"Rolf is my brother's son. I do not be disloyal to family."

"Well, that pretty much answers the question anyway." He looked from one to the other. "The two of you go get those sheep and herd them away from my pastures."

"Yes sir," they said, turning to go. Then Peter turned again. "Do you know when Marta will return from town?"

He didn't blame the boy. He was missing Rosemary too. A sense of camaraderie sprang up between them and evaporated much of his anger. "Mrs. Fischer has to remain bedridden and unmoving for a few more days, but I believe Marta is planning to bring the children back home in another day or so."

Peter's face relaxed at the news. "I am glad to hear this. Marta helps with the sheep."

Finn grinned. "You want her back because she helps?"

"Well, that is not the only reason."

"I'm sure she's just as anxious to see you, Peter. But please keep those sheep out of my fields from here on out."

"Yes, sir. I will." He glanced past Finn and suddenly his smile vanished and his body tensed.

"What is it, Peter?"

"Mr. Clayton. He is not a good man."

"Clayton?" Finn whipped around as the rancher rode toward

him, heedless of the new hay that hadn't been trampled or consumed. Peter was right about him; he was not a good man.

"Well, Finn, I guess now you'll admit I was right." Clayton pulled his sleek black horse to a halt. "It appears Miss Jackson's sheep have ruined one of your fields."

"And what makes you think that?" Finn asked, refusing to give him any evidence to use against Rosemary. The fact was, all Clayton would have to do was incite a few of the cattle ranchers over a fifty-mile radius and they'd run Rosemary out of the area just on rumor alone. He'd be no party to it.

"Well, just look at it." The man's face twisted in anger as he caught on to Finn's attitude.

"Believe me, Mr. Clayton, I have been. I'm thinking prairie dogs might have gotten to it." He raised an eyebrow, challenging Clayton to prove that Rosemary's sheep were responsible for his field.

"This isn't over," Clayton said. Staring at Peter, he asked, "What would you say got to this field, son?"

Peter kept his gaze leveled on the bully. "It is as Mr. Tate says. I believe I saw a prairie dog in this field one day. Could be he came back with his family."

Clayton glared at Peter but dismissed him, turning back to Finn. "I know you're sweet on that wild sister-in-law of yours, but let me assure you, I will get rid of those sheep one way or another. And it'll be a shame if she stands in my way."

"That sounded an awful lot like a threat against Rosemary."

"Call it what you wish." Clayton turned his horse and rode back across the field. Once he reached the road, he nudged his horse into a run and took off like a man with purpose.

Finn refused to let Clayton spook him, so he wasn't sure how concerned to be. He turned to Peter. "What was all that about with Clayton?"

The young man's ears grew red instantly.

"Don't bother denying it. Just explain to me how you know him and why he tried to get you to be an ally." Finn studied the boy's face closely. "Is Rolf involved with Mr. Clayton?"

Peter let out a heavy sigh. "He is. After Marta angered him, I believe he accepted Mr. Clayton's money to harm Miss Jackson's property or sheep."

"But why would he do that?"

"My mother and father live on Mr. Clayton's land. My father works his cattle. He has tried to bribe my family before, but we are not interested. The only reason Mr. Clayton keeps Papa working after we work for Miss Jackson is because he is very good and works very cheap. I believe Rolf will profit highly for turning the sheep into your field."

"But what good will it do to turn them into my land? Other than ruining my fields, it doesn't do anything for him." With a sense of unease, Finn recalled when his anger had run so hot just minutes ago that he would have had strong words with Rosemary if she'd been standing in front of him when the sheep were in his field.

"Mr. Clayton is using this incident to make a point that the sheep are destructive to cattle grazing and farmer's fields. If he can get all the farmers and the ranchers to come against Miss Jackson, she will not be strong enough to withstand the pressure, I'm afraid."

Finn guffawed. "Clearly he doesn't know Rosemary."

The despicable man just couldn't leave Rosemary alone. She

would never let her sheep graze on another field on purpose. And after this morning, he'd be putting up his own fence so it would never happen again, accidentally or from sabotage. And if it *did* happen again after he put up his fence, he would know for sure that sabotage was involved.

He dreaded having to tell Rosemary that Rolf had ceased to be loyal to her. He would go to town later to see her. For one thing, he missed her. And he missed Sarah, whom Rosemary insisted upon keeping with her so that he could work in his fields. So far the baby had kept down the food that the doctor had given them, so Finn was hopeful that soon he could bring his daughter home.

He mounted his horse. With Rosemary gone and Rolf a traitor, he didn't feel comfortable about leaving her home unattended. The men had completed the barn, collected their pay, and gone back to Williston.

Everything was quiet when he arrived. Too quiet. He tethered his horse to the house railing and climbed the steps to the porch. He heard scuffling inside and didn't have to guess who it could be.

Flinging open the door, he watched with grim satisfaction as Rolf jumped, his eyes wide. "Mr. Tate. Vat are you doing at Miss Jackson's house?"

"Are you seriously asking me that? You little traitor!"

Rolf had clearly been going through the papers on Rosemary's desk in the sitting room, and he had tucked one hand behind his back.

Finn nodded toward the hand. "I'll see what's behind your back."

Rolf frowned and took a step backward, his eyes shifting toward the door as though gauging whether or not he should make a run for it. "There is nothing there, Mr. Tate."

"Don't take me for a fool, Rolf. I've had a bad feeling about you from day one." He stepped closer, his hand on the butt of his pistol. He wouldn't draw it unless he had no choice. But Rolf didn't know that.

Rolf's blue eyes blazed with anger as he produced a paper from behind his back. He held it out for Finn.

"Step forward and give it here, easy-like." Finn took the paper from Rolf and examined it. "What were you planning to do with the receipt from Rosemary's land claim?"

Rolf shrugged.

"Did Mr. Clayton put you up to this?"

Shaking his head, Rolf averted his gaze. "I did vat I did."

Finn drew his pistol. "Drop your gun belt," he said. "We're going to town to pay a visit to the sheriff."

For the first time since Finn had known the young man, Rolf's arrogance failed him and his eyes showed fear. To his credit, he didn't beg Finn not to take him, doing instead as instructed and dropping his gun belt. Finn left it where it had fallen and motioned for Rolf to walk toward the door. With his gun leveled at Rolf's back, Finn fell in line behind him.

They mounted up and headed for Paddington.

* * * * *

Rosemary nearly burst into tears of relief when Agnes greeted her with a smile and sat up on the third day after her surgery.

Dr. Richards followed them into the room. "Children, don't get too close. She's in a good deal of pain yet."

"Doctor." Agnes's voice was still thin, but her tone was firm. "My children must come and give their mama hugs."

Rosemary stepped between them quickly. "One at a time." She eyed them with such stern admonishment that they obeyed instantly. "Afonso, you first. Gently."

He tiptoed to the bed and stood unmoving at his mother's bedside.

"Well?" Agnes said, her eyes smiling.

"I don't know what to do," the boy said.

"You haf forgotten how to give your mama a hug?"

"Gently," Rosemary reminded.

Agnes smiled at her son. "Yes, gently."

At the first touch, the rough-and-tumble boy burst into tears. "I miss you, Mama."

Agnes released her own tears, and each child in turn wept until there wasn't a dry eye in the room, including the doctor's.

After a few minutes, the doctor stepped up. "You should all go wait in the chairs while Miss Jackson and your mama talk."

The children left, and Dr. Richards regarded Rosemary. Fear gripped her stomach. She braced herself for bad news.

"Agnes is doing well," he said.

Wilting with relief, she frowned. "I thought you were telling me something very different."

"No, no. She is doing well." He pulled off his spectacles and pinched the bridge of his nose.

"What is it, Doctor?"

"The doctor is saying I must recover in peace and quiet."

"What do you mean?" Rosemary looked from the doctor

to Agnes and back to the doctor. "Whatever you need me to do, I'm willing. Just say what's on your mind, Dr. Richards."

"I would like to keep Mrs. Fischer as still and quiet and worry-free as possible for the next two weeks. If she stays quiet and can regain her strength, then she can go back to your homestead."

"Ach, I do not vish to be trouble."

"Agnes, please." Rosemary took her hand. "You are far from trouble." She turned back to the doctor. "What can I do for her?"

"There is no good place for her to convalesce in my office. I'm not set up like a hospital. And there is no hospital within a hundred miles."

"What do you suggest?"

"The boardinghouse is the only decent place."

Agnes let out a gasp. "Herr Richards, Doctor." She looked at him earnestly. "I am in your debt. You haf saved me, and now I must find a vay to pay you for your surgery to me." She closed her eyes and opened them, and Rosemary could see that her pain had returned. The doctor must have seen it as well. He walked to the cabinet, unlocked it, and pulled out a bottle of white, milky liquid.

He brought it to her, but she shook her head. "Not until I say vat I must."

"All right. But no more about paying my fee."

She turned to Rosemary. "This is a very stubborn doctor. How vill he pay for his medicines and equipment if he vill not accept payment?" She turned to him. "You are very goot doctor, not so goot head for business."

He chuckled. "I'll never get rich by fixing people up. That's the truth."

Rosemary squeezed Agnes's hand. "I think what she's trying to say is that she can't afford to stay in the boardinghouse."

"Yes," Agnes said, her chest rising and falling. "This is true."

The doctor spooned the liquid into her mouth, no longer heeding her protests. "Let's lay you down now." His soft words and gentle manner touched Rosemary. He glanced at her and she smiled. In turn, his face reddened and he cleared his throat. "Help me please. She has been sitting up long enough."

"Thanks to you two," Agnes said. Her breathing was beginning to slow.

Dr. Richards patted her hand. "You'll be more comfortable once you're settled in at the boardinghouse."

"I can't..."

"It'll be taken care of." Rosemary nodded at the doctor. "I'll speak with Dottie today."

"Rosemary, you mustn't." The laudanum was already beginning to take effect.

"Shh," Rosemary said. "Concentrate on getting strong for those babies."

The doctor walked her to the door. "The best thing is for Marta to stay with her and the other children to go to the homestead with you. Otherwise, I fear that Mrs. Fischer will not be able to keep from taking care of them."

"I don't mind taking the children home with me. The boys can help with the younger children. And even Elsa is good with Sarah."

"That's good. Good." He pinched the bridge of his nose again then looked up at her as though he had been trying to remember another detail. "Agnes can't climb steps. Under any circumstances. She will pull her stitches out."

"I'm sure Dottie wouldn't mind setting up a room for them downstairs."

Rosemary smiled as the children filed toward her. "Is Mama coming home today?" Elsa asked in the soft voice Rosemary had come to love. She reached down and rubbed the girl's blond curls. "Not today, honey." She reached out to take Sarah from Marta. "Can you please get the children to the wagon?" she said. "I'll be out there in just a minute."

"When should Agnes move to the boardinghouse?" she asked the doctor, glancing at the wagon through the door the children had left open. "I don't see how she will even bear to be moved."

He nodded. "We will need Finn and perhaps the sheriff again."

Rosemary's heartbeat sped up, but she wasn't sure which man had caused the increase. "I'm sure either man would happily agree."

"She will, of course, have to be carried."

"But what about her pain, Doctor?" No matter how careful the men were, they would never get Agnes to the boardinghouse without jostling her beyond her pain threshold.

"I'll make sure she's asleep during the transfer."

"That'll be for the best."

The doctor looked past her, and his brow creased. Curious, Rosemary turned and followed his gaze, just as the children began calling out, "Hi, Finn." "Hi, Rolf." "What are you doing?"

Rosemary stepped onto the porch and Finn lifted a hand to her. "I'll meet you at the boardinghouse when I'm finished," he called.

Watching him ride with Rolf, his horse slightly behind the young man's, Rosemary couldn't stop a feeling of dread from washing over her. The feeling amplified when they reined in their horses in front of the jail. Rolf had shown violence and anger a few times, but she couldn't imagine what might have happened to cause them to go to the sheriff's office. Everything in her wanted to rush over there and demand an explanation, but she had the children to attend, and she had arrangements yet to make for Agnes.

She pressed her palm to her aching head and walked toward the wagon. What else could possibly go wrong?

Chapter Twenty-Two

....

Finn could picture Rosemary pacing inside Mrs. Franklin's parlor, stewing as she awaited an explanation. He regretted that she had spotted him riding into town with Rolf in the first place. At first Rolf had kept quiet, confessing only to trying to steal the land-office receipt that proved Rosemary had filed a claim for her plot of land after the previous homesteader forfeited it.

He wouldn't say why he'd tried to steal the receipt, only that he thought a woman had no business owning land without a man to run things for her. At first Finn misunderstood and thought that Rolf had been rejected by Rosemary. Perhaps the act was the revenge of a spurned lover. But he quickly realized that wasn't the case. Rolf resented Rosemary's position, her wealth, and her generosity. He denounced everything from her land ownership to her bringing the Fischers into her home. As Rolf paced the cell, jumping angrily from one topic to another, he finally revealed the heart of the matter— he didn't believe Rosemary was a good example of womanhood for Marta. "She has poisoned Marta's mind against marrying me."

Finn chuckled at the ridiculous statement. "Rolf," he'd said as calmly as possible, "from what I heard, you were unkind to Marta. What woman can love a man who doesn't treat her with kindness?"

Rolf stopped pacing long enough to twist his lips in contempt. "It is a woman's place to obey, not to be treated with kindness."

The sheriff laughed. "Well, now we know why little Marta turned from you to your brother."

Finn agreed with Sheriff Mayfield but couldn't help but feel that now wasn't the time to bring up Peter's name. Rolf was too angry as it was. Why add gunpowder to an already roaring fire?

"Rolf," Finn said, keeping his tone calm, "I believe you that you're angry with Rosemary for Marta's behavior. I believe that you don't think a woman should own land. I believe all the things you've said here today. But I believe something you haven't said, as well."

"And what is that?" Finn realized he'd hit on the truth when Rolf's eyes narrowed, as though he was waiting to hear whether Finn truly knew the entire story.

"Rosemary's sheep went into my field when you were supposed to be watching over them last night."

He shrugged. "I was alone. They got away from me. The woman does not have enough intelligence to have a dog to herd the dumb sheep away from danger and your fields."

"She wouldn't need a dog if her supposed right-hand man hadn't sent away a couple of men who should have been out there in the first place."

Anger flared in Rolf's eyes. "And who told you this?"

The sheriff motioned to Finn. He closed the door to the room containing the cells and expelled a heavy breath.

"Do you have any proof that Rolf did more than break into Miss Jackson's home and try to steal a receipt?"

"Only the word of his brother Peter and his uncle. But they won't be much help."

Mayfield shook his head. "Then I can't do much to him."

"What do you mean? He was in her house."

"Yes, but he works for her. You said it yourself—Rolf is her right-hand man."

"Not for long."

"All you have on this kid is that he was looking for a receipt. Whatever his motive, if he's not willing to confess, no judge is going to convict him. There's just no real crime."

"No crime? He broke into her house."

"And if you'd caught him with a handful of money, I could probably keep him and force him to go before a judge." Leaning back in his chair, Mayfield stretched his long legs out in front of him and laced his fingers across his chest.

"So that's it?"

Mayfield shrugged. "I can keep him locked up overnight just to scare him, but in the morning, I'll have to let him go."

Finn scowled. "I should have known you'd be a worthless sheriff."

"Come on, Finn. You know I'm right. Don't let your jealousy talk for you." Mayfield grinned. "By the way, what kind of flowers does Miss Jackson like? I'm thinking I might pick her a bouquet for our outing tomorrow."

"What outing?"

"Didn't she tell you?" Mayfield's smug grin was beginning to grate on Finn's nerves. First he was a terrible officer of the law and now he was trying to take Rosemary? "I'm taking her on a picnic by Willow Lake."

Finn felt like he'd been punched in the face. Stunned by the news, he left the sheriff's office without a word. He grabbed his horse and led him toward Mrs. Franklin's boardinghouse, not bothering to ride. The walk helped him to burn off some of his frustration. He was upset that he'd been unable to obtain a confession from Rolf, and annoyed by Sheriff Mayfield's lack of concern about the incident at Rosemary's homestead, not to mention the sheriff's admission—boasting was more like it—that he was having a picnic outing with Rosemary the next day.

He blamed Rosemary for the latter. How could she share such an intimate kiss with him and the same day begin courting the new sheriff? She had never been this way back in Kansas.

He tethered the horse to the hitching post in front of the boardinghouse and climbed the steps, but the door opened before he could knock. Rosemary stepped onto the porch, closing the door behind her. She held Sarah in her arms, and the baby grinned as soon as she saw him.

"Here, for mercy's sake, take her. I've been holding her for thirty minutes waiting for you to get here."

Finn held out his arms and was thrilled when Sarah reached for him.

"Gracious, Finn. Don't keep me in suspense any longer." Rosemary stomped her tiny foot, looking every bit the image of a petulant child. "What on earth happened with Rolf? Where is he? Is he in jail?"

Finn's anger melted away. "I caught him going through your desk."

Rosemary frowned. "But he does that all the time. It's why I gave him a key to the desk."

"Yes, but he was holding a receipt behind his back when I caught him."

"A receipt? For what?"

It bothered Finn that she seemed so completely unbothered by this news, as though it had never even occurred to her that Rolf might be up to no good.

"The receipt you got when you filed your claim."

"I wonder why he'd be looking for that."

The day was beginning to warm up to a typical late-July day, with high sun and blue sky. Rosemary's skin glistened as a sheen of perspiration began to appear on her forehead and neck.

Finn sat down on the rocking chair and held Sarah on his lap. Rosemary took the chair next to him. "All right. You have to tell me what you're not telling me, Finn. This is driving me mad."

"I guess you have the right to know." He drew in a breath and told her everything, about finding her sheep in his field....

She gasped. "I'll repay any damage they caused."

"Let's discuss that later. The point is that both Peter and Ian implicated Rolf. He deliberately got them out of the way so he could lead the sheep toward my field."

"Why would he do that?" She frowned and her blue eyes darkened as she tried to make sense of the revelation. "Is he upset with you for some reason?"

"You should be asking yourself if he's upset with *you*."

She laughed. "Why would he be upset with me? I've given him a position with a good salary. He's free to do whatever he feels is right concerning the sheep—as long as he lets me know what he has planned, of course. I hired his brother Peter and their uncle Ian. I've literally done everything he's suggested or requested." She angled her head and stared into the sky. Then she shook her head. "No, I can't think of anything. Unless…"

Finn nodded and smiled. "Marta."

"You mean because I took up for her and made him stop being a bully?" She shuddered, and her eyebrows pushed together in a frown. "I can't abide a man who believes a woman is his to possess! I don't think the Lord ever meant for it to be that way."

"Well, don't yell at me," Finn said. "I don't think a woman should be treated poorly either."

She cut her gaze toward him and sent him a guilty smile. "I'm sorry. I just get so riled up when I think about mean people." She paused and then asked, "Finn, who is watching my sheep if Rolf isn't there running things?"

Finn shrugged. "As far as I know, Peter and Ian. Although I have to tell you, I don't trust Ian. I never have. Once you get back home, I suggest you let him go."

"Honestly, Finn." She stood and walked toward the door. "I can't imagine Rolf being guilty of sabotage. And why would he want the receipt? It wouldn't do him any good anyway."

"Maybe he didn't want it for himself. What if someone paid him to steal it?"

She laughed again, and this time Finn felt his pride take a hit.

"Suit yourself, Rosemary. But I'm trying to keep you and your land and your sheep safe. According to Peter, Mr. Clayton isn't giving up. He paid Rolf to sabotage my field."

"But that doesn't make any sense. How would sabotaging you hurt my sheep?"

"I think he means to use my field as an example of the harm that sheep can do to farms if they get loose."

"But they won't get loose if they're herded properly."

"They wouldn't have gotten loose if you'd put a fence up."

"But I didn't want there to be a fence between our properties."

"Why?" Finn smiled at her little pout. He knew she didn't mean to look adorable, but she did just the same.

"Because, Finn. What if Sarah wants to run back and forth between the properties when she's a little older?"

"There won't be a fence in the road."

"But there's something special about her cutting through your property and then cutting through mine on her way to my house. Or the other way, when she goes to your home."

Finn contained his disappointment. The reason he hadn't put up a fence of his own, despite her insistence that there shouldn't be one there, was because he believed she knew that eventually they would merge the two homesteads into one.

Her reason was probably no less valid, wanting Sarah to be able to run between the properties and feel equally at home without a fence to keep her out. He looked at his daughter, who had learned to blow bubbles on her hands and was now doing so with wild abandon, drooling all over his sleeve.

Rosemary reached for the door. "I'm going to let Dottie know I'll be back in a few minutes. I need to go and speak with Rolf. I can't let myself believe he would deliberately try to hurt my land or my sheep, much less try to steal from me. There just has to be a reasonable explanation."

"I'll go with you."

To his chagrin, she shook her head. "I think your presence might make things worse since you're the one who found him in my house and jumped to conclusions in the first place."

Anger burned inside him once more. He wished she would stop putting up a wall between the two of them. He hadn't been able to reach her since the day of their walk together in Paddington. He had been telling himself that the reason was that Agnes had become ill and Rosemary had been busy taking care of the children—and that might have been part of it—but he had come to town every evening this week after the chores were finished and still she kept her distance from him. As a matter of fact, this conversation on the porch was the first of any real depth in days.

Before he could do any more contemplating, Rosemary returned to the porch wearing her bonnet and carrying a Bible.

"Are you planning to preach to him?"

She smiled and her dimple flashed. "I might."

"He'd love that. He ranted that a woman should not have her own homestead. Imagine what he'd think of a woman wanting to preach the gospel."

"Don't worry, I have no desire to deliver a sermon. The Bible is for Rolf in case he gets bored and wants something to bide his time. He couldn't do better than to bide his time with God's Word." She bent over and pressed a kiss to Sarah's head. "Bye, sweetie," she said. "Auntie Rose will be back in a little while."

It was all he could do not to grab hold of her waist and pull her down to his lap next to Sarah. She was so tiny, there would be plenty of room for both. But she moved away before he had a chance to think it through. Then he realized he wouldn't have anyway. He had

no rights to her body. She wasn't Rachel, and until she believed that he could truly care about her in a completely different way than he'd cared for Rachel, he would never have the right to draw her close, kiss her, marry her.

He had wrestled with his own thoughts and feelings about his motives. He believed that he loved Rosemary for herself, but if he were honest, there were nights when his dream-self begged Rachel to come back. She always stood in her white nightgown, looking like an angel. And then Rosemary would walk in. At first he would think Rachel had returned to human form, but his heart would sink as he realized it couldn't be Rachel. The woman who looked just like her was, in fact, Rosemary. And Rosemary would look at him with disappointment and say, "You can't have both of us in one body. I want a man who sees me and loves me."

Finn watched the real Rosemary until she disappeared inside the jailhouse. He wasn't sure why he wanted Rosemary. He only knew that he did. And the thought of Sheriff Mayfield, on the other side of that door with her, tightened his gut.

It took every ounce of discipline he had to keep himself on that porch, holding his daughter and minding his own business.

* * * * *

Rosemary smiled at Sheriff Mayfield as she walked into the sheriff's office. "Hello," she said, "I'm here to see Rolf."

"Well," he said, sitting up straight in his chair, "I can't say I'm not disappointed. I'd hoped you were here to see me."

"I'm sorry." Rosemary's heart always felt lighter around the sheriff. He made her laugh. And she liked that about him. "I am truly here to see Rolf."

He stood and walked around to the front of his desk, leaned back, and folded his arms. "I'm sorry, Miss Jackson. He isn't feeling well."

Rosemary frowned. "He seemed fine when Finn brought him in this morning. Maybe I should take a look at him." She hurried to the door of the room with the cells, but as she reached out to grasp the latch, Sheriff Mayfield's hand grabbed onto hers. She glanced down and noted fresh cuts and bruises on his knuckles. "What on earth?" Shaking loose from his grasp, she quickly swung open the door and went inside. Rolf lay curled on the floor of his cell. Rosemary knelt on the floor. "Rolf," she said softly, "it's Miss Jackson. Can you hear me?"

A groan of pain answered her. She stood up and swung around. "What gave you the right to harm him? You had no right to accuse, convict, and punish him. No right at all."

The sheriff's face filled with shame. "I apologize, Miss Jackson. I admit I got angry."

"Well, you should learn to control that particular emotion then. 'Be ye angry, and sin not.'"

"You're right, of course." He reached out slowly and cupped her cheek. "But when he confessed to me that he was working for Bart Clayton and the man wants to run you and your sheep off your property, I overreacted."

Rosemary felt the weight of the words he'd spoken. "H–he confessed to sabotaging me? Turning my herd into Finn's field?"

Sheriff nodded. "I'm afraid so, Miss Jackson. I'm so sorry. I know

how much you trusted him. But he isn't to be trusted. He has been working for Clayton all along."

"And the receipt? What was the point of that?" Rosemary couldn't stop asking questions, though she knew it wasn't right to obtain her information through violence any more than it had been for the sheriff. But she had to know.

"That's still a little sketchy. I'm guessing that if Clayton has your receipt, he can claim you gave up the homestead the way the other fella gave it up to you."

Rosemary looked down at Rolf. His face was beginning to swell and bruise. "I'm going to get Doc Richards to take a look at him."

"Even after he sold you out?"

Rosemary smiled. "He didn't sell me out. He tried to, but I'm still here. My sheep are fine. The boys are watching the herd." She walked toward the door. "Get him on the cot, please. And don't hurt him anymore. If you do, I'll speak to the mayor about having you removed."

"I give you my word, I won't hurt him anymore."

Something in his tone didn't sit right with Rosemary. "On second thought, I'll stay here with Rolf. Will you please go after the doctor?"

"You don't trust me even after I gave you my word?"

"I don't know you well enough to trust you yet, Sheriff."

"But I just defended your honor."

Rosemary leveled her gaze at him, and he drew in a sharp breath, keeping his eyes locked on her. "The fact that you thought I needed my honor defended is sweet, and I appreciate the gesture, but that you could beat up a boy in such a fashion and call it defending my honor proves that you don't know me at all."

"Something I am hoping to remedy soon."

She lifted her chin. Thinking he'd have a chance to court her after she discovered him capable of this sort of senseless brutality confirmed that Sheriff Mayfield would never understand the sort of woman she was. "Please bring the doctor."

Ten minutes later Dr. Richards blazed through the door, carrying his bag. "Why are you in the middle of all my emergencies lately, Miss Jackson?"

"This is only the second one. And you can't really compare the two, can you?"

He turned to Sheriff Mayfield. "Open this cell and get him on the cot so I can examine him."

Fifteen minutes later, the doctor exited the cell and shook his head. "He's bruised, but nothing is broken, and as far as I can tell he's not bleeding internally."

Relief flooded over Rosemary. She turned to Sheriff Mayfield. "Is he free to go?"

"I was going to keep him overnight." He frowned. "You know, I like you a lot, Miss Jackson, but I'm not accustomed to women telling me how to conduct my sheriffing."

"I thought I liked you a lot too, Sheriff," she said through clenched teeth. "But that was before you beat up a boy."

"Good heavens." The doctor headed to the door. "He'll heal best if he spends a couple of days resting in bed. Otherwise, he's not too bad off."

When the door closed, Sheriff Mayfield smiled down at her. "You were saying?"

"I was saying that unless you plan to bring charges before a

judge, you can't keep him here. It's not fair. I think he's suffered enough, don't you?"

His lips twisted into a scowl. "I reckon. If you say so. And as long as you're not too angry with me to cancel our picnic tomorrow."

Rosemary shook her head. "I'm sorry, Sheriff, but I am going back home tomorrow. As a matter of fact, we could use your help this evening with taking Agnes over to the boardinghouse. She and Marta will be staying there for a few more days while Agnes continues to recover."

"I can't say I'm not disappointed," he said. "But of course I'll be happy to help with Mrs. Fischer." He walked her to the door. "And I deeply apologize for allowing my anger to override my judgment with Rolf. That only happens when someone I care about is hurt."

"Sheriff Mayfield," Rosemary said, surprised at his audacity, "you don't know me well enough to speak to me that way. And besides, I wasn't hurt."

"That you know of. Mr. Clayton is a slippery fella."

Rosemary narrowed her gaze. "How would you know? You've only been in town a little while."

"The mayor told me all about the richest man in the township. Clayton's had some questionable dealings with homesteaders much like you, and he's come out better off than those he swindled. Why do you think he owns over a thousand acres?"

"If he is such a crook, why not arrest him?" Besides, something about the sheriff's statement didn't quite ring true. The mayor and Clayton were friends. It was doubtful that the mayor would malign his friend's reputation, no matter how deserved.

He gave a short laugh. "A man like Clayton is a little smarter than your boy in there. He doesn't get caught."

"Every evil deed done in darkness will eventually be brought to light."

"Is that in the Good Book you're holding?"

"It certainly is. And it wouldn't hurt you to read about the peacemakers."

"You win, Rosemary Jackson." He reached out and brushed away an errant strand of her hair. "He can go when he wakes up."

"Wonderful." Rewarding him with a smile she knew showed her dimple, Rosemary walked to the door. "I'll ask Finn to bring the wagon round and drive Rolf back to the bunkhouse before he goes back to his own fields."

The sheriff's jaw dropped. "Are you saying you're taking Rolf back to your homestead? Are you daft?"

"I just believe in second chances, that's all."

He shook his head. "If I'd known you meant to take him back to your place, I'd have beat him up worse so he had to stay close to the doc."

"Don't say that, Sheriff."

Rosemary left the office, disappointed by her discovery of Sheriff Mayfield's true character. Finn might not love her the same way he loved Rachel, but at least in asking for her heart, he was honest about it.

Chapter Twenty-Three

....

Finn could barely contain his anger as he unloaded Rolf from the wagon and helped him into the bunkhouse.

"Please be gentle with him, Finn," Rosemary said. Her kindness was almost more than he could bear. "Just remember, you put me out of your house and I still forgave you."

"Rolf betrayed you. That's different from asking you to leave. I didn't exactly toss you into the cold." He shook his head at the comparison. "I even made sure you would have a place to live. It just wasn't where you wanted to live."

She grinned at him teasingly. "I was raised to have my own green pastures. How could I have lived in a boardinghouse?"

"Many women do."

"Not this woman." She touched his arm. "Thank you for agreeing to take him home."

He agreed to be kind to Rolf—although he couldn't help but be a little glad the sheriff had taken the initiative and beaten him. At least now he knew that two men were looking out for Rosemary, whether she wanted them to or not.

Rolf could barely walk, so great was the bruising to his midsection. But the doc had said there were no broken ribs.

"Why is she allowing me back?" he asked Finn.

"Because she doesn't think you really meant to betray her." Finn's voice dripped with sarcasm. "She is certain you're sorry now and will come back to her side and be more loyal than ever."

"She is right." He struggled to speak through cracked, swollen lips.

"She'd better be." But Finn had his doubts that Rolf could actually stop working for Bart Clayton. Men like that didn't just let a person leave their employ—especially not a spy and saboteur like Rolf.

Peter entered the bunkhouse. His eyes grew big at the sight of his brother, then he turned and glared accusingly at Finn.

Finn shook his head. "I didn't touch him."

"After Mr. Tate left, I thought you would be in jail," Peter said to Rolf.

"Not enough evidence to keep me," Rolf said.

His words brought Finn's anger back. He wanted to pound the guy into the ground. "A real man would have confessed," he growled.

Rolf nodded. "Probably. But not if he wishes to stay alive and to keep his family alive. Which I do."

"Miss Jackson will allow you to keep your position?" Peter's tone sounded incredulous—exactly the way Finn felt. Personally, he felt she should publicly humiliate the boy and then fire him. That way no one else would hire him.

Observing Peter, he couldn't help but wonder how the two brothers had turned out so different. "Are you keeping the sheep out of my field?" he asked.

"Yes. They are on the other side of the land."

"Ian is with them now?"

Peter nodded.

"Get back out there, then, and help him keep the sheep out of my field. We'll start building a fence tomorrow."

"Mr. Tate…" The hoarse words drifted up from Rolf's bunk.

Finn wanted to ignore Rolf, but he'd promised Rosemary that he would be kind, and for that reason alone, he turned his attention to the boy.

"Do you need something, Rolf?"

"I need to tell you about the receipt."

His interest piqued, he walked to Rolf's bunk and bent down. "Talk, then."

Rolf explained why he'd taken the receipts, at the same time revealing Clayton's scheme to steal Rosemary's land. Sabotaging the sheep was only meant to be a distraction as Clayton worked out his plan.

Finn's gut tightened with urgency. "If you're telling the truth and we avert this thing," he said to Rolf, "you've just absolved yourself."

He ran outside the bunkhouse. "Peter!"

The boy ran back. "Yes, Mr. Tate?"

"Take care of Rolf. And be nice to him." He swung around, pulled Charity from her stall, hastily saddled the mare, and galloped into town at breakneck speed.

* * * * *

Rosemary hugged Agnes, and Agnes's eyes misted as her children sniffled their good-byes to their mother. "You be very good for

Fräulein Jackson," she said, her voice still so weak that Rosemary wondered if she truly should be out from under Dr. Richards's constant care.

Dottie Franklin had readily agreed to give Agnes one of the downstairs rooms and had brought in a cot for Marta to sleep on so she could be near her mother.

Rosemary was almost sure the elderly woman was disappointed when she discovered the children would not be staying. When the children were there she seemed livelier and less cranky, and baked treats every day. The children had taken to calling her "Miss Dottie," and as each one hugged her good-bye on the porch, she gave them a treat.

"You children promise you'll come back and see Aunt Dottie sometime."

"We will," Heinrich said. The young man had been quite a help to her, working in her garden and running to the general store for this or that. Rosemary knew he would miss town and Dottie as much as the elderly woman would miss him.

"I promise we'll be back in a few days to visit," Rosemary said.

Horse hooves pounded down the main street, kicking up dust.

"Land sakes. Someone's in an all-fired hurry," Dottie said. "Must be a fire or a new baby."

Rosemary frowned and peered through the dust. "That's my horse, Charity, and Finn is riding her." Her chest tightened. "Something's wrong."

Charity was lathered and heaving as he pulled her up fast. In one fluid movement, he slid from the saddle and handed Afonso the reins. He grabbed Rosemary's arm and pulled her away from the others.

"Finn, what is it?" She could barely breathe as she pictured the new barn burning, the sheep dead, her house demolished. "Tell me!"

"Do you trust me?"

Without hesitation, she nodded. "You know I do."

"Then you and I need to leave right now, but not past the land office or anywhere Clayton's people can see you, and that includes Sheriff Mayfield."

"Tell me."

"We have to leave the children, and you need to come with me to Montrose."

"I can't leave the children, Finn. Agnes is too ill. Dr. Richards said they will slow her recovery."

"Fine, then. They'll just have to come along."

"Why do we have to go to Montrose? Everything in that town is right here in Paddington."

"Everything but the preacher. He went from here to there, and he's leaving in the morning."

Rosemary stopped short and pulled her arm from his hand. "Finn Tate, stop this instant and explain yourself. Why on earth do we need to go to Montrose and find the preacher?"

Finn took hold of both her arms, pulled her to him, and kissed her hard on the lips. He held her out from him. "Because you, Rosemary Jackson, and I, Finn Tate, are getting married today. If you trust me, then just trust that I'm doing the right thing. I'll explain on the way."

Knowing there had to be more to this than Finn's stubbornness, Rosemary didn't argue anymore. By the time they reached Montrose and located the preacher having supper in the home of a

Mr. and Mrs. Smith, he had explained everything and done any with all her objections.

The children fluttered about in excitement, and Mrs. Smith sat them all down, insisting that they eat. When the meal was over, Finn bent down and whispered something to Elsa. She ran outside and returned a couple of minutes later with a bouquet of wild roses, handing them shyly to Rosemary.

"Wait," Mrs. Smith said. She reached into a drawer and drew out a pink ribbon. "A bouquet needs a ribbon."

Rosemary took the wild-rose bouquet and smiled up at her groom.

They stood before the reverend with Heinrich Jr., Afonso, Elsa, Gerta, and baby Sarah as witnesses. They recited their vows and said, "I will." Then the reverend pronounced them husband and wife. Finn bent down and kissed her softly on the lips.

Rosemary knew her cheeks were blooming, but she didn't care. Everything had happened so fast that by the time they climbed back into the wagon and headed to her ranch, the sun had set, the children were asleep in the back of the wagon, and Rosemary cuddled Sarah to her, trying to take it all in.

Finn seemed tense next to her, and Rosemary didn't know what to say. "I appreciate this, Finn," she said.

"Don't say it like that," he said, his tone gruff.

"Like what?"

"As though I'm doing you a favor. Like this is a business arrangement." He stopped the wagon and turned to her, slipping his arm around her. "When Rolf told me exactly how Clayton planned to waylay you next week on the day before you turned twenty-one, I realized that the very thought of him taking your land, stealing something you loved so much, was unacceptable. I also realized that if he won and you lost the land, I would lose you."

Rosemary shook her head. "No, you wouldn't have, Finn. I would have married you."

He nodded. "I know I would have had you physically. But your fight would have been gone. You'd have always been disappointed. You would have helped me tend my land and build a home for our daughter and whatever children God blesses us with, but inside, you would be empty."

Mindful of baby Sarah, who slept peacefully in her arms, Finn pulled her closer. "When I look at you, I see the only woman who could have stood her ground and taken that land and made me want to help her save it. It's for you, Rosemary Tate. When I look at you, there's only you. When I kiss you, it's you I'm kissing. When I hold you, my arms are surrounding you. Only you, for the rest of our lives."

As the moon glowed big and round overhead, Rosemary lifted her face for her husband's kiss. He obliged, leaving her breathless and flushed and happier than she'd ever thought possible.

* * * * *

A week later, on the day before Rosemary's twenty-first birthday, she and Finn drove the children into Paddington to reunite with their mother in the boardinghouse. Then they returned to the homestead. Rosemary missed the children, but she had to admit, it was nice to have her husband all to herself. Except for Sarah of course.

That evening they were sitting on the porch in the rocking chairs Finn had crafted for her as a wedding present when Mr. Clayton and his four men rode up to the house. The sheriff also rode with them. Rosemary and Finn stood and stepped to the edge of the porch. Finn was poised with his rifle, but they both hoped and prayed there would be no need for it.

The men approached, and the sheriff climbed down from his saddle.

"Sheriff Mayfield," Rosemary said, "this is quite a surprise."

At least he had the decency to look ashamed as he approached with papers. "Rosemary, according to these documents that Mr. Clayton has obtained, you are not old enough to legally make a claim on this land."

Rosemary took the papers, which stated that at the time she'd made the claim, she had been only twenty years old—which was true. She hadn't known that one of the questions in the paperwork indicated she was supposed to admit she was underage when she filed the claim.

"Yes, unfortunately, I became aware of this a week ago." She met Sheriff Mayfield's gaze. "Sheriff, I didn't know I wasn't of age to file."

"I believe you." He smiled at her. "But I'm afraid I'm duty-bound to ask you to pack up and leave the homestead."

Finn eyed Sheriff Mayfield. "What Rosemary means, Sheriff, is that we discovered a week ago that Clayton learned about Rosemary's age and meant to remove her from the land the day before she was of legal age, just to be cruel."

Clayton smiled his wooden smile. "Whatever my intentions, the law is clear and Miss Jackson can no longer file. I have put in my name on this plot at the land office. But I'm not an unreasonable man. I can give her twenty-four hours. That should be enough for her to simply move her things next door and for you two to go find the preacher. He can't have gotten far."

"Actually, Mr. Clayton," Rosemary said, "my name is Mrs. Tate now. Not Miss Jackson. And I'm afraid you got to the land office for nothing. You see, my husband and I went to the land office in Williston the day after our wedding last week. As we explained our dilemma and showed my receipt, my husband Finn was able to file on the claim. You know they'll let a man file twice as many acres now. So all we have to do is plant some trees and keep the improvements moving forward, and by the time our children are grown, we'll have a virtual forest on this land."

"I don't believe you!" Clayton's face turned purple with rage. "I demand to see the paperwork and the marriage certificate."

"Certainly, as soon as you show us the proof of ownership of every acre of land you lay claim to, Mr. Clayton."

The sheriff stepped forward, and Rosemary could see the humor in his eyes. "May I?" he asked, looking at the documents in her hand.

Rosemary nodded and he climbed the steps to the porch as she held out the documents. "Be my guest."

Sheriff Mayfield perused the papers and turned to Clayton. "Looks legitimate to me. If you have any more complaints, you'll have to take them up with the land office in Williston, because this is signed and stamped."

"I'm not leaving here without seeing them put off this land." Clayton stared hard at the sheriff. "Now you get to it and do what you were hired to do, or so help me, I'll have your badge."

Clayton's men stood poised to fight, their hands resting on their pistols.

Mayfield stood next to Finn and pointed at the group. "Now, you listen here. I went along with your little scheme, and I'm ashamed I did. But these people are legally married and have legally filed on this land. Clayton, if you know what's good for you, I suggest you turn around and ride off and forget about this claim. It's not going to be yours."

Rosemary held her breath, and she felt Finn's tension beside her. She didn't want land at the risk of her husband's life. *God, please intervene!* she prayed.

Clayton stared hard at Rosemary. "You think you've won, little miss?"

Without batting an eyelash, Rosemary shook her head. "The only one fighting was you, Mr. Clayton."

For a few tense seconds, he continued to stare. Then he nodded. "Then I guess this is over for now. But I intend to go to Williston. If there's even the tiniest detail out of order, I'm coming back."

"There won't be."

Finn slipped his arm around her waist, drawing her close to him, as they watched Mr. Clayton and his men ride away in a cloud of dust. Sheriff Mayfield turned. "Well, you two took the wind right out of his sails, didn't you? Congratulations."

"Thank you for standing with us, Sheriff Mayfield," Rosemary said. "You might not have a job in Paddington after today."

He shrugged. "It's time for me to move on anyway. I don't think I'm cut out to be a lawman." He tipped his hat to Finn. "Well, it looks like the best man won."

Rosemary laughed. "He's the best man for me. And he always has been."

Finn pulled her close as the sheriff got on his horse and rode away. "It looks like this land is all yours now."

Rosemary wound her arms around his neck and pulled his head down to hers. "Ours." Their lips met, and Rosemary would have happily stayed in his arms the rest of the day, but a sound inside the house pulled them apart.

"Did I hear Sarah?" Finn asked. The two inclined their heads toward the door, smiled at each other, and entered their home together to answer their daughter's cry.

Epilogue

....

The trees had struggled this year, but by the grace of God, they'd made it. There was nothing to keep Finn and Rosemary from proving they had met all the requirements for this 160 acres, as they had Finn's original homestead three years earlier.

"You about ready?" Finn asked Rosemary.

She nodded and grabbed the picnic basket from the rocking chair on the porch. "I've been waiting for you since you asked me not to walk out there alone."

Rosemary rubbed her protruding belly and looked across the land she and Finn finally owned. Five years of sweat, tears, joy, and sorrow had brought them to this moment. Finn caught her hand with one of his and held their two-year-old son, Roland, in his other arm. Sarah raced through the field toward their picnic spot in the exact middle of the land, between Finn's homestead and Rosemary's homestead, where they had built a pond to sit beside, cool their feet on a summer day, and fish to their heart's content.

"Are you sure you want to walk?" Finn asked, looking down at her belly.

"Yes, I feel good. Tired, but strong." They set out from the house,

Finn adjusting his stride to hers as she labored to keep moving forward.

A wagon approached just as they reached the creek. "They're here!" Sarah called out. She ran to the wagon to greet Gerta, who, at seven years old, was only two years older than Sarah.

Agnes and Dr. Hiram Richards climbed down from the wagon. They had become Finn and Rosemary's closest friends over the years. They arrived with all of Agnes's children except Marta, who had moved with her husband, Peter, to Bismarck two years earlier.

"How are you feeling, Rosemary?" Agnes asked as Hiram helped her from the wagon.

"I think it's a good thing your husband is here today," Rosemary said, laughing. "I feel like this baby could be born any second."

"Then maybe ve shall haf new baby." She smiled. "My Hiram is very goot at bringing babies."

Rosemary laughed. "I hear the new teacher is staying at Dottie's," she said, laying out the blanket.

Dr. Richards chuckled. "Heinrich is smitten with the pretty young thing. I have a feeling he's not going to be single much longer."

"It is true. My Heinrich is smitten. He is much too young, though." Agnes sighed, lifting food from the basket. "I still cannot believe Miss Dottie haf gone to be vith the Lord."

Dottie had succumbed to heart failure during the winter, but not before amending her will, naming Agnes as the sole owner of the boardinghouse. Agnes and the children had never left after her surgery. Dottie had begged Agnes to stay and help her run the place. When Hiram asked for Agnes's hand, she insisted they live at the boardinghouse and not leave Dottie alone.

The day progressed beautifully. The children played, the boys fished. Hiram and Agnes went off hand in hand to see the new lambs, and Rosemary watched, smiling, as the two families dotted the fields much like the sheep.

Catching her mood, Finn grabbed her hand and brought it to his lips. "Rosemary, look. The first of the wild roses of the summer."

Rosemary followed his gaze and smiled. "They're beautiful."

"We'll get some for you to set out on the table while you recover from having the baby."

She shook her head. "Let's not. These are the first." She took in a breath of clean summer air and watched the breeze blow against the soft petals. "Let's leave them alone and let them grow as wild and free as they want."

"Like you?" He pressed a kiss to her temple.

She shook her head. "I never wanted to be wild and free." She closed her eyes as weariness washed over her. "I wanted to be captured and loved."

"And so you are, my Rose. So you are."

Author's Note
....

Dear Readers,

Thank you for coming along with me for *Love Finds You in Wildrose, North Dakota*. I have to tell you, while researching this book, I fell in love with this part of the country. Wildrose is so far north, it's almost Canada.

Because the name of the town is so beautiful, I desperately wanted to set a story here. But here's the thing. Trying to settle such a place was almost impossible, and my research kept bringing my story to a standstill. So in order to bring you the story of these characters I grew to love so much, I had a long talk with my editor, and we ultimately decided that the story and the town of Wildrose were worth a little creative license. To that end, I grabbed the existing historical truths and backed them up a decade or so.

Please forgive me, North Dakotans, who know better than to think there were homesteaders in Wildrose as early as 1889, when the first homesteader didn't file his claim until the 1900s. And in fact, Wildrose wasn't an incorporated town until 1913 and a Great Northern Railroad terminus until 1916. Three years seems sadly short-lived to me, so perhaps that's why I had to lengthen the time frame of the surrounding area. You are also much too wise to think the town of

Paddington (which I *had* to use, because if I were ever to build my very own town, this is what I would name it) was as built up as it was in my story almost two decades before it truly was. As a matter of fact, Paddington, built on the shore of Willow Lake (another name I love), only came along in 1909. As the railroad chugged into the area, two cities became one: Paddington and Montrose. Their two post offices merged and were supposed to become the city of Montrose. However, because the town of Montrose already existed as a stop along the railroad line, the railroad men noted the beautiful wild roses and suggested the name Wildrose. For many years afterward, Willow Lake, on which the town of Paddington was built, was used as a resort of sorts for ranchers, homesteaders, and railroad men.

Why, you might ask, didn't I just set the story later in time? Well, I could have, but I didn't want my characters to add the tragedy of World War I to their already-harsh existence. Quite plainly, I wanted their love to have a chance, and I wanted to write a prairie romance rather than a World War I romance.

So, yes, I took some license with the historical accuracy inasmuch as dates were concerned and a name or two of towns that might not have existed quite as early as I asked them to come to life for my story. I hope the time-traveled facts will not be a distraction for the average reader. I beg you to bear with me, to suspend just a tiny bit of disbelief, and lose yourself within the pages of this story I fell in love with.

God bless you as you live, move, and have your being in Him.

—Tracey Bateman

About the Author

....

Tracey Bateman is an award-winning author with nearly one million books in print. Since publishing her first novel in 2000, Tracey has written more than thirty books, including *Love Finds You in Deadwood, South Dakota* (published as Tracey Cross). She's also the author of *The Widow of Saunders Creek* (releasing in 2012), *Thirsty, Tandem,* the Westward Hearts series, the Kansas Home series, the Drama Queens series, the Claire Everett series, and the Penbrook Diaries series. Tracey is an active member of the American Fiction Christian Writers and has served as the organization's president.

Tracey loves living in the beautiful Missouri Ozarks. When she's not writing, she reads, watches sci-fi, and tries to catch up with friends on Facebook and e-mail. She also loves to cook and is thrilled to create culinary works for her family members—who sometimes even like what she creates.

Tracey and her husband, Rusty, have four children, and they love to watch God's faithfulness to the next generation of Batemans. More than anything, Tracey is grateful for her family and the ability to write for a wonderful God.

Want a peek into local American life—past and present?
The *Love Finds You*™ series published by Summerside Press
features real towns and combines travel, romance,
and faith in one irresistible package!

The novels in the series—uniquely titled after American towns with romantic or intriguing names—inspire romance and fun. Each fictional story draws on the compelling history or the unique character of a real place. Stories center on romances kindled in small towns, old loves lost and found again on the high plains, and new loves discovered at exciting vacation getaways. Summerside Press plans to publish at least one novel set in each of the fifty states. Be sure to catch them all!

NOW AVAILABLE

Love Finds You in
Miracle, Kentucky
by Andrea Boeshaar
ISBN: 978-1-934770-37-5

Love Finds You in
Snowball, Arkansas
by Sandra D. Bricker
ISBN: 978-1-934770-45-0

Love Finds You in
Romeo, Colorado by Gwen
Ford Faulkenberry
ISBN: 978-1-934770-46-7

Love Finds You in
Valentine, Nebraska
by Irene Brand
ISBN: 978-1-934770-38-2

Love Finds You in Humble, Texas
by Anita Higman
ISBN: 978-1-934770-61-0

Love Finds You in
Last Chance, California
by Miralee Ferrell
ISBN: 978-1-934770-39-9

Love Finds You in
Maiden, North Carolina
by Tamela Hancock Murray
ISBN: 978-1-934770-65-8

Love Finds You in
Paradise, Pennsylvania
by Loree Lough
ISBN: 978-1-934770-66-5

Love Finds You in
Treasure Island, Florida
by Debby Mayne
ISBN: 978-1-934770-80-1

Love Finds You in
Liberty, Indiana
by Melanie Dobson
ISBN: 978-1-934770-74-0

Love Finds You in
Carmel-by-the-Sea, California
by Sandra D. Bricker
ISBN: 978-1-60936-027-6

Love Finds You
Under the Mistletoe
by Irene Brand and Anita Higman
ISBN: 978-1-60936-004-7

Love Finds You in
Hope, Kansas
by Pamela Griffin
ISBN: 978-1-60936-007-8

Love Finds You in
Sun Valley, Idaho
by Angela Ruth
ISBN: 978-1-60936-008-5

Love Finds You in
Camelot, Tennessee
by Janice Hanna
ISBN: 978-1-935416-65-4

Love Finds You in
Tombstone, Arizona
by Miralee Ferrell
ISBN: 978-1-60936-104-4

Love Finds You in
Martha's Vineyard, Massachusetts
by Melody Carlson
ISBN: 978-1-60936-110-5

Love Finds You in
Prince Edward Island, Canada
by Susan Page Davis
ISBN: 978-1-60936-109-9

Love Finds You in
Groom, Texas
by Janice Hanna
ISBN: 978-1-60936-006-1

Love Finds You in Amana, Iowa
by Melanie Dobson
ISBN: 978-1-60936-135-8

Love Finds You in
Lancaster County, Pennsylvania
by Annalisa Daughety
ISBN: 978-1-60936-212-6

Love Finds You in
Branson, Missouri by Gwen
Ford Faulkenberry
ISBN: 978-1-60936-191-4

Love Finds You in
Sundance, Wyoming
by Miralee Ferrell
ISBN: 978-1-60936-277-5

Love Finds You on
Christmas Morning
by Debby Mayne and Trish Perry
ISBN: 978-1-60936-193-8

Love Finds You in
Sunset Beach, Hawaii
by Robin Jones Gunn
ISBN: 978-1-60936-028-3

Love Finds You in
Nazareth, Pennsylvania
by Melanie Dobson
ISBN: 97-8-160936-194-5

Love Finds You in
Annapolis, Maryland
by Roseanna M. White
ISBN: 978-1-60936-313-0

Love Finds You in
New Orleans, Louisiana
by Christa Allan
ISBN: 978-1-60936-591-2

COMING SOON

Love Finds You in
Daisy, Oklahoma
by Janice Hanna
ISBN: 978-1-60936-593-6

Love Finds You in
Sunflower, Kansas
by Pamela Tracy
ISBN: 978-1-60936-594-3

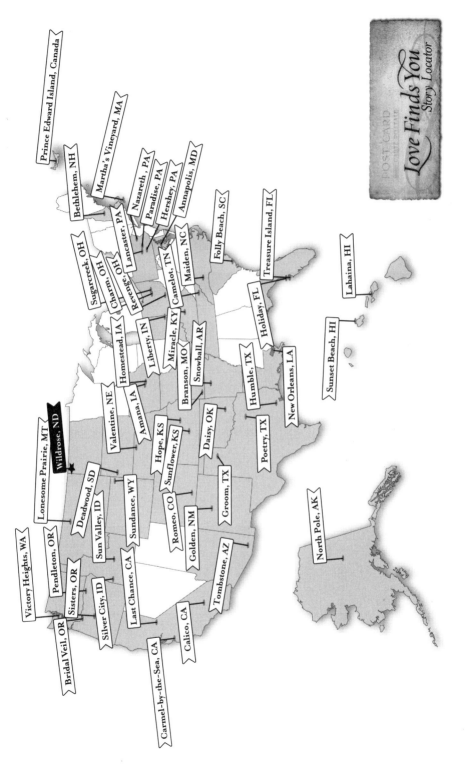